REVENGE IS A FISH BETTER SERVED COLD

SEBASTYEN DUGAS

GET TWO FREE BOOKS

Get two **FREE** short novels from this author. Discover two of his book series by visiting Sebastyen's website.

Download them for **FREE** by subscribing to Sebastyen's newsletter by clicking on this link: https://link. sebastyendugas.com/frontlafseng

ONE

I've been chasing this purse-snatching bastard for ten minutes now. Although he's not exactly a rocket scientist, he runs like the wind. Probably a former long-distance runner. He goes through the neighbourhood's backyards, forcing me to leap over fences like a Greyhound in a dog show, minus the fancy-dressed lady running alongside and holding on a leash. I'm not twenty years old anymore, you jerk.

Come on, Martin, hurry up. You've got to catch up with that vile moron who must laugh at you losing ground with every passing minute. Jumping over the fences like a horny grasshopper, the thief casts a few furtive glances behind to assess the distance between us. Moving confidently, I land in a yard where a couple is enjoying a steak with baked potatoes. There's no denying it, it smells like heaven. Nothing to boost my motivation to catch up with the other imbecile. Especially since I don't really care that much, to be totally honest with you. I wink at the woman for good measure, and her idiot husband points me in the direction the idiot is heading. That is where I was going, anyway.

"Thank you, Sherlock," I say snappishly.

Another jump, a new backyard. This time, four pretty young women are splashing around in an in-ground pool, while

1

another one tries yet again to take a satisfying selfie. She will eventually get one, I guess. I slow down.

"Hello, sweethearts."

The naughty girls chuckle.

"What do we have here? A dip between girlfriends, am I right?"

The least attractive of the group looks at me sternly.

"What do you want, Grandpa?"

"But... you little bitch... I'm chasing a criminal while you—"

Shit, the robber.

I take up my run as the girl insults me. Then, I jump into the next courtyard, grabbing one of the pork chops from a plate on the table and sinking my teeth into it. I head for the other yard. Holy shit, the chop tastes like nothing. I stop dead in my tracks, sitting astride the fence and turning to the pot-bellied cook in the dirty apron.

"Hey, poor man's Gordon Ramsay. Two words: Spice. This crap is disgusting."

I throw the rest of the pork chop at him and run across to the neighbour's yard amidst the insults of the junk cook. Granted, I won't catch up with the jackass by stopping so often. Thanks to the silly little girls at the pool, and the crappy cook, the thief lost me easily. But since I know the area like the back of my hand, I can guess where he's going. This asshole will probably try to reach the shabby industrial buildings on the east side. I'm sure he will. He'll think he's safe and check out the fruits of his labour. And who will be there to kick him in the nuts?

Your humble servant.

I make a quick right turn and cross the street like a flash, nearly getting hit by an old beige Buick Regal. If there's one insulting death, it's getting killed by an idiot with no taste in cars. He honks at me. I answer by pointing to the sky with my middle finger, and I keep running. Arriving near the old pulp and paper factory that now houses a handful of crystal-meth-doped squatters, I cross the field and bingo; the jerk comes towards me with a light step, unsuspecting. I slow down to await him at the corner of the old bakery.

"Come on, kid. Don't be afraid. I won't hurt you."

I laugh like a madman. Oh, how this right punch in the face will be delightful.

BAM!

I don't have time to swing before this jerk gets hit by a car crossing the street. He's tossed a few feet in the air and falls flat on his face behind the car. Holy shit, he's dead. He still has a firm grip on the purse strap.

A+ for determination.

I jog over to find out what this is all about, but he staggers to his feet. He plunges his fingers into his mouth to pull out a tooth, which he casually tosses to the ground.

"Wow, buddy, you impress me. You are not the sissy I thought you were," I shout.

Seeing me, he gets scared and turns to flee when a second car hits him.

Good Lord!

This time, he goes about twenty meters further in the air and crashes in front of the car. He's finished. He won't make it. I signal the driver to stay put, and I run to the corpse.

My goodness, he gets up again. He has an open fracture in his right leg. He shrieks with pain as soon as he puts any weight on it. I clench my jaw in disgust as I hear his femur crack.

"Listen, pal, you have to do something about your leg, your teeth, in short, your whole body."

But instead of admitting defeat and accepting his fate, this moron picks up the handbag from the ground and tries to run away by hopping on his left leg while the other drags behind him. Then, Jesus Christ! You'll never believe it. I laugh, but it's not funny. This sucker gets hit by a garbage truck. Life is hanging by a thread, huh? Or in his case, a ligament. One minute you're stealing a granny's purse, the next minute you're getting hit by two cars and a garbage truck.

You have got to be kidding. The bastard is crawling. He's now on the sidewalk and speeds up when he sees me coming.

"Will you die for the love of God?"

"Hunh... argh... huuuu..."

"Yeah, yeah. This is awful, isn't it, big guy? I mean, you're out on the lawn, you think nothing can possibly happen to you, but with your terrible luck, a Cessna will hit you in the face."

He's still crawling at my feet, thinking he has a chance to escape. I watch him with, I confess, a pinch of praise.

"Bud, if you had put that kind of dedication into studying and getting a decent job, you'd be a millionaire by now." I look at the purse. "Aren't you curious to see what's in it, if it was worth the trouble?"

"Fuuunng kiouuuu."

"I'll take that as a yes. So, what do we have here? Lipstick, tissues... Oh crap, maxi pads, for heaven's sake. Isn't she menopausal? Peppermints, of course. A senior citizen card, a McDonald's senior discount card, and, yes, a wallet. That's what you were after, you rascal, right? Okay, let's open it up. Credit cards, and a whopping... wait for it... twenty-one dollars in cash."

I scan him up and down, a smirk hanging on my face.

"You wouldn't have gotten far with that, would you, Clyde? Farther than you did with your torn-off leg, you might say. You got a point there, buddy."

Ambulance sirens blare as they approach. I tell the paramedics the entire story. They refrain from laughing, but our complicit looks don't lie. It's quite burlesque. If he survives, of course, what kind of monster do you think I am? If he dies, obviously it will be tragic. For his family, anyway. Although maybe not. What I'm trying to say is maybe his loved ones don't care for him, and that's why he is the way he is. I'm psychoanalyzing him live for you, so bear with me. He causes a lot of trouble to the paramedics by fidgeting to untangle himself, so much so that he wobbles the stretcher he's on and crashes face down on the pavement. His right leg is dangling in the middle of his back. He is crying like I rarely see anyone cry. I didn't think it was possible to be so unlucky in such a short amount of time. Finally, they get him into the butt of their ambulance, and they drive away. I just have time to wave at him. I can't guarantee it, but I'm pretty sure he motioned for me to go jerk off. It wouldn't be the dumbest idea ever, to be honest. On the way to give the granny her purse back, I think back to that miserable fellow on the stretcher bawling at each bump as he was being wheeled into the ambulance. Poor guy. He thought little of me laughing at his bad luck, but his ragged looks coupled with his bad luck were too much for me. That he is still alive after getting three consecutive bumpers to the face is a miracle.

Here is the grandma whining like a widow at her husband's funeral when she spots me coming in with her treasure. I hand it to her casually.

"There you go, Granny, it's all there."

"You are my hero."

"Yeah sure."

I am about to leave when she addresses me with her rough chain smoker's voice.

"This is for you."

Am I insane or is this fool handing me a quarter?

I look at the coin; I look at her.

"Really, Grandma? Really?"

She's digging in her purse to, I presume, reward me better. She searches a little too long for my taste.

"But—my gold watch is missing."

She stares at me, waiting for an explanation. Since I didn't pay too much attention to what she was doing, I say,

"What's that?"

"My gold watch. Where is it?"

"How am I supposed to know?"

"It was in my purse."

"Then it must still be there."

"I'm telling you it's not."

"So, the only logical explanation is that it's now at the Montreal General Hospital."

The old lady squints, as if trying to understand what I mean. I sigh.

"It's at the hospital," I repeat.

"My watch is at the hospital?"

She handpicks her words to show how absurd what I'm telling her is—how it makes no sense.

"No, I know, it sounds absurd. But yes, your watch is at the hospital, probably in the thieving bastard's pocket."

"You took it from me."

"I beg your pardon?"

"You took it from me, give it back."

I can't believe what I'm hearing. Fury is rising in me like a creeping syphilis.

"For lack of a better word, and with all due respect, are you completely stupid? Why would I steal your cheap ass watch?"

"To sell it."

I cross my arms and look down at her.

"You do realize I just ran three miles to catch the thug who stole it from you in the first place, and bring it back to you, don't you?"

"I don't give a shit. Give me my watch, you thief."

Now it's on like Donkey Kong. I return the favour.

"Listen to me, old fart, read my lips. I. Do. Not. Have. Your. Damn. WATCH!"

"I want my watch back."

"Piss off. Your filthy watch is at the Montreal General Hospital in the pockets of the thief who snatched your purse. Now get lost."

I leave her hanging, ignoring her distressed screeches, and then I hear the thunderous voice of a man in the distance. A mountain over another mountain. A hulking monster.

"Hey asshole, give her back her watch."

"I don't have her watch, for the umpteenth time. She's delirious."

"Her watch or it's gonna go south for you."

"I don't have it. Are you dumb or what?"

Well, I must admit I kind of regret saying that as soon as I do it. He puffs up his chest and lunges at me. The hell with that. I take off, too. It will be easier than trying to reason with him.

This is the last time I help an old lady. I swear to God, this is the last time ever.

TWO

After a day of practicing with her improv team at school, Lauriane Derome is hopping on her way home. She's becoming more and more confident that somehow, she'll be Samuel Blais's girlfriend. After all, didn't he choose her as his teammate when they needed to team up for one exercise? She doesn't want to get ahead of herself, because we're talking about the best-looking guy in school, but her heart races as she moves forward, a wide smile hanging on her lips. She's had scattered lovers, of course, but she's never experienced what she feels for him. Might as well say she has never felt true love. Life can be so sweet sometimes.

She got all fancy by putting on her makeup right before her improv class. Subtly enough that it didn't look obvious, but enough to make her look good. Her aunt, a makeup artist, gave her some pointers on how to enhance her features without looking like an embalmed corpse. Lauriane is the official makeup artist for her friends on all occasions. She will also be in three months when all these fine people will gather in their gowns for their graduation ceremony. And of course, for the graduation ball right after. In her wildest dreams, she and Sam would make a remarkable entrance arm in arm, to the guest's amazement, and the jealous gaze of her rivals.

Her mother suggested that her friends should pay her for

this, if only to cover the raw material cost, but Lauriane does it for fun. She loves to help and feels valued when her friends, on the verge of tears, swoon over the results. Often, they wrap their arms around her neck, thanking her a hundred times over. She has a certain know-how, but she does not wish to make a career out of it. She has always sought to be a lawyer. She's worked very hard to get her academic rating high enough to get into the university of her choice. To honour her father, a young lawyer who passed away when she was still in her mother's womb. By pursuing the same career as him, she wishes to pay tribute to him while feeling closer to him. She carries a picture of him in her wallet and talks to him often. She is not religious, but she asks for his help in the hardest times. She wears a white shirt, the top button carelessly undone, and a dark skirt. She ties her ashen hair in a ponytail behind her head, and she gets ready to stroll through the park, the last stretch to the apartment she shares with her mother.

She enjoys listening to Adele, her favourite singer, through the headphones she received for Christmas. She loves the British singer's powerful voice and was blown away by the 21 album. She pumps up the volume to soak up every note of the surrounding harmonies of the artist's melodies. Who knows? Maybe one day she'll take care of Adele's legal business? Lauriane has these thoughts that some would find unattainable, but she believes it is healthy to dream. She's a devoted positive thinker, and believes that by reflecting on positive thoughts, she reinforces her chances for them to happen. It comes from the cosmos, or whatever force is running our lives.

A little stiff wind makes her shiver, but the sunlight streaming through the tree branches like spotlights warms her bones. She would like to sing loudly, to scream her joy at having spent an hour with her beau, but she would look like a fool. So, she just smiles blissfully. She doesn't notice the motion behind her or the man who has been watching her for the last few seconds, hidden in the woods. She thinks she'll have a heart attack when a force grabs her from behind and lifts her firmly from the ground. She looks around to get help, but no one is around. She would scream if it weren't for the big hand crushing a rag over her face. She thrusts her heels backwards, hoping to hit something, but to no avail. The one holding her strongly in the air against him is quiet, besides the sound of his breath. Then, as if she's intoxicated, her sight blurs. Energy fades from her body; the trees of the forest melt into each other; her breathing becomes muffled, and she plunges into darkness.

The man holding Lauriane's inert frame in his arms drags her towards the wooded expanse. He has to be cautious since anyone could emerge from nowhere at any moment. He puts the young girl in an enormous case on wheels that he left in the woods, scans the surroundings one last time, then walks the few meters away to his truck in a clearing away from prying eyes. His accomplice waits for him patiently. He slips the massive suitcase in the back of the vehicle and settles on the passenger side whilst removing his ski mask. He puts the bottle of chloroform in the glove compartment and sticks the cloth soaked with the liquid in a *Ziploc* bag, as he was told to do. It's not in his nature to mess with people, but this is the job they hired him to do. It was too much money to refuse.

"What's in that suitcase?" his partner asks as he starts the engine.

"I told you, you ask too many questions. Just take us back to the house."

The accomplice presses gently on the gas pedal, and the truck heads towards the street, then increases speed to get to the junction where the driver will then turn right. The passenger breathes a long sigh of relief as the vehicle pulls onto the boulevard. Everything has gone well and will soon be over. At least, that's what the boss keeps saying.

THREE

I wear perfume, knowing what is coming. Philippe is not exactly subtle. I know he didn't ask me over for dinner for pleasure. He hasn't craved my company so far, and I certainly haven't sought his, so let's not kid ourselves. There's something fishy. I foresee this fish will be a hot chick, freshly showered, so that I can enjoy her at home. Please, don't make a big deal of it. I'm not the misogynist you imagine I am. It's my colourful language. Don't go snowflake on me. You'll ruin it.

Melanie, Phil's girlfriend, must have appreciated my extraordinary potential as a girlfriend in need of a real man, and thought, "You know who's a real man? The alpha male of alpha males? Martin Lafs." Like a farmer groping a bull's testicles to identify the best breeder for his herd, she got it right. Hand it to her. She has a knack for reading people. I would have paid good money to see Phil's face when she introduced the idea. Poor guy, reality must have hit him square in the face. He must have been so mad. To have such a hot boss would throw anyone off. I don't blame him.

I confess I can hardly wait to find out about the fat fuck dump. I can picture it: a functional video game chair, action figures still in their boxes that he will one day sell for 1% of the profit he thought he would earn when he bought them. I imagine half-eaten bags of potato chips lying around the apartment, and Melanie yelling at him to pick himself up and stop arguing with fourteen-year-olds while playing a debilitating video game online. And the floor. What can I say about the floor except that it will be carpeted with a grey industrial rug covering the piss stench of a cat marking its territory in every corner of the apartment. I gag as I imagine the latent litter smell that will reek through the kitchen as I am served a meal of warm, beige pasta with canned tomatoes poured over it.

I fucking hate canned tomatoes.

That's it. I don't want to go anymore. I will call to cancel. Damn it, I gotta see this horror of an apartment. I must see who they picked out for me. We'll see what they really think about me. You can judge what people think about you by the quality of the mating candidates they present to you. If Phil wants to keep his job, it better be someone hot. I'm not looking for a relationship, so I'm less picky. And I'm not expecting a Yvonne either, if you know who I am talking about. There's a middle ground. I ring the bell. She opens the door. Wow, Melanie made a genuine effort. She dressed up, and I must say she is far from disagreeable to look at. She smiles at me and does her best to pretend that it delights her to see me. I know you don't like me, Melanie. You're deceiving no one with your courtly grin and your straight teeth. I'll play along.

"Holy shit, Melanie, you look great tonight. Remind me why you're so into Phil?" I say, laughing like a donkey and pushing her in.

I'm almost sincere. Her smile morphs into an awkward grimace, and she stammers something I couldn't care less about as she shuts the door behind her. First thought? Not as drab as I expected. No fetid cat litter smell, and by the scent, I'd say Melanie cooked us meat. I thank all the gods in heaven that she's not one of those damn vegans. I'll take a quick look in the recycling bin later to see if there are any empty canned tomatoes.

"It smells fantastic," I say, scanning the place and casually handing her my coat as if she were a maid.

The melamine cabinets are aligned with the image I had of

the apartment. I watch Phil walk in, also poshly suited. They go all-in for the blind date.

"The rumour is true, Phil," I say, extending a limp hand. "You sure can dress up when you put your mind to it."

He looks at Melanie, begging for solace that won't come. I pat his shoulder with a solicitous hand, telling him I'm just kidding. Even though I'm totally serious. I know how to behave. You don't just show up and act like a jerk. Does the concept of diplomacy mean anything to you?

"Are you showing me around your apartment? Or should I say your rented flat?" I said, sneering like a lunatic.

"Oh, we bought the place, my dear," Melanie replies in a self-assured tone. "We purchased this condo ten years ago."

Congratulations on the condescending remark.

"What about you, Martin? When did you buy your apartment?" she says with an equally disdainful smile.

Bitch, she knows I'm a tenant. Well played.

"Is this the living room?" I say, pointing away to change the subject.

"Yes, follow me," Phil says in a deadpan tone.

Even if it kills me to admit, Phil's place isn't too crappy. Of course, Melanie decorated it, but it's nice. I think about my apartment and how it's a piece of shit. I've lost some of my enthusiasm, to be honest. Bummed out, to put it mildly, that I can't find anything to criticize.

I smile as I notice a cat popping out from behind the couch. I knew it. I shudder, thinking about all the naughty things Phil must put that feline through when Melanie is not around.

"Where's the chair?"

"What chair?"

"Come on now. The video game chair?"

Phil looks at me with a frown. "I don't have one."

I scowl to show that I don't understand what he means by "I don't have one".

"I don't have a video game chair. I'm not a gamer. I play

games once in a while, but I haven't picked up a game controller in eight months."

"Your hands are busy doing other stuff, aren't they?" I say, nudging him in the ribs, winking playfully.

"I don't get it," he says most seriously.

"I know you don't."

What? You don't either? Holy shit, I meant he's jerking off. Are you as slow as him, dammit?

Once I get to the dinner table, I only notice three place settings.

"She's already eaten?" I ask as I sit down.

Melanie stares at me, her eyes filled with incomprehension. "She?"

"Yes, the girl."

Phil and Melanie share a confused look for a few seconds. They're messing with me, those scoundrels. I sigh, irritated.

"The girl. The blind date. I guess you didn't invite me to chat about the weather."

Melanie leans forward, a weird look on her face.

"You thought it was a blind date? Really?"

"Yes, no. Actually, yes."

She bursts out laughing.

"What makes you think I hate someone enough to pull a stunt like that? "

I admit, she knows where to strike to hurt. I try to keep it together. She looks at me, eager for my reaction.

"Oh, you're waiting for an answer?" I said, stunned. "We all hate someone, don't we? Like you, Martine—"

"Melanie."

"Whatever," I said, grinning, "you don't really like me. So, you can hate people too."

"I don't hate you, Martin. It's just that—"

"That what?"

"Actually, it's something else."

"Keep talking?"

"It's what you think, but worse."

"Which means?"

A timer rings by the oven.

"Oops, I have to check on the food. I'm sorry."

She jumps up and hops off to the kitchen. I look at Phil, who couldn't be more bored if he was attending a knitting tournament.

"Saved by the bell, huh?" I say, giggling like a hyena.

He purses his lips and shakes his head. After having spoken about everything and nothing, eating a decent salad niçoise, and of a roast beef by God, delicious, Melanie gets to the heart of the matter.

"We didn't ask you to come here for a blind date, as you now know, but I wanted to talk to you about something very important. Before I do, I ask you to be open-minded. You don't need to give me an answer today."

Wait, they want me to impregnate her? Phil shoots blanks? I'll bet he does. That prick is impotent. Holy shit, this night won't be so bad after all. I'll do her in a New York minute, no sweat. I can do that for a friend. I've got my heart on my sleeve after all. The answer will be quick. It's yes.

Melanie stops talking and looks at me, puzzled. "Yes, what?" she asks.

"What?"

"You said the answer is yes."

"Did I say that out loud?"

"Yes."

"Shit, I'm losing it," I say, scoffing like an idiot. "But yes, I'm willing to do that for you guys."

"We haven't told you what it is we want yet."

I look at her, as if to say, "Stop beating around the bush, girl. You want my seed. I'll give it to you. I'm that generous."

I'm already thinking about all the positions I'll take her, so it won't be awkward. Will I be able to look Phil in the eye if I take her doggy style? Will Phil ever speak to me the way he used to if Melanie has an orgasm for the first time in her life?

"What exactly do you think I was planning to ask you?"

"Well, if you need me to say it, I'll get right to the point. You want the Martinator."

"The what now?"

"The Martinator. My cock. My sperm. You need my sperm."

Phil chokes on his wine. Melanie is speechless. A noteworthy feat in her case.

"A blind date, and now your sperm. What the fuck is wrong with you?" she says.

"If it's not that, what is it?"

"Oh my God," she says, burying her face in her hands.

She looks at Phil and shakes her head.

"I can't do it Phil. Forget the whole thing. It makes no sense."

"Ask him anyway. We'll see."

"I can't trust Josiane's hopes to that jerk."

"I can hear you, you know?" I say, aggrieved.

They ignore me.

"I'll be working on this as well. Come on. As soon as the initial shock wears off, he'll be okay. You'll see. That's the way he is. Get past his first reaction."

I grab my plate and stand up.

"While you're talking about me as if I'm not here, I'll get a refill, if you don't mind. Cool? Alrighty then."

I head for the roast beef casserole warming up in the oven, toying with the idea of leaving, pretending this shitty evening never happened. Thinking that I cancelled an invitation to spend the night with one of my girlfriends, thinking that I would have something better to do tonight. The proverbial "a bird in the hand is worth two in the bush" has never been truer. I eat another portion of roast beef while listening to them debate my case. I've already rolled my eyes thirteen times so far. Good Lord, what a drama.

"You know I can just walk away and forget the whole thing. I'm totally fine with that. I'll just have another serving of roast beef to take out."

"Stay right there," Melanie commands me.

I shrug and go for a second piece of that juicy meat. I'll have to ask for her recipe, which will complement my collection of things I'll never cook. But just knowing it's there keeps the hope alive that one day I'll actually do it. After about fifteen minutes, they turn back to me.

"I guess there's no harm in telling you why we asked you here. My friend Josiane's daughter has been missing for five days. The police are working the case, but Josiane doesn't feel it's a priority for them."

"Pfff, no kidding," I say with my mouth full, spraying some brown sauce on the white tablecloth in front of Melanie's panicked eyes.

"So," she says, "she's wondering if there's anything you and Phil can do to help."

"Sure, she can come by the office. We're taking on new clients. Phil will take care of it."

My mouth is still full. I can't seem to finish a bite without popping another one into my mouth. It's delicious.

"She's a little desperate, so—"

"Say no more. She needs the Martinator."

Melanie throws her arms in the air.

"You and your shitty Martinator."

I was going to make an anal sex joke, but I restrain myself.

"If she doesn't want the Mart—This. What does she want?"

Philip straightens up in his chair.

"We are hoping that the firm will take the issue pro bono."

Stunned, I stare at them both. "That we what now?"

"That we work pro bono on this one."

"Pro bono? You know I hate U2."

Philippe stares at me mischievously, not sure if I'm bullshitting him or if I'm serious.

"Wait, you don't know what pro bono means?"

"Yes, of course I do. Who do you think I am? I was just kidding."

Like you, I don't know what it means. No need to pretend you do, it's OK. Don't feel bad about it.

"So, do you accept?"

I'm trapped. I have little choice.

"Yes, I do."

I watch their reaction; they are happy. Melanie suddenly develops a new affection for me. We are far from her harsh retorts from a few minutes ago. She thanks me and goes aside to call her friend. I assure them it's nothing. It's normal. Phil looks at me with a pleasantly surprised look. It worries me. What have I gotten myself into? What is this pro bono bullshit? Once Melanie is back at the table, ready to open a bottle of Mumm Napa champagne, I excuse myself and head to the bathroom. I grab my smartphone and type "what does pro bono mean" into Google.

It loads.

Well, that's it... blah blah blah... short for the Latin term pro bono publico... OK... blah blah blah... non-interested commitment—That's true, I'm not interested—blah blah blah... VOLUNTEER? Son of a bitch.

"Are you okay, Martin?" the traitor Melanie, asks from the dining room.

"I'm fine."

I hear Phil snicker.

"I think he just figured out what pro bono means."

FOUR

I'm still pissed that Phil has played me for a fool. I had too much arrogant pride to ask what pro bono meant, and now I'm stuck working for free for a woman that won't sleep with me in return.

That's not the kind of bullshit I started my private investigator business for, believe me. I wanted to make money and retire at a young age to an island paradise, John McAfee style. To bleach my hair and ride around on my boat armed with three Kalashnikovs. Working pro bono won't get me any closer to my goal, quite the contrary.

I'm sitting at the café near the office, brooding over my misfortune. This coffee factory that allows me to observe the patrons as a microcosm of society. You can meet all kinds of people in a thirty-minute horizon: the harried businessman who spits out his order while talking on his cell phone, the careerist who treats the clerk as if he were his minion, the student who drinks a latte she can't afford, the hipster who wears a toque in the middle of the summer and doesn't even like coffee, but thinks it's cool to be part of the gang by hanging out in this sad place. Coming here is the equivalent of smoking when you were young. You don't know why you do it; you know it's probably not good for you, but everybody does it and you want to be cool, too. I like coffee, and I don't give a shit about being cool. Yes, I know, you roll your eyes thinking no one is cooler than me. I would never dare to say it myself, but I won't argue with you. I'm sipping my cappuccino and moping around when a young woman draws my attention as she desperately tries to take a selfie, pretending to drink her coffee. By desperately, I mean she is on her thirtieth attempt to take a satisfying selfie. She brings her cup to her mouth, extends her other arm as she turns the camera of her phone towards her, puts down her coffee, evaluates the result, shakes her head, and tries again.

I don't think there's anything more pathetic than this contemporary spectacle. I have nothing against a quick selfie to show friends where you are. Some people have this irrepressible need to tell others about their every move. But when you're still trying to take the perfect selfie after fifty attempts, it's just sad. Give up, do something else. It's obviously not for you. I get it, she's lonely. As lonely as I am right now. And her goal is to portray herself as someone living her best life on social media. Look at me, see how happy I am, with my coffee, surrounded by friends. She wants to trick her followers into thinking it's a candid photo, and push the obnoxiousness to the point of using the #LifeIsBliss hashtag.

Another attempt, another failure.

"Keep it up, you'll get a good one soon," I tell her, giggling like an idiot.

She turns towards me, insulted.

"I beg your pardon?"

"How many times have you tried? Forty, fifty times?"

"Go fuck yourself, old man."

The ugly girl goes back to her phone after staring at me as if she was hoping to kill me with her eyes. I lied to you. She's not ugly at all, she's beautiful and she knows it. I'd do her right now, but all that artifice makes her ugly. She's ugly on the inside, you understand? After another ten minutes of watching her, totally discouraged by her failures, I say: "Do you want me to try? Maybe it will be less complicated?" She turns once again, staring at me, and that's when it happens. Her eyes get sad. She looks down for a few seconds, tightens her lips and tells me that yes, it wouldn't be such a bad idea after all. Suddenly, I feel sympathy for her.

I stand up and position myself in front of her, working a forty-five-degree angle. I ask her to move to her side, to get a little more into the sunlight. "That's it, my pretty. Give me more, come on. Make love to the camera, swallow it all, I mean, your coffee. Yes, that's it, baby." Sometimes I think I'm a professional photographer, you know? Maybe it has something to do with the "ten ways to take a perfect selfie" article I read in a woman's magazine, which I memorized for some reason. I have this immutable knack for retaining garbage for absolutely no good reason. I hand her the phone, and she browses through the dozen pictures I took. Then her face lights up. She has found the Holy Grail. She looks at me as if I were a frozen Leonardo Di Caprio in the ocean, giving her the wooden plank in Titanic. I saved her life.

"Thank you very much, sir."

"Martin."

"Thank you very much, Martin."

She says it with a slightly teasing eye. Her name is Anne-Marie. I smile at her and wish her a good day. I could have tried to invite her back to my apartment for a quickie, but the pro bono thing has messed up my mood since yesterday, so I'm not particularly fat, dumb and happy, if you know what I mean. I wave my hand at the clerk, who looks at me with disgust. Fuck him. My cell phone vibrates in my pocket, and, as usual, I take three seconds to figure out what's going on before I answer. It's Nicole and her hoarse ex-smoker's voice, expressing with far too much enthusiasm that Josiane Derome is waiting for me at the agency.

The pro bono girl.

I see a Greyhound bus in the distance, and I suddenly feel like running with all my might to get on it and let it take me God knows where. Anything not to deal with this weeping chick at the office. Especially since it's probably just about an ungrateful teenage girl who got her kicks by running off with a bum, just like in the movies. She plays Bonnie and Clyde, just long enough to realize that it's not as cool as she thought it was, and she'll come back, low key, to her privileged life.

I've finally come to my senses and look at the woman bawling in front of my very eyes. I'm on the verge of a nervous breakdown as I watch her snot menacing to spill out onto my leather captain's chair that I snagged at a bargain basement store in Rosemont. I slide a box of tissues towards her to urge her to stop demolishing the work of art on which her quite nice butt is sitting. It's funny how you can throw tissues at a woman for totally different reasons depending on the situation. I tap my fingers on my desk as I sigh loudly, just to make her stop her whining and get to the point. I have little time for that. Normally, I would say I get paid by the hour, but that's not the case here. I don't get paid at all.

Shit, don't make me think about it. If you knew the rage this puts me in…

"She's my little girl. She disappeared six days ago. I swear to you, Mr. Lafs, this is not—"

"Martin."

"I beg your pardon?"

"Call me Martin. If you keep calling me Mr. Lafs, it will annoy the reader in ways you can't imagine. So please, call me Martin."

My tone of voice is anything but cordial. Behind Derome, I see the acrimonious looks Nicole gives me. I signal her to get off my back with an angry wave of my hand, and I continue to listen to the tearful woman's story. She swears her daughter is not the kind of person to leave with no news; they are very close; the father died a long time ago. I stop drawing concentric circles in my notepad to write "Daddy issues". She tried to call her several times on her cell phone, no answer. And as of yesterday, her voice mail is full. That never happens.

"Maybe she lost her phone. I don't know," I say with the detached demeanour of someone watching a B-Movie.

Josiane stares at me as if I just said something outrageous. A teenager, living for more than an hour without her cell phone? What, am I crazy? She has a point. I ask her to continue.

"Her friends haven't seen her in days. They are as concerned as I am. And given that there are already two missing young girls in the last few weeks, it's alarming."

"You know, there are teenagers missing every day. Nothing unusual."

"It's not my daughter's style."

"I've heard that a lot, too," I say, giggling.

I am referring to my former mothers-in-law, none of whom understood what the apple of their eye was doing with a guy like me. Mothers-in-law are a drag. Josiane doesn't appreciate my half-assed joke, so I ask her to go on as I glance at a watch I forgot to put on this morning. I'm three-and-a-quarter hairs away from kicking her out.

"I've been to the police, but I don't feel they consider this with any urgency. They're treating her disappearance as a fool-hardy escapade."

"Assholes, it's anything but that," I say, standing up with a theatrical gesture.

I know I'm contradicting myself from one second to the next, but when it comes to making cops look bad, you know me; I have no pride. I walk slowly in a circle asking questions she assures me she has already answered with Philippe. It pains me to admit I haven't read her interview report. I look over to Phil's office and see him huddled on the edge of his door while he enjoys a breakfast burrito. I give him a bemused grin.

"When was the last time you saw," I open the file "Lauriane?"

I just learned her name. That tells you all you need to know about my interest in this case, doesn't it?

"When she left school last Friday."

I count on my fingers like a jackass who would have dropped out of school at twelve.

"So, it's been six days."

She looks at me in dismay. She doesn't need to say more. I

know that she already told me that before. I really need to listen when people talk to me. It's embarrassing. I remember hearing about the missing teens on the news, but I didn't really pay attention, but now I'll have to learn more about them.

"What do the police say?"

"That she'll come back, that they all do that at least once. They fall in love with a small-time punk, and have a fling, and then come back when the guy messes with them."

I must admit it shakes me to my core that they told her exactly what I think. I have to snap out of it. I'm getting sloppy like these fucking state servants. I rub my hands together, seeing the opportunity to make them look bad. I now have a motivation. If her disappearance were to be linked to a human trafficking ring, and I were to dismantle this criminal organization, you have no idea how I would strut in front of these incompetents to shove their deep ineptitude up their ass.

I laugh. Oh, am I laughing. God, I almost have a hard-on.

"Uh, Lafs?"

Phil is in my office doorway. I realize I was giggling out loud like a madman. Josiane looks at me, dumbfounded. Nicole doesn't know where to stand.

A dead silence.

I clear my throat and sit down. I speak in a calm tone of voice.

"Mrs. Derome, it will be my pleasure to take your pro bono bullshit."

I offer her a hand that she ignores.

"I'm going to find your kid."

She cries again. Phil looks at me with the corners of his mouth upwards. Good God, is he smiling? Nicole sits back down, huffing and puffing as if she's just figured out the ending to her soap opera.

That's fine, but where do I start?

FIVE

I wait for my ham and cheese sandwich, thinking about Josiane Derome. Something about her obsesses me. Is it her perfect body? Her bouncy ass or her generous breasts? No, there's something about her face, but I can't quite figure it out. Anyway, it wouldn't look good to sleep with her right now, would it? I'm not the monster you imagine. I have a certain decorum. It's variable from situation to situation, I agree, but I have it. After crossing the street without getting killed, a significant feat in Montreal, I am about to enter my office building when I hear something horrible, the sound that irritates me the most deeply in the world: a harmonica. And I know very well who is behind this shitty sound.

Marcel Lafleur.

Curiosity prevails over logic, and I step into the alley between the two buildings. He's there, leaning against the brick wall, with his grimy lips brushing his rusty musical instrument, or rather, his instrument of torture.

"I hear you work pro bono?" he says without looking at me, a trickle of drool stretching from his lips to his harmonica.

I feel like throwing up. How does this jerk know what pro bono means? Is this a joke? Am I the only one on this fucking planet who didn't know that?

"What do you want, Lafleur?"

"To help you."

For the record, Marcel Lafleur is the owner of the Flower PI agency (yes, I know, it's a terrible business name coined by a collective of fourth graders) who always wanted to partner up. He wants to stand next to the master and learn. I'm not bragging, that's what he told me. Well, not necessarily in those terms, it sounded more like "joining forces", but that's what it meant. You'll agree.

"How many times do I have to tell you I work solo? I don't need partners, especially not one with Tourette's syndrome."

The problem is that Lafleur yells expletives or, should I say, citrus names.

"I have this very well under control."

I cross my arms and smile.

"You do?"

"Yes."

"..."

"..."

"LEMON."

"There it is," I say, laughing.

I am about to leave him hanging when he throws a bomb at me.

"Are you working on the three girls' case?"

I come back to him, looking suspicious.

"What are you talking about?"

"The three missing teenagers."

"What do you know about them?"

He looks at me, realizing that I know less than he does.

"Enough to help you. Come on, let's work together on this one, Lafs."

I am about to refuse when the devil on my left shoulder appears: "Come on, it's pro bono. Let him do the dirty work. If he wants to work for free, why do you care?"

I admit it right off the bat. I don't.

I consult my watch-less arm, then look at him with a sigh.

"Go to Phil. Tell him what you know about the three girls. It's probably not related, but we can't rule anything out."

He takes off running toward the office, arms in the air like Rocky climbing the stairs at the Philadelphia Museum of Arts. What a jerk! I chuckle as I go the other way. I pass a beautiful woman who comes my way. She has that smug look of those who've figured out that men will do almost anything in the book to screw her.

"Good morning. Delightful afternoon, isn't it?" I say.

"Go fuck yourself."

"Right away, thank you."

She goes on her merry way, and I go on mine, trying to pick up the bits of self-esteem that I have left. Not a fan of the weather, obviously. Back at the office, I come close to spitting out my coffee when I see Phil's helplessness against Lafleur's overflowing energy. Nicole listens to them with a keen interest while pretending to sort out the same pile of sheets for half an hour. Lafleur yells citrus names like he does every time he gets hyper-excited, and I drink my coffee while watching Phil with a mischievous smile. You tried to make me work for nothing to impress your chick, pal? Suck it up. I enter Phil's office and put my exquisite butt in the chair next to Marcel Lafleur, who doesn't see me coming.

"One of them is Lea Briand, sixteen years old. Blonde with blue eyes. She studies at the Saint-Henri high school and... GREEN LIME—I startle him when he sees me sitting next to him —you scared me, Lafs."

I signal him to continue.

"Lea is not your typical serial runaway, so her parents think something bad has happened to her."

"Or she really ran away," I say, taking a sip of coffee.

They both shrug, and I rub my temples. I'm in big trouble with these two idiots.

Lafleur continues:

"The other teenager, Rashida Lafleur—"

"Ha ha!" I yell mockingly.

"No relation."

I look at him, wanting to say, "stop messing with me, man."

"Clementine," he whispers.

"What do you mean?"

"I'm not related to Guy Lafleur, but I would still look for him if he was missing."

Tears come to my eyes as I think about this national hero. He is a monument, this man. His goal against the Boston Bruins in 1979 was simply masterful. Of course, if he vanished, everyone would go out of their way to find him. It's just a fact of life. I take the last sip of a coffee that has become cold from not drinking it. I grimace, and I look at Phil, who is waiting for me to finish so he can hear the rest.

"OK, and what's Rashida's deal?"

"Also sixteen, high school senior, blonde with green eyes, tall and slender, athletic. Has never run away from home before. Her relatives are mortified. President of her class, many friends, loving parents and... ORANGE... no reason to run away."

"When was the last time they heard from her?"

"The 16th."

"About eight weeks ago," I quickly calculate in my head.

"Two months," he says, correcting me.

I'm going to rip the cantaloupe off his shoulders.

"Why isn't anyone talking about this?" I ask, really caring about the explanation.

Lafleur scratches his head.

"It's getting people talking. And if we spread the word that there's another—"

"… blonde teenager missing," I say.

"... right," he replies, offering me a high-five that goes unanswered.

Once Lafleur leaves with the task of getting the story out to the media, his brother-in-law works on The Gazette's dog-eat-dog column. I give Phil my most wicked smile.

"You didn't think it would go down like that when you ambushed me, did you?"

He frowns.

"Ambushed you?"

"You know very well what I mean."

He scratches his head and smiles.

"Because you didn't know what pro bono meant, I'm dishonest?"

I admit I didn't think before I spoke.

"No, because... uh... Melanie's dinner was scrumptious, so you—"

There's that shit-eating grin again.

"Fuck you, Phil."

SIX

I drive like a madman and Josiane Derome grabs anything for dear life. She has asked me at least fifteen times to slow down, but I dismiss her with an impatient wave of my hand.

"I was the undisputed champion of the St. Edmond Karting Club two years in a row when I was a teenager, missy, so I think—"

"Watch out!"

I narrowly avoid a jerk who has double-parked on our right.

"Can you please, for the love of God, slow down, Martin?"

I may have overestimated my driving skills a bit like a young douchebag in a jacked-up Honda Civic. My heart beats loudly in my chest like a John Bonham drum solo on acid. The rest of the drive is more respectful of official speed recommendations. I am furious with that asshole Guy Lefebvre, the Montreal police sergeant. I asked Phil to come by and ask about what they have on the Lauriane Derome case. You'd think they'd be happy to have us help them, especially since they don't seem to give a damn, and our involvement frees them from an insistent and weepy mother. But no, Lefebvre is being a jerk again, throwing roadblocks at us. And let's be honest, Phil is not like a pit bull who would rather die than give up his bone. I am. It's going to be a bumpy ride. I'll tell you that.

I storm into the police station and demand to see Lefebvre.

"Well, he's here," says the cop at the reception desk.

"Of course, he's here. Where else would he be? In the field doing his job?" I reply, cackling like a brontosaurus.

Lefebvre rolls his eyes when he sees me in the waiting room. Then his face contorts in fear when he recognizes Josiane behind me. He suddenly loses his swagger.

"What can I do for you?" he asks in a voice that would have been mellow if he wasn't such a douchebag.

"Do your job, or else get out of our way," I say in a nasty tone.

I can see that he wants to jump to my throat, but he keeps himself under control in front of the civilian.

"What are you talking about?"

I approach him.

"Are you going to keep us on the doorstep as if we were a bunch of Jehovah's Witnesses on a Saturday morning, or will you let us in out of respect for this woman who is going through a horrible ordeal?"

Yes, I know. I'm happily rubbing it in, using the grieving mother to stifle him. What is he going to do? Chase us away? I don't think so. He sighs heavily and nods for us to join him. Josiane follows in my footstep, speechless.

"Where is your darling? What's his name again... Morin?"

"Go fuck yourself," says Lefebvre in a low voice.

"I beg your pardon?"

"I said help yourselves."

He extends his hand to invite us into a tiny interview room.

"That's what I thought," I say, looking defiant.

"Can I get you coffee, a bottle of water?" he says, looking at Josiane.

"A black coffee, thank you."

"I'll have a cappuccino too, but with a drop of milk."

He leaves the room mumbling. I thought I heard him say, "I'm going to shove it up your ass", but maybe I misunderstood.

Josiane looks at me, puzzled. I gently pat her shoulder with a reassuring smile.

"You don't like each other, do you?" she says.

"Not so much, but that's not important. What is important, however, is to know what they have collected so far."

"Precisely," she says, staring at the ground, "I'm afraid it won't work because of your feud."

You must hand it to her. Despite her angelic allure, Jojo doesn't sugar-coat it one bit. Lefebvre comes back with, obviously, only one cup of coffee in his hands that he gives to the tearful woman while looking at me with a malicious glance.

"You wanted nothing, right, Lafs?"

I hiss an insult between my teeth, but don't bother.

Lefebvre explains, or should I say, lectures us, that they don't really have anything more than they did a few days ago, that for them, Lauriane ran away until proven otherwise, but assures us they are walking the streets with the pictures of the runaways and keeping an eye open as they always do.

"In short, you do nothing thinking that she will go back home, right?"

"That's not what I said," Lefebvre replies, squirming in his chair.

"That's exactly why Mrs. Derome hired us, to—"

"Hired you?" Lefebvre says with a sarcastic demeanour. You're not doing this pro bono?

I stand up straight, formal.

"You'll learn, dear friend, that many famous lawyers work pro bono. That's called having a heart, man. A concept that eludes you, considering that you're incapable of doing your job, even when you're paid for it, so I can imagine how you'd be dragging your feet if you weren't. But I'm made of a different cloth, little guy. The one that they made the great ones of—"

"I'm going to cry, Lafs."

I was about to compare myself to Martin Luther King, Gandhi and Mother Teresa, so I'm slightly annoyed that I didn't get to do that. My speech was brilliant. I'll save it for another time.

"So, if you don't want to work on it, give us the information you have so far, and we'll take it from here. You can go back to dealing with purse snatchers and solve nothing, as usual."

Josiane speaks up, realizing that we would spit on each other's faces for hours. She puts on a show, tears sliding down her cheeks, her hands trembling, her eyes imploring.

And the Oscar for the best actress of the year goes to...

For the first time since I've had the displeasure of knowing him, I see a chink in Lefebvre's armour.

"Listen, Mrs. Derome. I understand your pain. Believe me, I do. But there are, year in and year out, between ten and twenty teenagers running away from home every day. And over nine out of ten go back home after a while."

"We're going to do more than just keep an eye out, Lefebvre. We're going to comb every corner of the city, we're going to talk to everyone on the street, we're going to—"

"Oh yes, with the help of the alcoholic hanging out in front of your office?" he says, interrupting me a second time.

Is that jerk talking about Serge? My Serge? You can say what you want about me. I can take it. You can say what you want about Phil, too. He doesn't care, but Serge? Oh, no sir, that doesn't fly.

A huge fight ensues and Josiane tries to reason with us, but she can't do anything. We are both standing, pointing at each other with our index fingers, shouting. All the rage I've built up over the years of putting up with this Guy Lefebvre crap finally comes out. I scream at him everything I've ever hoped to say, everything I've ever imagined myself saying to him when I was at home talking to myself in front of a mirror after having had one too many glasses of Scotch.

All the while, I know for a fact that this is not the time or place to do this, that I am destroying the little bond of trust I have with Josiane. I can see the look on her face as if to say, "who the hell is that dumb fuck?" I know that she bitterly regrets having me on her side, even for free. At this point, she is firing me with her acrimonious sigh. I understand I am not serving my cause, but I can't help it. I'm trolling Guy Lefebvre; I'll deal with the consequences later. I am trolling him at the expense of Lauriane and Josiane. I am aware of that. Then the door of the room opens with a bang. It's Lieutenant Tremblay. Lefebvre's boss.

"What the hell is going on here? What the fuck is wrong with you, you morons?"

We stop talking. I realize that I'm so close to Lefebvre's face that I could kiss him. The thought of it makes me retch violently. Tremblay sees Josiane behind me.

"And in front of a civilian, too? Are you nuts or what?"

We look at the floor without saying a word, like two kids caught with their hands in the caramel jar. He orders us to follow him into his office. The common room, where the other investigators' offices are located, is deathly silent. They stare at us, giggling like idiots. It's awkward for me, but I can't imagine the shame Lefebvre must feel right now. I give a comforting glance at Josiane, but she glares at me furiously. She doesn't understand. It's normal. She doesn't realize that Tremblay's intervention will provide us with what we want. Tremblay is a sensible guy, apart from the protection he gives to that idiot Lefebvre. I'm sure we'll come to an agreement. He asks her to wait for us in an empty room next to his office. I know I'm going to get the shit kicked out of me, and so is Lefebvre. Tremblay is terrifyingly calm. I wouldn't be so scared if he were yelling. He speaks in a calm but acid voice. He challenges our professionalism, condemns our inability to work with each other like adults. That we look like two morons in a pissing contest. I would win since I've got a leg up in the game. I explain the pro bono story, the mother's plight, and that I just want their help, so I don't start from the beginning. I say the right things in the right order, which I'm not familiar with, you'll agree. So much so that I can feel Lefebvre liquefying in his chair.

The way I present my request really makes him look like what he is, which is a complete idiot. I leave Tremblay's office thirty minutes later and signal to Josiane to follow me. She walks behind me angrily. Her step is intentionally heavy, so that I know she's furious and that our relationship ends right here. Sorry, my dear, but this is personal now. I want to find Lauriane, if only to shove it in Lefebvre's scumbag face. And anyway, I'm all she has. A heavy silence fills the cabin of my car as I drive her home. Once in front of her apartment building, she addresses me in a restrained voice, trembling with rage.

"Martin. I am extremely disappointed that you would rather harm my cause and put my daughter at risk for your own personal vengeance. This is incredibly reckless, and I can't—"

"We'll have it all tomorrow."

She looks at me, puzzled. "I'm sorry?"

I look at her with a tight smile.

"We'll have everything the police have on Lauriane's disappearance tomorrow. I knew what I was doing, Josiane. I'm sorry I put you through this, but it was the only way they would react."

She frowns.

"Or you could have simply gone over Guy Lefebvre's head and addressed Lieutenant Tremblay directly."

Indeed, that would have been smarter, but far less enjoyable.

SEVEN

The next morning, I can't take it. Not content to sit through Lefebvre's bullshit and fight the system, Phil finds nothing more interesting to do than wasting his time smoking and chatting with the homeless man near our building. First, who the hell still smokes these days? I mean, there aren't enough campaigns about the harmful effects of smoking for everyone to grasp? And no, your grandmother didn't smoke until she was eighty-five and still had pink lungs when she died. That's just your justification for shoving a pack of smokes daily in your face. I walk up to them, looking stern, and Serge, the homeless man himself, looks at me with a smirk. At least he looks in shape, which means he didn't gulp down a six-pack of Jack Daniels before daybreak.

"Speak of the devil," he says to Phil.

"Nice modern expression Serge," I say as I keep walking toward them. "I forgot, you're a hundred and thirty-nine years old."

"Still as charming as ever," he says to Phil, still ignoring me.

Phil shrugs, as he takes another puff of nicotine. Man, do I enjoy when they talk about me like I'm not there. For those of you not so quick on the uptake, I'm being sarcastic.

"Glad you're with us Serge. Are you running out of money to drink yourself silly?"

"Why are you so jumpy this morning, Lafs? Don't worry, I'm simply waiting for the liquor store to open."

"That's the spirit."

Serge giggles like a donkey. You have to hand it to him; he is very hard to insult. On the other hand, what could I throw at him that would be worse than his life? I am about to walk away when I hear his hoarse voice telling me something. I'll never learn. My curiosity will be my undoing. I turn back to the two jerks.

"What's that?"

"Did you find Lauriane already?"

I glare at Phil.

"Have you tipped off the entire town, Phil? Didn't we agree to play it cool?"

He frowns.

"We literally never said that. Besides, in what universe would that make sense? If anything, we want as many people as possible to know about it and to look for her with. Imagine how the cops will look if we find her before they do."

The struggle I wage against the rising corners of my mouth is arduous. The bastard is right. I approach Serge. He might be useful after all. That damn bearded man has a lot of contacts in the city. That's the only reason I tolerate him around here.

"Listen, Serge, if you have two minutes to spare," I say this sentence without laughing, "I think it would be a good idea for you to keep an eye out for the girl. I assume Phil has already given you her picture?"

Serge strokes his shaggy beard, as if he were really thinking.

"Okay, but I want fifty per cent of what you get for this warrant."

"You can go fuck yourself—"

I stop. It's pro bono. He can have one hundred per cent of zero, after all. But the smile on his face shows he knows about it. He said that just to taunt me.

"I know you know it's pro bono, Sergio."

He frowns.

"That it's what?"

His face gradually changes, turns scarlet, and then the two jerks laugh so hard they slap their thighs.

"Bunch of nitwits."

"I'm serious Martin, tell me what it means. Does it have anything to do with U2?"

He spews out his last line with great difficulty while trying to catch his breath. He laughs so hard he can't hardly breathe. Anyway, if it can bring him some joy in his shitty life, I'll have contributed to something. I rush into the office building front door, overhearing them asking me not to get angry, that they're just pulling my chain. As I climb the stairs, I realize I'm the only one in town who didn't know what the hell that Latin word meant.

———

Phil puts his arm around Serge's shoulder. They both wipe away their tears as they do everything in their power to regain their composure.

"See what I told you, huh?"

Serge has an admiring pout.

"You know your boss well."

"That's the thing about Martin. If you make him think it's his idea, he'll go for it. But if you suggest the same idea, he'll stare at you like you're the biggest asshole on earth and dismiss it outright."

Phil hears someone shouting citrus names in the distance.

"Lafleur, what brings you here?"

"Is the boss here?"

"He's licking his wounds in his office," Phil says, pointing to the second floor of the building.

Marcel Lafleur propels himself over there, shouting "grapefruit" with all his might. Serge stares at Phil, flabbergasted.

"I'll never get it. Why shouting citrus fruits?"

"No idea, man."

They decide Serge will talk to his contacts in town. Someone has definitely seen the girl. If she ran away, someone must know where she is.

Nicole stiffens when she hears "tangerine" as Lafleur climbs the stairs. Her motherly spirit takes on a life of its own every time she bumps into him, even though he's older than her. He is so sweet and vulnerable. She would take him in her arms and cradle him. When Lafleur turns the corner to enter the office, he smiles.

"Splendid Nicole, it's been a while."

She blushes. "Not really. I saw you last week."

"That's what I mean, way too long," Lafleur says, proud of his retort.

Even if she knows his reply is intended, Nicole looks at the floor like a glowing schoolgirl.

"Hey ho, get a room!"

Lafs's voice rattles her. He comes out of the bathroom, still securing his pants while walking to his office.

"For God's sake, Martin, please get dressed before you get out of the bathroom."

"I don't have time, Nicole. You know me, always on the run."

"Of course, two more seconds would be too much." Nicole says, looking at Marcel Lafleur.

He grins. Lafs signals him to come into his office.

I sit back and sigh in despair, unsure of what I'm up against. Life in general, I suppose. Probably also at Lafleur for his body of work. He heard that the other two girls have a similar profile to Lauriane Derome, top of the class, popular with their peers and teachers, pretty, blonde, between 5'5 and 5'7.

"As if the guy has a specific type," I say, scratching my chin.

"Lemon, boss, you are good," Lafleur says, whistling admiringly.

That's what's bothering me about Lafleur. Besides the fact that he calls me boss, I never can tell if he's fucking with me or if he's serious. He always has a shit-eating grin on his face. He talked to his brother-in-law from the newspaper's crime section. He's interested in the story. He wants to meet me. But why does everyone always want to meet with me? Don't they understand how much I hate humans in general with grand passion? Nature did not privilege Marcel Lafleur, to say the least. Apart from his fixation on citrus fruits, he is short; he has a limp in his right leg because it is shorter than the other. He has a huge wart on the left side of his nose, or on the right side, if you are facing him. He gets bald but insists on keeping some kind of crown that goes around the back of his head, circa your grandfather in the seventies. But he's happy. You've seen no one happier than him in your entire life. A permanent smile on his face, the playfulness of a demented spaniel. There's nothing you can throw at him that'll get him down. I think that's why he pisses me off so much. He underlines my misery.

The son of a bitch.

EIGHT

Waiting by myself in a meeting room at the police station, I look at the electronic equipment as I tap the wooden table with my index finger. If you are wondering where your taxes go, the vast majority of them go here. I know because I had my conference room done at the office, and I couldn't afford this kind of gear. You will argue that I don't get any tax dollars; you are not wrong. You'll also state that I should get some; again, you're spot on. Can't you see we are made for each other, you and me? I wonder what they want from me, and why they asked me to come here. Does Lieutenant Tremblay want to go back on his promise to grant me access to the Derome file? If so, I won't let him get away with it. I will not accept any concessions whatsoever. I've already put in way too much bono time to give it all up. OK, you're right, I have put little effort yet, but the cops don't need to know that. Phil wanted to come with me, but I was told to show up by myself. At least, that's what I told him. Phil has the misconception that we are equals in this agency. Like two partners who invested fifty per cent each in money. Sometimes I have to put him back in his place, bless him.

Partners? That's hilarious.

I text Josiane, asking her to be ready. If I must pull the tearful mother card again, I'll do it. No one can resist a whiny mother sniffing like a Saint Bernard. I stiffen as I see the three men enter the room. There's Tremblay and Lefebvre, of course, but also, Mayor Jean "call me Johnny" Ouellet. Some call him The Big O because he thinks he's bigger than the Olympic Stadium. Others, more cynical, call him The Big Zero. You can guess which side I'm on. Personally, I've always had a good relationship with the municipal magistrate. I won't pretend that I hang out with him regularly, but I run into him occasionally and I thought he was the only one who didn't look at me like a parasite. However, in the last few months, I guess he ended up thinking he really was The Big O. He's much haughtier, suddenly treating me like crap. Actually, no, it's worse. He ignores me. He rules the city like a king and master, a surprising change of heart. He is far too extravagant, and far too tanned. He looks like a poor man's George Hamilton. Young people, check the Internet to see who I'm talking about. Google is your friend, after all. Plus, he smiles too much with his ultra-bleached teeth that, I assume, are soaking in a glass of water at night with a Polident capsule. Again, youngsters, you'll want to search on Google for Polident. I will not educate you in every subject, right?

"Please, give me the address of your tanning salon, Mr. Mayor," I say with a chuckle as he sits down on my left.

I extend a hand, which he ignores. Is it just me or is the mood shitty? Even Lefebvre is impassive, a rarity in my presence.

"Martin, the mayor wants to know what is going on with Lauriane Derome's disappearance. That's why you're here today because I told him that the mother hired you."

"Indeed," I say. "We want to see if there is a link between her disappearance and that of some other girls."

I hear an unpleasant hiss to my left. I understand it is the mayor, who looks away sarcastically. Okay, I don't mind a scant of decorum and playing the politic game, but don't get overly cocky. I let it go, but I can already feel rage growing in me. After stating what they have, which is nothing I didn't already know from reading the documents they gave me, they look at me. It's awkward because I haven't progressed that much. I'll have to improvise.

"Our team is on the ground scouring all the places where runaways normally hang out. Probably one of the three girls—"

"What girls?" The Big O says, rudely interrupting me.

I give him a sinister glare. Is he making fun of me, or am I being a little too touchy?

"Yes, the three teenage girls who have gone missing lately."

The mayor pouts with bewilderment. "I thought it was about Lauriane Derome."

"Lieutenant Tremblay opened the conversation by referring to young girls in the plural."

"Exactly," says the chief magistrate.

I must admit that I'm lost. I sink into my chair and sigh. I watch the lieutenant, looking for some kind of support that won't come. The mayor looks at me with a smile so arrogant I could rip his little head off with a baseball bat.

"You see what I mean, Tremblay?" he says, keeping his eyes on me. "He's incompetent. He doesn't understand shit. He can't even handle a simple discussion about missing girls. Yes, Lafs, several young girls. Why are you only focusing on three? Why ignore the others? Because they are not as pretty?"

Tremblay does not say a thing. He and Lefebvre look at me stoically.

I pick myself up. "It's really easy, Johnny. May I call you Johnny?"

"No, you may not."

"It's very simple, Johnny. All three disappeared in a short period; all three have a similar profile; all three look curiously alike, and when it's strange, I'm in."

I immediately regret the wording of my sentence. Lefebvre has a sly smile, and the mayor laughs like a piglet. A piglet that would have curled up in its own feces for hours, but a piglet, nonetheless. That would explain his permanent tan.

"No one doubts you get in on the act when things get weird, Lafs. But you're off the case. Tremblay, get this asshole out of here. I don't want to see him anymore."

"Should we call the mother, Johnny? Tell her you insist on

sidelining the detective who works for her pro bono? Do you want to show her just how shitty a decision you're making, putting her daughter's life at risk?"

The mayor leans in with his elbows on the table and looks into my eyes terrifyingly.

"Are you threatening me, Lafs? Would you be that stupid?"

I don't answer.

"Let's call her," he finally says, pushing the intercom towards me.

He signals Lefebvre to close the door.

"Come on, let's have some fun," he adds.

I dial the number slowly, feeling that something is fishy. I don't understand why he's so keen to call Josiane. It doesn't smell right. Upon hearing her feeble voice answer the phone, the mayor speaks up.

"Hello, Mrs. Derome, it's Johnny Ouellet again."

Again?

"I'm sorry to bother you, but Detective Lafs insists on burdening you once again. Lafs?"

The three men look at me and smile. The only sound in the room is the crackle of the line coming from the intercom. This is an ambush.

"H—hello Josiane," I stammer like a moron. "I just want to tell you that the mayor is asking me to withdraw from Lauriane's investigation. You and I both agree that this is irresp—"

"I agree with him."

A stab deep in my chest. I take a few seconds to wrap my head around it. Her tone is so dry, so stern. The mayor's triumphant gaze, and so is Lefebvre's, who offer me a condescending smile to boot.

"What's that?" I say, doing everything in my power to keep my heart from bursting out of my chest.

"I agree with him, Martin. Originally you weren't really excited about it, and the mayor told me you're not a good private eye, and that you will be more detrimental to the investigation than helpful. I apologize for the lack of finesse. He guaranteed he would put every resource available to find my daughter. Do you see what I mean? That's all I asked for in the first place. But if you want to be of help, I would be more than happy to—"

"Thank you, Josiane, that will be all. I'll get back to you with the progress of the investigation. As I told you this morning, I'll personally take care of it. Have a nice day."

He hangs up and looks at me, crossing his hands on the table.

"Any others you'd wish to call?"

Lefebvre laughs under his breath. I glare at him.

"You know just as well as I do you won't do a thing, right, Johnny? That's just talk, but you just want to take me out of the picture. Another promise you won't keep."

"How dare you question my laudable intentions?" he says, pretending to be offended, hand on his chest and all.

He smiles to make me understand I am right. That he won't do shit! That I can go fuck myself.

"I know you like to pretend to be a cop, Lafs. But you're not. Let the pros do their job and go back to dealing with husbands screwing their nannies."

Ouellet stands up, tying up his jacket. The discussion is over. I don't have the strength to fight. Josiane's right hook knocked me out.

"And besides," Ouellet adds before leaving, "why would I put any effort into helping a woman who didn't vote for me?"

He storms out of the room, followed by Tremblay. Lefebvre remains seated for a moment.

"I guess you agree with that?"

He purses his lips.

"A hundred per cent."

NINE

Lauriane Derome slowly opens her eyes, totally lost. Everything is blurred around her, and she cannot recognize where she is. She rubs her temples to get rid of the stabbing pain from her migraine. Is she in a hospital? What is this creepy place? The more time passes, the clearer things become. It is not a hospital, but a gloomy concrete room. She is lying on a bed that squeaks with every move she makes. Her heart races as recollections of the previous day's events come flooding back. The park, the force grabbing her from behind, then a blackout.

And now this.

She quickly braces herself against the wall behind her, kicking her feet into the mattress as if she is fighting something unseen. She takes a deep breath and blinks to best see what's around. She gasps when she spots silhouettes lying further away. She rubs her eyes to identify what they are. They look like shapes of sleeping teenagers. She glances at her hands and feet and realizes that nothing is binding her to her bed. Farther on, a thick chain lies on the floor with some kind of open collar at its end. Down the center of the room on her right is a huge, closed, metal gate. Lauriane quickly gets up to rush towards the door, but her legs give out, and she collapses heavily against the icy concrete floor. She winces in pain, and her eyes fill with tears. She rubs her scraped knee and carefully gets up to regain her balance. She wobbles, but eventually gets to her feet. She moves toward the door in measured steps, leaning against the wall. Her heart beats so fast that it soon becomes uncomfortable. As she stands in front of the huge grey metal door, she glances behind her at two sleeping teenage girls in white shorts and t-shirts. Lauriane wears her own clothes. It doesn't matter if she wakes these girls up, she must get out of here.

"Help! Please open the door!" she says, yelling and banging at the door.

It absorbs her blows with an insulting ease. The last blow induces a sharp pain in her right wrist.

"Fuck."

She screams again, but this time she stamps her foot on the door. In vain, as it's a thick door, obviously designed to resist shocks, and sealed tight enough that no sound can get through. This place looks like a dungeon. Lauriane panics, then jumps at the sound of a hoarse voice coming from behind.

"You're wasting your time. Nobody will come."

Lauriane backs up against the door, her eyes wide open. A girl of her own age sits up in bed, rubbing her eyes.

"We tried it all, believe me."

She is blonde, thinner than Lauriane, and she speaks with an impassive tone, typical of people who have given up. Lauriane wonders if she is on drugs. Otherwise, how can she be so calm?

The teenager smiles.

"Don't be afraid; we're all in the same boat," she says, pointing to the girl waking up next to her. She too is blonde, but with ginger highlights, and a small snub nose with freckles. She seems more fragile and shyer than the other girl.

"My name is Rashida Lafleur," says the first young blonde, "and she is Lea Briand."

Lauriane calms down a bit but keeps her distance. After a few seconds of staring at her, Rashida giggles.

"And you? What's your name?"

Lauriane looks around, scanning her surroundings.

"Lauriane. Lauriane Derome."

Rashida sits on the edge of her bed, letting her long legs sink to the ground.

"Well, poor Lauriane, I'm afraid we are now the most precious thing in your life."

"What do you mean?" Lauriane asks in a muted voice, not sure she wants to know the answer.

"Sit down, you're about to faint," says Rashida, pointing to Lauriane's bunk.

She complies and walks slowly towards her bed.

Rashida tells her she was the first one to end up in this creepy room. You can imagine what went through her head. She didn't have a reception committee like Lauriane's. Then, about two weeks later, Lea arrived, also unconscious at first. The two needed to learn to live with each other. Then Lauriane, almost a month after Rashida.

"Who did this to us? What do they want, exactly?"

Rashida shrugs. She does not know, but she collects clues here and there. A huge lunatic named Blondi guards them. They don't know his real name. He's not very smart, but extremely devoted to whoever or whatever is behind this. Loyal and scared. Rashida senses he has a perpetual dispute in him. He acts nice to them, but at the same time, he is their jailer. Rashida has never seen the other people involved if there are any. She tries to get Blondi to talk, but he is not very forthcoming. All she has gathered is that their captors won't hurt them, that there is a plan in the works.

"But I noticed something," Rashida says, lowering her voice and leaning a bit towards Lauriane. "I think he has a crush on our freckled friend."

Lauriane looks at Lea, quietly sitting on her bed. Lea shyly waves at her with a tight smile. Lauriane greets her back unconvincingly.

"I can't stay here," Lauriane says, "I have an improv class every night."

Rashida laughs loudly and straightens up.

"Forget about it, my dear," she says in a condescending tone.

"You have a new project now. And believe me, you will need to improvise like you have never improvised before."

Lauriane stares at Rashida with a puzzled look. Rashida rolls her eyes.

"To get us out of here."

"But that's impossible," Lauriane says, pointing to the gigantic door that must weigh a few tons.

"We won't get out by force, but with this," says Rashida, pointing at her temple with her index finger.

Lauriane observes her in silence. Rashida sighs.

"Our brain."

"Yes, I figured it out," says Lauriane, insulted.

"I hope so," Rashida says, "because we're going to need all the brainpower we can get."

Lauriane wrings her hands. "Do you have the beginnings of a plan?"

Rashida broadly smiles. "Yes. The only way we can get out of this shithole is to outsmart Blondi. To use his apparent affection for beautiful Lea to get us out. Or better yet, have him help us get out by himself."

Lauriane looks at Lea, who is still sitting upright in her bed and waves once again.

Lauriane tightens her lips. "Yeah, well, that's easier said than done."

Rashida glances at Lea who grins and shrugs. She stares at the ground, sighing.

"Indeed."

TEN

I don't know what's going on with Phil lately, but he is particularly insistent and persuasive. I won't lie to you. When I left the meeting with the Big O and the two other bums, I said "Fuck that". Why would I continue to work for free for some fool who doesn't want me to, against a crooked mayor doing everything in his might to get me out of this investigation, and against Lefebvre who giggles like a little girl standing next to a boy band, anyway?

So yes, "fuck that."

You wonder what I'm doing here, by myself, in a dingy delicatessen, waiting for Josiane Derome? Because of Phil. The jerk has a knack for toying with my feelings.

"Aren't you intrigued by why someone stands in our way? Why is the mayor getting concerned, and seems so reluctant to let us help?"

"No, Phil. Fuck that."

I'm telling you, I said fuck that. Not only to prove that I'm not bullshitting you, but also because I had made it my goal to say "fuck that" several times in the same minute. Check. But Phil struck where it mattered. "You don't want to shove that down Lefebvre's throat? I thought you were more persistent than that. Well, if you think the cops will do better than us..."

Son of a bitch.

"OK, I'll talk to her one on one and tell her that whether she likes it or not, I'm going to carry on with my investigation, but I'd rather get her blessing. We'll have a better chance of success if we work as a team, and nothing prevents the police from working on their own as well. The more people looking for Lauriane, the better the chances of finding her."

"Perfect, that's the Martin I know," said Phil with a triumphant look.

"Don't overdo it, big guy."

He laughed, walked out of my office, and gave Nicole a high-five. I glared at her like I do every time I realize she's behind Phil's shenanigans. Which is almost all the time, because let's face it, Phil isn't the woolliest sheep in the pasture. If you know what I mean.

I like delicatessens. Some people label these places with silly names such as "greasy spoons." Looking at the utensils on my white and red-printed placemat, the place lives up to the reputation. I love delicatessens because my grandmother worked in one for all her life. This incredibly kind woman, God rest her soul, always lamented that she didn't see me enough as a teenager. I knew she'd treat me to lunch, and she'd chat with me during her break, which I thought was a worthwhile fifteen minutes to invest. It was a good balance between not seeing her and seeing her too much. I liked to do what I'm doing now, which is people-watching and focusing on regulars complaining about their lives, their failures, and their regrets, with their favourite waitress listening to them while buttering toast. These ladies are not only waitresses, they are also psychologists, financial advisors, nurses...

But what I cherish the most in all this is watching them work their asses off, doing the same gestures several times a day with disarming precision. All those years of performing the same task have programmed their brains to move economically. Experience has shown them that if they do this or that first, they will save two seconds, and in the end, they will be more efficient.

"More coffee, sweetheart?"

I jump out of my thoughts.

"Yes, Johanne."

Johanne could be my mother, and she acts like it. She calls me sweetheart, just like my grandmother used to do. She has a smile on her face even though she has worked here for years. Normally, waitresses' lips curl downward as the years go by. They scribble your order quickly in their notebook, as if to say they don't have all day. So, when they are ready to take your order, you better be ready too. They will greet any hesitation with a sigh of exasperation and will promise to come back later, only to check back much later. With time, you learn to point out what you want to eat as soon as possible, and not to ask for too many changes to the menu if you don't want to get your plate thrown at you. I told you; I love delicatessens. There is no bullshit here. If strip clubs are on one end of the bullshit spectrum, delicatessens are on the other. Nothing is being dangled in front of you. No false promises. You eat and leave. Simple as that. But when you are a repeat customer, you break through that shell. Then the waitress who used to scare you more than a Hells Angels chief becomes friendlier and sometimes even flashes a quick smile.

And if you run into a Johanne, or even my grandmother at the time, then you've won the lottery. They feed you some "sweetheart" all day and grant you a piece of vanilla cake cut from the corner, where there is more sugar coating. Those little extras others don't have, and as a result, you are part of the elite. Johanne is in her early sixties with dyed hair in a toque. Her temples show blonde isn't her natural colour. She has thin round glasses, a friendly chubby face, and large calves. She has a pair of white orthopedic shoes that go "squick squick" when she walks. She took me under her wing. She rolls her eyes and smiles when Giuseppe, her gruff boss, hollers from the cash register. Only Giuseppe can work the cash register. He greets you as if he is overwhelmed, mechanically asking you if you enjoyed your meal without caring about the answer. He punches in his old box bought in the sixties. For a trip back in time, there's no better place than this restaurant. The look on Giuseppe's face when one day he'll realize we're in the 2020s.

I wave at Josiane Derome, who has just arrived, looking confused. She doesn't notice me at first, so I stand up and wave energetically, pissing off the patrons at the next table in the process. She sits down in front of me, smiling shyly. I thank her, and she smiles at me again with a tense pout.

"I wanted to see you to discuss what happened the other day."

"I've said what I had to say, Martin."

"Let me ask you a question. It's been four days since the conference call. How many follow-ups have you had from the mayor? Or even from the police?"

She looks down without answering.

"That's what I thought. None. Do you think it's right not to have a daily call while Lauriane is God knows where with God knows whom, and every day that passes decreases our chances of finding her alive?"

"No," she says, in a dead voice. "I'm messed up. I just want my daughter back."

"And that's what I want, too. I said yes so quickly to Philippe and Melanie when they told me about Lauriane that they were surprised. I really wanted to support you, pro bono or not."

Yeah, well. Shut up. She doesn't have to know the truth.

"I know."

"When we hung up the other day, I challenged the mayor and said that he basically had no intention of doing any of what he said, and you know what he replied? He went: Why would I help someone who didn't vote for me?"

This hurt her more than I thought it would. But it takes what it takes to snap her out of her slump. I take a sip of coffee, wincing as I realize it's cold. I glance desperately at Johanne, who comes hopping in with her coffeepot.

"Shall I warm it up for you, sweetheart?"

"Yes, please."

I look at Josiane.

"Would you like one?"

She shakes her head, still in shock at what I've just told her.

Johanne leaves and I can't help but be moved by her swollen ankles. This woman is the last of the Mohicans. I grimace as I burn my lips on the boiling liquid. Clearly, coffee makes me cringe in some way or another.

"I'll be very forthcoming with you, Josiane. I will work to find Lauriane, no matter what you say. When I take on a case, I don't drop it until I complete it."

Another blatant lie, but this is not the time for honesty. I need to crack this case in order to shove it in Lefebvre's face and that of his dumbass colleagues.

"I've got a great team with Nicole, who bakes great muffins, and Philippe who, uh... well. Who can help, I guess."

We've seen better sales pitches at flea markets, but there are limits to making up facts. I don't mention Serge, not sure she'd be thrilled to hear that a legendary drunk is on the case, too.

"I don't know what to think anymore," she says after a while.

"My advice? Take any help you can get from anyone who wants to work on bringing your daughter back home. I don't think you can turn anyone away. Even if a notorious alcoholic wants to help, you should accept."

She gives me a strange look, proving that I was right not to mention Serge. I snap my fingers at the man sitting two benches away from us. He stands up, looking annoyed.

"I'm not your dog, Lafs."

I smile.

"Josiane, do you know Mike Blanchard? Reporter for The Gazette?"

She nods.

I slide down my seat to make room for Blanchard. We have a love-hate relationship. I use him to get things done, but I also slept with his former girlfriend while they were still together. It's been over five years, and he has yet to forgive me. Some people hold grudges, don't they? Five years is an eternity. I don't even remember what she looked like. He is not quite ugly, nor quite handsome. He speaks in a radio-like voice and wears a long jacket as if he is a detective. He ends his sentences with "Roger" as if he were talking to you on a police radio. He has the perfect image of what you would imagine a street reporter would look like. A wrinkled, poorly buttoned shirt, beige corduroy pants that he must have bought just before Kurt Cobain died, hair combed loose. But he is efficient, and above all, counts on a vast network of informers. So, we have a kind of partnership of reason. And since he's Lafleur's brother-in-law, it's a forced union, so we might as well make the most of it.

I ask Josiane to share her story. Hesitant at first, she ends up confiding. The stalling of the case, the lack of police follow-up, and everything in between. I chuckle as I envision the Big O and Lefebvre's faces tomorrow morning when they pick up the paper.

I tell Josiane that they won't be happy and that they'll probably call her. She only needs to repeat what I told her, that she doesn't have the luxury of turning down any help, that she hasn't heard from them in four days, and that she just wants to locate Lauriane.

I proudly show them the three cream-coated sides of the cake Johanne brought me, but they couldn't care less.

People really have no taste for good things.

ELEVEN

A sunbeam wakes Serge Côté, who was sleeping under an overpass. He looks around and notices familiar faces, brothers-in-arms who not only carry all their gear with them but also the burden of their lives. All of them have the same issue; a more or less severe psychological problem that keeps them from living a normal life. Serge, like all the others, says that he likes the freedom that vagrancy provides him, and this is somewhat true. But it is not his choice, as he claims it is. Rather, homelessness has chosen him. Still, it has allowed him to meet many interesting people. There are all kinds of characters in the business. Aggressive ones that you'd rather stay away from. Comedians, intentionally funny or not. Serge is the patriarch. Even if he is not the oldest, he is still part of the cast. He has taken on the role of talking young people out of the streets, to get their act together, to get help. It's too late for him, but there is still hope for them. What he tells them, they have heard a thousand times. From their parents, from their friends. Therefore, he faces painful indifference coupled with an anger that bursts from the first sentences. "What do you want from me, Gramps?", "Leave me alone—you're not my father". Granted, he is not their father. He hasn't even been one for his own children, so who is he to lecture them?

But he can't help it. He can't let a teenager or young adult go down that road without trying to talk him out of it, even if his success rate is next to nothing. But when it works, then it's worth all the failures in the world, and he feels alive again. That's what motivates him so much in Lauriane Derome's case. If he can track her down and convince her to go back to her mom, he'll at least feel like he's doing something useful for a few moments. That's no small feat. It's more powerful than any bottle of gin he might pop to start his days.

He reaches into his coat pocket and finds a thin, sharp object. He pulls out Lauriane Derome's picture and looks at it. He doesn't realize he's smiling as he checks out this healthy young girl with rosy cheeks and a bright eye. She has long, ashy hair and big, expressive eyes. She is beautiful and looks confident. Although he has seen bright people end up on the street, he does not believe Lauriane ran away. The impression he gets from the photo does not suggest that she is looking for happiness where it is not. So, if she's not on the run, then what? There are multiple runaways every day. There are repeat offenders. But he always ends up spotting them, whether on the street, or smoking a cigarette, or trembling with fear behind a strip club. Otherwise, he sees them on the street, dressed as girls their age should never be. He pushes his rusty steel cart towards the brown building he usually hangs around. He hides his things under an immense ash tree in the next lot and sets out to find young Lauriane. But first, he must gulp down his fuel. He knows very well that he will die from this. Nobody needs to remind him. But without it, there's no way to go on.

Several hours later, he talks to an acquaintance who claims to have never seen the girl in the photo. His search is unsuccessful so far since no one has bumped into her. If she really ran away, then someone must have seen her. No one benefits from keeping this information secret, as other homeless people, too, would do everything in their capacity to prevent their reality from becoming that of a young person. Especially a young and vulnerable woman.

"Hi, Serge."

He turns and recognizes James Romano, a former homeless man who has fallen off the radar. In his mid-forties, Romano roamed the streets of Montreal until he faded away. Although at first everyone thought he was dead, he actually got his life back on track. No one would have bet on that, considering he wasn't the smartest of the bunch, and he was drugged out of his mind. Serge often saw him sitting on the floor, looking dazed, staring straight ahead, as if waiting for his demise, or some kind of deliverance that miraculously came. One day, he left and was better dressed, clear minded like never before. Of course, he still looks like an idiot. Serge figures he has the IQ of an elementary school kid, but he's quite a big guy. At least six feet three inches tall, shoulders as broad as a refrigerator, but as gentle as a lamb. Despite all that, everyone feared him. There's something not reassuring in his gaze. Except that for some reason, he worships Serge.

"James, long time no see," Serge says, slurring his speech.

He over drank this morning. He blinks to adjust his vision.

"What are you doing?" Romano asks.

"Nothing. I'm walking around, talking to the guys. But what are you doing here? I've seen little of you lately."

James lifts the two bags in his hands. "I'm shopping."

"I see your wife still treats you like a slave."

This statement confuses James, and Serge laughs loudly.

"I—I don't have a wife."

"I know, James. I'm teasing you."

Every time someone talks about women, he blushes so much that he looks like a ripe tomato.

"I have to go, Serge. It was nice to see you."

"It was nice to see you, too."

Romano is about to leave when Serge stops him. James pauses and turns back with his good-natured smile.

"Have you seen this girl?"

James stares at the photo for a few seconds. "No, I haven't. I don't know her."

Again, red as a tomato. Really, he must have had some kind of trauma with a girl. Serge shrugs and walks away.

Romano quickly moves in the opposite direction.

TWELVE

Lauriane Derome is baffled. She assumed the girls would know why they are in this dump, but clearly, they don't know any more than she does.

"I don't think they're planning to kill us, but I don't think they want what's best for us either," Rashida says.

"No shit," Lauriane says, ruffling her jail buddy's feathers in the process.

Lauriane doesn't want to have bad blood with those who are now her only allies, but she freaks out. She doesn't need to hear platitudes right now. Her life is a nightmare since that fateful day when everything flipped. She lost track of time, and she weeps thinking about her mother, who should be worried sick. It breaks her heart. Lea doesn't talk much; she just listens to Rashida. She is clearly terrified too but resigned to her fate. She is as fragile as a porcelain doll, Lauriane thinks. If the trio's hopes rest on her shoulders, then they're screwed. Lea has milky skin, big expressive green eyes and reddish-blonde hair tied up in a knot using her own hair. Lauriane immediately notices that they all have complementary strengths that could eventually get them out of this predicament if they play their cards right. Rashida is cerebral, detailed and calm, Lea is shy, charming and secretive, and Lauriane is a tigress, aggressive and determined. She feels the rage boiling inside her as she understands the extent of her misfortune. She closes her eyes and takes a deep breath. Now is not the time to be deterred.

"If you had to guess what they want from us, what would you say?" she asks Rashida.

Rashida glances at Lea, who listens attentively, and shrugs.

"I would say they want us to be their slaves. You know, like those girls in the United States who were kidnapped and spent decades as servants and surrogates for a family of morons? I'm sure they're a couple of toothless illiterates who think they can do whatever they want with us."

Lauriane frowns.

"I'd rather die. I will be no one's slave."

Rashida raises her fist sarcastically. "Girl Power."

Lauriane is offended. Rashida seems to think she's a naive girl who's always had her way, but she's wrong. She's made it through several critical issues because of her determination, and she views this shitty one as another opportunity to do so. A thud from the huge metal door startles her.

"Sit down on your bed," says a deep and hollow voice.

The instruction comes from behind the sliding crack at the door's top. Lauriane's heart is beating fast. She will finally know who is behind her misery. The girls sit upright on their beds while Lauriane stands still, thinking. Rashida signals her to sit down.

"He won't enter unless we are all seated."

Lauriane complies, too curious to see what this is all about. She needs more information to form a picture of what's going on and to assess her options. The enormous door opens with a gallows squeak, and a huge man enters, pushing a beige plastic cart with three plates on it covered with a sealed plastic bell. Lauriane looks at Rashida, who mouths the word "Blondi." Rashida glances at Lea, who nods before collapsing into tears. Blondi looks at her as he carefully closes the door.

"What's wrong, Lea?"

She sobs loudly, her face buried in her pillow. Blondi instructs the other two to take a plate and walks softly towards Lea. He sits down on the end of her bed, then asks again what is wrong. Blondi's soft voice surprises Lauriane. Obviously, he is empathetic to Lea's distress.

"You're mean," she says through her tears.

"I'm not. I'm just doing my job."

"You're mean because you won't explain what we are doing here. I want to know why we're here."

Blondi sighs. Lauriane believes that this is not the first time the girl has wept in front of him.

"You know I can't tell you."

Lauriane jumps up and walks towards him. "Tell us what the hell we're doing here, you bastard," she says, screaming.

Rashida jumps to intervene. "Sit down now," she whispers.

"But—"

"Lauriane, sit down right now." This time, the tone is unequivocal.

Lauriane looks at Blondi, who is swinging and grabbing his head.

"Tell her to stop. I will be nasty, tell her to stop."

"Look now, she's back in bed. It's over. Please calm down," Rashida says to comfort him.

After a few minutes of the same merry-go-round, Blondi stares at Lauriane, then gets up. He grabs his cart and leaves the room without speaking another word. Lea punches on the mattress.

"What are you, stupid?" she yells.

The sweet young girl is not so sweet after all.

"I—I don't get it." Their behaviour completely baffles Lauriane.

"Do you think we haven't tried screaming, crying, throwing tantrums?" Rashida asks. "None of that has worked. The only thing we can exploit is his fondness for Lea. That's the only chink we have found to break through his armour."

So, Lea is a freaking actress? Crying on demand like that requires a definite talent, Lauriane thinks. She couldn't do that, even in her improv classes.

"Do you think I'm not trembling with rage?" Rashida says. "Don't you think I want to jump on him and rip out his windpipe with my teeth, gouge his eyes out?"

"It's a bit intense," Lauriane whispers to herself.

"So, we must take advantage of the crack provided by our pretty freckled friend and figure out what the hell he wants from us, find a way out of this rat hole."

Lauriane nods in awe. It is indeed a good plan.

"Blondi isn't dazzling," Lea says. "So, if we act like we're his friends, he'll end up believing it and let his guard down and that's when—"

"... we'll tear out his windpipe and gouge his eyes out?" Lauriane says.

Rashida has a disdainful pout.

"Jesus Christ, calm down. We're not animals."

THIRTEEN

Phil shows up in my office, looking embarrassed.

"Martin?"

I look at him, and I know before he even says a word.

"There is stuff missing from the file, isn't there? And you hoped the cops would give you more, but they dismissed you?"

Phil looks down.

"Negotiation isn't your strongest suit, is it?" I say, chuckling.

I can imagine that his girlfriend Melanie wins all their arguments and gets her way with her pet of a boyfriend. He looks at me defiantly.

"Because maybe you were more successful?"

"Shut up, Phil."

To impress him, but mostly to put him back in his place. I could tell him the plan I've had in mind for the past few days, because I knew the police wouldn't just hand over everything they had just like that. Phil looks at me strangely.

"What's so funny?" he asks.

Oops. I didn't realize I was laughing out loud.

"Nothing. Listen, I have a plan."

He rolls his eyes. I have no patience for that this morning.

"Would you listen to what I have to say before you react like a pimply, spurned teenager?"

He smiles and sits down in my big brown leather chair in the corner of my office. I wince as I watch the furniture lose most of its value as soon as his huge ass touches it.

"Of course, I have plenty of time," the bastard says, crossing his arms.

Once I tell him my idea, he bursts out laughing like a psychedelic hyena. "Can I roll my eyes now?" he asks, his face flushed.

"Yes."

So, he does.

"What's going on?" Nicole says, walking excitedly into the doorway.

I signal her that nothing is going on and to go back to working on her crossword puzzle, but the asshole recounts my plan interspersed with giggles that anger me to the point where I sense it'll end badly. She doesn't get it. He can't put two words in a row because he's laughing so hard.

"Are you done?" I say to him, infuriated.

I explain the idea to Nicole. Maybe she will have more common sense than this idiot. She laughs so hard that her whole body wobbles as if she has Parkinson's during an earthquake.

"Anything better to suggest, jokers?"

They just laugh and shake their heads.

"Then shut up. Nicole, call for the costume. Phil, get out of here if you can't help."

Both walk hunched over towards the exit of my office, as they are still laughing.

"Idiots. I'm surrounded by idiots," I say with a grunt.

I sigh in annoyance as I hear Marcel Lafleur's nasal voice asking what's going on. He has just come in.

"Lafleur," I shout. "Come here."

I won't let these fools make a mockery of my plan.

"Lemon, boss. What's wrong with them?"

"They are assholes, that's what's wrong with them," I say loud enough for them to hear. This only sends Nicole into a convulsion from which, my goodness, I don't think she'll come out alive.

"You know Pierre Mondesi, don't you?"

Lafleur nods and sits down in the chair in front of me. Intrigued.

"Did I ask you to sit down?"

"No," he says, but remains seated.

The hell with that. He pisses me off, but I need him, so I let it slide.

I describe my plan, and although he tries to talk me out of it, he agrees to help. He'll contact Mondesi so I can meet him in a few hours.

I park in front of the police station and open the bag Nicole gave me. What an idiot! She got me an absurd costume. I scream in my car against the woman I will fire tomorrow. I've already dressed in Mondesi's beige uniform. And since I have no other option, I put on the huge black glasses attached to a big pink latex brandy nose, not to mention the silly moustache. I wonder which cat was killed to make this hideous stache. It reeks of dye.

I need to focus on the task at hand. Find Lauriane Derome's file. Phil told me it was a shitty plan because there will be people inside the precinct, and I have no chance of succeeding without getting caught. Isn't he aware of my ninja moves and resourceful side yet? Disappointing.

I practice my Mexican accent in the car.

"No, I don't know what you mean," I say with a Spanish accent.

Well, this will do.

Mondesi told me what I had to do. It's a good thing someone called in sick with the flu.

"If you get caught, I will deny you work here," Mondesi told me acrimoniously. "I only agreed because I owe my friend Marcel one."

"All right, James Bond."

"What's that?"

"Nothing."

I walk into the precinct and grab a yellow cart on wheels. It has all the cleaning supplies, a big empty trash bag at the edge. I must admit, it's pretty clever. My mother would laugh like a turkey at seeing me cleaning. God rest her soul. She's still alive, but I'm gearing up for her to leave at any moment. The damn woman won't be around for twenty more years, will she?

My fellow co-workers, three low-slung Hispanic women, look at me with a blank stare. One tells something to another, giggling. Fucking Nicole, even these idiots can see through my disguise. After getting our instructions and assignments in dubious English from the so-called team leader, I push my cart towards the back of the room. I know the place a little, and I know where the file cabinets are.

I say "Buena sera" to everyone so that people think I'm Mexican, but I can still hear the women laughing in the distance. Those bitches, they can't even speak a word of English, and they laugh at my Spanish? Fuck them with a pinata. I see a cop I don't know sitting at his desk reading something on his computer.

"I won't bother you long time," I say with a smile in a Mexican accent.

He doesn't flinch.

"I'm just passing by."

He looks up at me, then a smile appears on his face.

"Is it Halloween?" he asks.

No, you idiot. I smile as if I don't understand because I don't understand. "What?"

He laughs and goes back to his computer screen, shaking his head. Then I realize he was referring to my ridiculous costume. Nicole, I'm going to kill you.

It looks like they dimmed the lights for the evening.

"You dimmed the lights like at a restaurant?" I say, laughing to another policeman further away.

He looks at me with a surprised look and goes back to his screen.

"Get lost, hombre."

My accent counterbalances Nicole's shitty costume. I'm a pro. "Grazie."

"I thought you were Mexican," he says.

"I am."

"Then maybe you should stop speaking Italian."

He laughs loudly. A colleague joins him, and I slip away.

Shit, it's Gracias, not Grazie, you asshole.

I'm summarily dusting the tops of the cabinets, and when I say summarily, I mean I'm barely removing any dust, too busy glancing behind me. As time goes on, I think Phil was right. This is a shitty plan. But I'm here, so I might as well find what I came for. The cabinets are in a secluded corner of the offices. I can snoop around to my heart's content without attracting too much suspicion. I push my cart slowly in that direction, pretending to carelessly dust some desks along the way. No one cares about me, and I am extremely hot. My fake moustache is getting wet, and my fake glasses are fogging up. How do they work in this furnace? I see my reflection in a window overlooking the darkness and I look absolutely foolish. No time to daydream. I open the first drawer but find nothing. Fucking hell, this is going to take me all night. No wonder those stupid cops can't find anything. Their filing system sucks balls. Then, in the third drawer, a file catches my attention. It says Roger Zadinar. I open it out of curiosity because I have the attention deficit of a Chihuahua, and I feel my heart break. I didn't think that after all this time, it would still get to me to see the pictures of Zadinar screwing Yvonne. The pictures that Lefebvre had used to taunt me after the arrest of that crazy woman and her man mountain. I put the photos back in their file as tears well up in my eyes and, you have got to be kidding me, a swelling in my crotch. What a sick bastard I am. How can this possibly turn me on?

"Excuse me," says a voice coming from behind.

I grab a rag and rub the top of the binder, hoping the person will move on. No luck.

"Hey, mister."

I answer without turning around.

"Schnell, Schell, I have to vash everyzing!"

Dammit, I sound like Schwarzenegger now. I'm mixing up my accents.

"Lafs."

I stop dusting. I recognized Lefebvre's voice. What the hell is he still doing here?

I turn over, looking sheepish, and a bright flash of light makes me squint.

The flash of his camera.

I open my eyes and see Lefebvre lowering the cell phone he is holding horizontally. I roll my eyes. My disguise has fooled no one.

Fucking Nicole.

He smirks.

"Sorry Lafs, but nobody would have believed me if I told them. Would you mind telling me what you're doing here, you idiot?"

I swear I entertain the idea of denying it by switching back to my Mexican accent, but since I already mixed it with the Austrian accent just a few seconds ago, what's the point?

"Ha, Lefebvre," I say nervously, removing my grotesque mask. "What can I do for you?"

The bastard laughs like a cow. So much so that two of his colleagues, who obviously have nothing better to do, join him, intrigued.

"You can't do anything for me, Lafs. I'll ask you again, what the hell are you doing here? Who exactly did you think you would fool with your clown disguise?"

"You," I say, laughing.

His face darkens. He looks behind me and has a sneaky smile.

"What year do you think it is, you moron? Do you really think we're still printing out records and filing them in those antiques? Everything's digital now. You should know that, detective."

"Listen, you jerk," I say in a voice that's much sourer than I want it to be. "I'm running out of money, and I need a second job to make ends meet. Are you happy now?"

He smiles his condescending shit-eating grin. I'd wipe off his face with a quick slap if we were both alone in a back alley.

"And you got a job at the precinct a few days after we gave you a half-assed file on the Derome disappearance. You're also snooping through file cabinets by accident, I presume?"

"Exactly."

"So, if I call the cleaning company owner right now, he will confirm that, right?"

I think for a few seconds. I have little hope other than to take a chance. "Definitely," I say, defiantly.

"All right, follow me."

I'll spare you the long minutes waiting for him to speak to Pierre Mondesi. The smile on that runt's face confirm that Mondesi kept his word. He denied hiring me. Marcel, you citrus-loving piece of shit. After his call, Lefebvre looked at me, a sly smile splitting his moon face.

"I hope you didn't have plans tonight, pal."

I frown.

"Breaking and entering a police station. I don't know how much it's going to cost you, but one thing's for sure, you can kiss your business goodbye, or what's left of it, anyway."

With a neutral face, he yells at a colleague who runs over like an obedient puppy. "Put this awful actor in a cell for the night."

I don't even give him the pleasure of begging. I watch him and defiantly stand up. But I have absolutely nothing. He's got me. I wonder who the rat is that tipped him off. I'm sure he wasn't on duty tonight. As the metal door closes, leaving me feeling awkward on an uncomfortable makeshift bed, I say something to myself that I rarely say.

I should have listened to Phil.

FOURTEEN

Now, it's ridiculous.

It's one thing to get arrested for breaking into a police station under false pretenses. In the end, I deserve it. But to the point of putting me in jail? In a maximum-security prison, to boot? What's wrong with these people? I thought I would be with losers here for their unpaid parking tickets. Instead, I'm with a scrawny cellmate who looks way too nervous for my taste. And by nervous, I mean horny. And by horny, I mean aroused. This creep looks at me like I'm a sixty-five-day-aged tenderloin. He salivates. Can you imagine anything more cliché than that? Fresh meat arrives, and all the guys stare at them like they would use them as a blow-up doll. I'm very handsome, but it's not my style. Nothing against it, though. To each his own. I feel sick that I need to say that, so as not to offend anyone's feelings. That's where we are in our society. We must apologize for everything we say, lest someone be hurt by a comment, and collapse into the fetal position, unable to control their tears. Convulsing. Big time pain.

"What's your name?" asks the salivating-mouthed moron.

I wave my hand and signal him to shut up. I ponder. I try to put the pieces of the puzzle back together. I'm sitting on the top mattress on this twin bed. My bed is at most six feet long, so I sleep with my feet propped up against the wall. Our cell is disgusting. It's about seven by eleven feet. There's only one table, and a stool screwed to the floor. I've never slept in anything so cramped. I wonder how people can endure this. My back would be a mess after a week of this abuse. Our beds block the only window in the cell, so the sun is on our face every morning. We can't hang curtains either. And since it is relatively cold at night, I need any blanket I can put my hand on. What about the single toilet in the cell? It's almost glued to the bottom bunk and has no flap. To hear, and especially to smell, the other retard go at it is too much for me. The worst part is that we can't flush the toilet at night because the pipes are so old that it might wake everyone up. So, we need to cover the toilet with a makeshift lid, but I swear it doesn't hold all the fumes that come out. That's just plain silly. Just before my first night in this shithole, I got a call. I informed Phil of the situation and asked him to get me out of there, presto. And also to get me Marcel Lafleur today, no matter what.

"What's your name?" the idiot asks again.

"Will you shut the fuck up?" I say impatiently.

"Come down and say it to my face!"

I jump off the bed to greet him. He moves back in his bunk.

I look at him and am struck by how sickly he looks. He's clearly abused Fentanyl. I could knock him down just by blowing at him. Which gives me a courage I wouldn't have in front of a bigger guy.

"Listen carefully, Twiggy—"

"It's Ruffles."

I pause, amused.

"Like the potato chips?"

He looks down.

"Yes, like potato chips."

"But how on earth did you get that nickname? Anyway, here's what's going to happen. I won't be here for long. So, get off my back. Do your thing, and I'll do mine. Comprendo?"

"I'm not Italian."

I glare at him.

"Yes, I understand. I just wanted to—"

"I don't give a shit what you wanted, buddy. Shut your mouth and everything will be fine."

Ruffles looks down.

"Oh yeah, and don't you dare grab my ass," I say as I climb back into my bunk.

He mumbles something I don't get.

"I beg your pardon?"

"You're not my type."

I chuckle.

"Come on, man. Of course, I'm your type. I'm everyone's type."

Total silence. I'll take that as a tacit endorsement.

Later, I hear that I have a guest. It's Lafleur. When he sees me coming, he laughs like a turkey.

"Lemon, boss, what the hell are you doing here?"

"You're the one who should tell me what I'm doing here. Your friend Mondesi acted like an asshole."

"What do you mean?"

"He's the reason I'm here. He ratted me out to the cops."

Lafleur doesn't really understand what I'm getting at. I tell him, and he lowers his head.

"Mandarin."

"Indeed. So Lafleur, do me a favour and tell that jerk to call the cops and say that he made a mistake, that he confused me with someone else, or that he misunderstood, whatever. He needs to tell them that, of course, I'm an employee and I work for him, because of my financial issues."

He looks surprised.

"You have financial troubles?"

"No, you idiot. It's justifying my work at the police station."

"Ha," he says, as if he's just discovered the cure for cancer.

He winks at me. What was I thinking, including him, to work on the case? Instinct. Always trust your instinct. When it tells you no, it means no. There's a reason I've turned down every offer to partner with Flower PI, besides the crappy company name. Listen to your inner voice.

"GRAPEFRUIT."

I flinch as he yells. I wave to the guard walking toward us, everything is fine.

"Will you stop screaming like a goat?"

"Sorry, it's my Tourette's."

I sigh.

"So, will you talk to that idiot Mondesi?"

"He won't lie. The man's a straight shooter."

"Well, that's your problem, pal. You told me to contact him. Get me out of this shit. Do you understand? You say you're resourceful, and that there's nothing you can't do? It's time to prove it."

He seems a little hesitant. I pull out all the stops.

"Every moment I spend here decreases our chances of finding Lauriane alive. If you won't do it for me, do it for her."

God in heaven, his eyes are watering. I'm a hell of a negotiator.

Then he sneezes.

"Excuse me," he says, wiping his eyes. "Freaking allergies."

Yeah, well. I'm sure my speech still had its effect.

As I walk back to my cell, I hear a voice behind me. A heavy, powerful voice. Gritty and terrifying. I would recognize it in a million. He calls me by my last name, a tinge of rage in his tone.

I'm in trouble, folks. I'm in deep trouble. I turn to him.

"Hey, my buddy Formenton."

I helped put this jackass away a few years ago for fraud, and he swore he would get justice one day. Since he was going to be in jail for several years, I wasn't too worried. But since I'm in here, and he's standing next to me with the big vein in his forehead about to explode, I realize he will eat his revenge cold. I look down at my crotch to make sure I'm not pissing myself. He looks even more huge than I remember.

In the end, Lafleur might not have time to get me out of here.

FIFTEEN

Jean Ouellet storms into the room where his crisis intervention team is waiting for him. He throws a copy of The Gazette newspaper on the conference table. The headline reads, "Mayor Ouellet blocks young Lauriane's investigation."

"Has anyone reached that jerk Mike Blanchard?" he says, yelling.

"We left a message," Pierre Dorion, the city's public relations director, says.

Ouellet stares at him blankly, his face flushed.

"Call his boss, call his mother, call his dog. I don't give a shit, but I want to know how he came to talk to that idiot, Josiane Derome."

Dorion is about to advise his boss it's not a good idea to disrespect the mother of a missing teenager, but he doesn't want to add fuel to the fire. He's never seen the mayor so angry. It's not the first time the media is hard on him, but obviously this is one time too many. Ouellet sits down and starts reading the article to make sure everyone knows what it's about. The text is certainly not flattering, but things have been worse in the past. People share stunned looks for what they think is an over-reaction.

"I'm sure it's that jerk Martin Lafs," the mayor mutters to himself.

Dorion's eyes widen.

"Lafs? The dim-witted private investigator?"

Ouellet smiles, as if he's found an ally.

"Yes, exactly. This piece of shit is utterly incompetent."

Ouellet describes the nature of his recent encounter with the private investigator and the cops. How he orchestrated an ambush using the teenager's mother. He relates how he learned that Lafs still hasn't let go and that he disguised himself as a Hispanic cleaning man to break into the police station. A bald man chuckles after hearing that.

"I'm telling you, he's a jerk," the mayor says triumphantly, thinking he's found another ally.

He describes how he lobbied to have Lafs sent to a prison, so he won't be a smartass anymore. Dorion squirms in his chair.

"That's not good, Mr. Ouellet."

Ouellet gives him a devastating look.

"Ooh, Little Peter is afraid? Little Peter is going to cry to his mommy?" he says, mimicking hands wiping tears away.

Dorion frowns.

"Am I supposed to be Little Peter in your fantasy?"

"Yes, you coward."

"It's unnecessary to—"

"Boo-hoo, Little Peter cries."

"—resort to this." Dorion wonders what the mayor's deal is lately. Their relationship was cordial in the past. Why has he suddenly become irascible and disrespectful? Quite a surprising change of heart. This guy, Lafs, must have done something terrible to him to get to this point. Did he sleep with a former girlfriend in the past? Dorion is a few months away from retirement, so he doesn't care. He takes a deep breath and settles back in his seat.

"You know, Mr. Mayor, it's your call. It's not my reputation that will be tarnished if your shenanigans come to light."

"Are you threatening me, Dorion?"

Pierre Dorion stares around the table to see if he's the only one who doesn't get it. He motions for everyone to leave the room, then stands up to sit closer to his boss.

"Johnny, I will ask you a very direct and delicate question. Are you on drugs?"

Ouellet sneers nastily. "You little fucker."

"I say that with all due respect, because you don't look OK, you don't look OK at all."

The mayor is about to reply, but Dorion raises his hand. "I will ask you to listen very carefully to Little Peter until the end, and then the decision will be yours," he says, proud of his remark. "You will call the police and request that they release Lafs. You must let no one know you had anything to do with his detention. Second, we'll hold a press conference denying everything in the newspaper, and that we are doing everything we can to track down Lauriane. And of course, we will accept help from anyone, even that crappy private investigator. If you do this, everything will go back to normal, and we can all move on. If you want to do anything other than this, it'll be without me."

Dorion leaves the room without waiting for a response and closes the door behind him. Ouellet reads the article again and screams with rage. He storms out of the room and slams the door back into his office.

A few hours later, Ouellet addresses a horde of journalists, including Mike Blanchard, whom he stares at for a long time, and reads out the statement that Pierre Dorion has written. Dorion stands next to the mayor to make sure there is no outburst. He has another matter on his mind—dealing with the mayor's attitude. How will he manage this issue that is much more serious than an unreliable article? How will he find out the reasons behind Ouellet's apparent irascibility? There aren't many things that can explain such a turnaround. He asked him about drug use, because he knows drug addicts and notices the same patterns in Johnny Ouellet. Or perhaps he has begun drinking again after thirty years of abstinence? He doesn't seem to have slurred speech. He speaks clearly, too much so. And he doesn't stink with alcohol. So, it can only be dope. He can't believe he's falling back into despair like this. Later, he calls his wife to discuss the matter with her but isn't able to reach her. Dorion will talk to her later. He will take care of that, and then retire to his condo in Florida, leave it all behind, and never hear from Johnny Ouellet again for the rest of his life.

SIXTEEN

Tommy Formenton walks up to me with a threatening look on his face, and although I wish I had more courage, I instinctively back away. He's flanked by two gorillas. I'm looking intensely for a prison guard to rescue me, but there are clearly none around. When it's time to do their job, I swear—.

"How are you doing, Tommy?" I say as I continue backing up, keeping my eyes on him.

"How do you think I'm doing? I'm in jail."

It's weird how angry he looks without looking furious. My dad always told me it's the quiet ones you have to watch. But since he thought it was a good idea to bet his paychecks on racehorses, I wouldn't give him too much credit as a life coach.

"You need these two men to fight me?" I point to the two tanks following him like obedient dogs.

"To fight you? I don't need anyone to do that, as you can guess."

I keep backing up, but I quickly realize that I'm nearing the wall behind me, and I might not have a chance to break away. Especially since we're on the third-floor corridor, so jumping down is not an option. Unless I'd rather die than get a severe beating, which is arguable.

"Because of you, I've been rotting here for three years. Do you know what three years means?"

"Between two and four?"

The two huge idiots laugh, but not Formenton. His face hardens.

"Still joking, I see?"

"Not so much, no." I try awkwardly to compose myself.

I'm doing everything in my power not to piss him off, to get out of this mess with my wits, but you know that's not where I normally shine. So, I'm kind of, how shall I put it, in deep shit?

He's a few inches away from me, and I see him taking a swing. I close my eyes, hoping to soak up the punch as best as I can. And that's where it gets weird. Instead of taking a beating, I smell his cologne mixed with a subtle scent of perspiration as he crushes his hairy, muscular chest into my face. Am I crazy, or is he hugging me? Is he going for a bear hug? Lift me up and throw me down the three levels?

"You changed my life, Lafs."

"I beg your pardon?" I say as I open one eye.

He grabs me by the shoulders and looks at me with a honeyed look. His two sidekicks look at me with astonishment. They, too, don't quite understand what's going on. Formenton wraps his right arm around me, spraying me with a whiff of his sweaty scent as he goes, and drags me along with him, walking in the opposite direction.

"You know Lafs, I was a real bum. I was riding high in the saddle, but deep down I was miserable."

"Why won't you girls get a room," says a filthy man from his cell as we pass.

"Shut up, Paquette, or I'll rip you a new one." Formenton says, screaming at him.

"Take it easy, Tommy. I was joking."

Formenton stares at the man, still gripping my shoulders.

"Yeah, shut up Paquette," I say in a very insecure voice.

Formenton looks at me and laughs.

"I'm telling you, this guy is a real comedian," he says to the two mountain men.

He leads me to a lower table where the four of us sit down. Tommy needs to talk, and I'm more interested in listening than getting my face smashed. So, I listen to him as if he were giving me the gospel. He tells me the sentencing devastated him; that he had one goal: to get back at those who put him in that hellhole. He swears I was at the top of his list, and I have no reason to doubt it.

"But I found Jesus while I was hanging out in the little chapel here."

"Jesus?" I ask

"Christ."

"Oh yes, that Jesus."

"It was while chatting with Father Kofipot, that—"

"Wait, you talked to a coffee pot?"

"Yes, Father Kofipot, why?"

"Go on," I say, stifling a laugh.

I will not piss him off when we get along so well.

"He made me understand that—"

"You were bitter. That life shouldn't be so black, but that you could gather all your beans? To go unfiltered, one cup at a time?" I say with a sneer.

Will I shut my big mouth, for God's sake?

"What's going on, Lafs? What are you trying to say?" he asks, slowly getting angry.

I ask him to carry on. He finally tells me that the priest made him understand he is the only one responsible for his misfortunes, and that he has the means to get out of his misery, by welcoming the Lord into his heart.

There's something endearing about seeing a huge moron display such sensitivity. It would bring a tear to your eye if you weren't still searching for puns with "coffee pot."

"And you, Lafs, have you accepted the Lord into your heart?"

"You bet I have," I answer without skipping a beat. "I've been on the same journey as you. I can relate."

I'm the most atheistic guy in the world, but I'd tell him I believe in the God of cotton candy if it meant I could get his empathy. He stares into my eyes and gets emotional. Holy shit, is he going to cry?

"Alea jacta est," he says.

"Alea jacta est?"

"Yes."

"That's Julius Caesar, buddy—" What the hell am I doing? "Alea jacta est, Tommy."

Who cares if he mixes up everything? As long as he doesn't crush my nose with his big hand, I'll say yes to whatever he says. I look at the other two, who are totally immersed in the conversation. I smile. In the end, it wasn't so bad. Except I have to get out of here before Formenton loses faith and decides that getting even with me wasn't such a bad idea after all.

A guard approaches.

"You still work here?" I say in an acrimonious tone, thinking back to earlier when I needed one of them.

"Pick up your shit. You're leaving."

"How's that?"

He shrugs, and obviously doesn't care to explain the reasons. And frankly, I don't really need one. If I can get out, then I'm out, that's it. I stand up and look at Formenton.

"Well Tommy, that was short, but very enlightening. How long do you have left?"

"Fifteen years."

"I mean, before you can ask for parole?"

"Fifteen years."

I hiss in amazement.

"Wow, they weren't very kind to you."

Formenton lowers his head and I see him contract his muscles, his jaw, and his complexion becomes a little more reddish. I try to calm him down.

"Alea jacta est, Tommy. Remember? Alea jacta est."

He stares at me. His eyes have changed. I see glimpses of the bad old Tommy. Before he ran in with his coffee pot. I say to the guard,

"Get me out of here at once."

He instructs me to follow him, and I glance behind to make sure Formenton is still sitting at the table. He will need some therapy sessions after this. I've brought out all the bad in him.

I have the unfortunate tendency to bring that out in people.

SEVENTEEN

I gave it my all, believe me. I want to impress Anne-Marie, the selfie-enthusiast from the coffee shop. I'm sure that guys who've slept with her haven't made the same effort as I have tonight. But they're young jerks. With experience, you learn that you must prepare for sex in advance. It's all about the mood, about taking the other person with you on this long, libidinous journey.

My God, what a poet I am! I could almost sob.

After the prison episode, I direly need a change of mind. And since there's no one like Anne-Marie in the slammer, there's no better way to do it. I was told that the mayor lobbied to get me out of jail, but I don't believe it. I'm pretty sure he's behind my prison trip, which could have killed me if Tommy Formenton hadn't converted to Christianity. But back to today. Since I suck at cooking, I asked a friend of mine, a caterer, to fix me a quick meal. I put everything in the oven to heat; I took out my fancy candles, the ones that smell a bit like ginger. I heard ginger is an aphrodisiac. I can't confirm it since I'm permanently aroused. What I'm trying to say is that I'm always ready, standing up like a soldier in the trenches. Anne-Marie is about fifteen years younger than me. Often at that age, they say stuff like "I don't want to sleep with my dad" which is totally justified. But I'm not her father, and I doubt hers had her at fifteen. But Anne-Marie didn't say any of that. Since I helped her take a selfie for her Instagram account, she's relaxed. She sees me for what I am: a gentleman, a valiant knight, a romantic. Shut up. You don't know that deep inside; I have a tender heart and a lot of love to give and to get.

I look at my watch, still an hour before her arrival. What could I possibly do? I put on Benjamin Grosvenor playing Chopin. Classical music has the documented ability to set the stage for an intimate mood. People think they are dealing with a scholar, not a moron. I leave a Charles Bukowski novel lying around, but not Women; I'd be afraid she'd get the wrong message. I casually place a copy of Kurt Vonnegut's Breakfast of Champions on the couch. Of course, I've read them, are you kidding me? A librarian I once knew gave me her list of fifty novels to read before I die. I've only read those two. Perhaps it's not much, but I'm not dead yet, so I have time. I have other priorities; you know?

Like what? Oh, come on, think about it. Anne-Marie, damn it! Lauriane? Oh yes, her too, but on a different level. Since the prison episode, things have calmed down, and the path has cleared a bit. The Big O hates me just as much, but otherwise it's business as usual. Phil is still doing what he can with the skills he has. Nicole is still eavesdropping, Serge is still dead drunk every other day, and Lafleur is still yelling citrus names like his life depends on it.

What a dream team.

I'm surprised that Anne-Marie agreed to meet me after I sent her a direct message on Instagram. After all, we don't know each other that well. We crossed paths at the coffee shop. We started by smiling at each other conventionally, then in a naughty way. I volunteered one day to take more pictures of her, which she said yes to, giggling like a grasshopper. This generation and their inclination to document every move they make. It's fascinating and distressing at the same time. People don't really live when they focus on their social media. They live a life made up for others.

For fuck's sake, tell me she won't take a selfie while I doggy style her, saying "Best. Fuck. EVER!!!"

Will she? Sex is a private matter, or so I hope. Although it would give me great clout with her equally hot and libidinous girlfriends. In fact, it all started the day I asked her about what she was scribbling. She showed me a very interesting drawing. She has some talent with charcoal pens. But why would she do that at the café? No idea. People like to hang out there and sit for hours enjoying the Wi-Fi and checking out each other. Strange times, I tell you. I think way too much for my own good. I should check out every room in my apartment to refine my staging. Since she's an artist, I pull out a big impressionist book I never opened. I quickly browse through it to register some painters' names. If she ever asks me whom is my favourite, I won't look too dumb. Okay, this one doesn't look so bad. Claude Monet—he must be a Frenchman. It will be easy to remember.

I jump at the sound of the doorbell. I'm suddenly nervous. For God's sake, pull yourself together, Lafs, and don't mention the Martinator. Obviously, few people are fond of this. She is even prettier than when I met her at the coffee shop. The delightful creature put in the effort. I kiss her on the cheeks, but close enough to the corner of her mouth to induce a small electric shock on our respective spines. I press her to sit down.

"Nice place," she says with enough sincerity for me to believe her.

Especially since the place is a shithole. Nothing impressive. It's not Phil's, but it's in the same range. She hasn't put on her hipster toque, revealing long, shoulder-length brown hair and a lit face that shows a little snub nose and big, expressive brown eyes. I find her both exciting and youthful, simultaneously pretty and bubbly. It's a far cry from the scowling face she displayed at our first meeting. She is wearing a short black sweater that fits her curvy body and ivory jeans that reveal a butt to die for.

"It smells good," she says, stepping closer to me as I pour us each a glass of white wine.

The liquor store clerk told me it was a very respectable wine in this price range. I fill my chest proudly and play it cool.

"Yeah, listen, I cooked us an osso bucco with what I found in the fridge."

I'm freaking out. I forgot to ask her if she's a vegetarian, or worse, vegan. Maybe she loathes eating lamb? Those girls are often like that. She doesn't eat meat thinking she's saving the earth, but failing to know that animal overpopulation exists and that it's harmful for the planet to let them gorge on pasture. I watch her, looking for any sign of discomfort or disappointment. I have pasta in the pantry, of course, but not a great wow factor. All I have mastered is a spaghetti with canned tomatoes. My mother used to call it dummy spaghetti. And she was as crappy as I am in the kitchen. The fruit doesn't fall far from the tree.

"I love osso bucco. How did you know?"

"I have my little secrets. I'm a private detective, remember?" I say, giggling like the lamb warming up in the oven.

I am a lucky devil. I take it as a sign that stars are aligned for a special evening with this ingenue who is more and more ravishing as time goes by. We sip our wine while discussing things and exchanging complicit glances. I love this pre-sex tension. This game of eyes and hands. The shifty looks and the smiles that are both awkward and naughty. That hand she runs through her hair, those long, penetrating glances with Fred Chopin and his violin as background soundtrack.

Dinner goes very well. My buddy outdid himself once again. I almost have an orgasm before my orgasm. Just like Anne-Marie, who moans with every bite like Meg Ryan in When Harry Met Sally, except she's not faking it. We go back to the living room to have another chat. I don't know why, but I'm reluctant to make the first move. I've come close a few times. I seem to have lost all my confidence. Something instructs me to wait. Then, after a moment of rare silence, she puts her glass on the living room table and says in a confident tone, "OK, let's get down to business now, shall we?"

She climbs on top of me, sitting on my thighs to face me, and she kisses me, forcing her tongue into my mouth. Of course, the first thing I do is grab her ass, which has had me drooling since she got here. My God, it's round and firm.

The Martinator wakes up promptly.

"I beg your pardon?"

Shit, did I say that out loud again? I really need to get checked out.

"Uh, nothing."

I grab her by the back of the neck and kiss her hard again. Just as she begins her descent toward my zipper, I stop her.

"Before we go any further, I have to settle something."

I stand up as she grumbles and go to my office to the sound of her impatient sighs.

"What are you doing?" she says in a voice that perfectly mirrors her exasperation.

She rightly wonders what could be so important as to break the moment we were living. I don't want to take a chance. I come back with a pen and paper.

"Just to make sure we're on the same page, we're going to fuck, right?"

She looks at me like, "No shit, Sherlock!"

"OK, so I just have a little contract here stating that this is voluntary sex and that, if you're not comfortable, I'll stop. If you could sign here next to your name? I don't have your last name, so please write it in. Oh yeah, and write your safe word here. May I suggest osso bucco?" I say, laughing with discomfort. She doesn't grab the pen I hand her. What is she waiting for?

"Are you kidding me?" she finally says, still refusing to comply.

"No, I'm not. Listen, I want more than anything to fuck like animals, but you'll appreciate that with my profession, I can't afford to end up in the news because a girl says I took her against her will, so this contract is just to protect us both and to put on paper the fact that we want to screw together, that's all. I won't have #metoo up my ass, and—"

She stands up angrily.

"You're a colossal moron. Can't you tell when a girl wants to have sex with you and when she doesn't? Do you really need a contract for that?"

"No, actually, yes, but—"

"You know what? You are right. I don't want to fuck you. So, you can stick your contract up your ass."

I spent three seconds thinking about how I would do that. Rolling it tight seems like the most viable option. She heads to the lobby and grabs her coat.

"Come on, Anne-Marie. Don't you see that I'm nothing but a gentleman who—"

"Fuck off," she shouts, slamming the door behind her.

There I am, sheepish with my pledge in hand, and the Martinator deflating faster than a friendless child's self-esteem. He realizes that I've screwed up once again and nothing exciting will happen. I'm sure he called me an asshole on his way down. I look at the contract and wonder if I overdid it. Maybe I went overboard in my attempt to be safe? If a guy can pick up on the right signals and is tuned in, there's no problem. After all, I'm not one of those idiots who takes a no for a yes. I'm not even taking a yes until it's a "yes motherfucker, shut the fuck up and do me right now." Or when a girl straddles me and says, "OK, let's get down to business now, shall we?" before kissing me languidly. I see you nodding, as if you're judging me from the top of your goddamn perfection. Like I'm the ultimate jerk.

Shit. You're right.

EIGHTEEN

Rashida stiffens as she hears a key flick into the huge metal door lock. She looks at Lea.

"Ready?"

Lea nods.

"Ready?" says Rashida, this time to Lauriane.

She nods.

As soon as the heavy metal door opens, tears slip quietly down Lea's cheeks.

Blondi sighs, seeing her sink her head into her pillow again. What a pain in the ass she can be. He places a tray with vegetable soup and two pieces of roast pork on Rashida's and Lauriane's beds. He then sits on the edge of Lea's bed and silently studies her for a few minutes, not knowing what to do next. Then, he asks what's wrong with her, patting her back. Lea instinctively braces herself but goes along with it. She finally gets up and sits on her bed. She notices Blondi looks a tad jaded. This is bad news. Lea's crying flabbergasts Lauriane. How the hell does she do it? But as soon as Lauriane thinks about her mother, about all the things she misses from her life with her friends or at school, about her crappy situation, she starts sobbing too. Blondi wrings his hands as he witnesses the two girls in tears. Rashida buries her face in her hands as if she is crying too, but no tears come. Never mind, she fakes it. If she rubs her eyes hard enough, they will redden. Lea urges Blondi to let them go. She says she knows he is kind deep down, that he has a big heart. He, too, can run away with them. She tries to convince him he, too, is there against his will. He doesn't blink, just quietly stares at the girls one after the other. Lea gets up, then takes two steps towards the heavy half-opened door. She watches Blondi from the corner of her eye to see how he reacts to each step she takes towards the door. He doesn't flinch. The giant's lack of reaction surprises Rashida. He is simply watching them in silence. She neither senses frustration nor concern on his face. He's rather blank, as if he didn't know how to react. The plan works much better than they had hoped. She is blown away by Lauriane's resolution to cry, too. Rashida had no choice but to jump in. Three young girls crying and begging him to let them go is probably more than this low IQ man can handle.

Lea is reaching the door and opens it slowly. She smiles at Blondi and goes out quietly. Lauriane follows her gently, as does Rashida. They find themselves in a concrete passageway similar to that of a jail. It's gloomy and echoing. The floor is cold. They follow the hallway and open every door they pass on their way. They are all closets with equipment inside, including a huge white freezer. They walk on to what appears to be a staircase built into the ceiling with a rope hanging down from it. The staircase obviously leads to the upper floor.

"Pull on this rope," says Lauriane, remembering seeing the same at her grandparents' house to get up to the attic.

They are too short. Rashida proposes to climb on Lauriane's shoulders, but she cannot stiffen up enough to reach the rope. Lea screams as Blondi walks quickly towards them.

"Hurry up, he's coming."

Rashida leaps, sitting on Lauriane's shoulders to reach the rope, but fails to do so. Lauriane nearly drops her every time.

"Damn it."

Rashida dismounts from Lauriane, and scans the surroundings, looking for a box or a chair, but nothing. Lauriane launches herself at Blondi.

"Let us go, you monster."

Blondi handles her with a disconcerting ease and holds her like a vulgar potato sack under his arm. She hits him everywhere on his body, but he doesn't flinch.

"Go back to your room," he says to them in a calm but firm voice. Lea implores him to open the door and to let them leave, but he wants none of this. The more they insist, the more he chokes Lauriane with his powerful arm.

"Go back or else I'll kill her."

His words hit home like a blast, and Lea falls silent. Rashida sees Lauriane is gasping for air, and wonders if she would sacrifice the girl's life to save hers and Lea's, but she gives in. She can't do that. She couldn't live with someone's death on her conscience.

"I can't breathe," Lauriane says faintly.

Lea notices the look of panic on Lauriane's face, and she pleads with Blondi to drop her. They will go back to the room, but he must release Lauriane. Lea takes a few steps towards the room, but Rashida doesn't move. Blondi holds Lauriane even tighter against him, and she passes out.

"OK, you fucking bastard," Rashida yells, before she follows Lea.

They enter the dorm with Blondie following. He puts Lauriane on her bed, limp as a rag doll. He looks harshly at the two other girls, breathing very hard. Lea keeps begging him to set them free, but he's no longer responsive. For the first time, Rashida breaks down in tears as the heavy door closes and the lock clicks.

"We'll never get out of here," she says. "This was our only chance, and we missed it. He'll never help us. We're screwed."

Lea also weeps as she watches Lauriane, still struggling to regain her senses. She is worried about her but calms down when she finally sees her breathe deeply. Lea is not as dramatic as Rashida. The roles are reversed. Rashida, normally the strongest of the group, is disheartened, while Lea, the sweet one, finds something positive in the whole situation.

"How can you possibly think this is good?" Rashida asks when Lea expresses her feelings.

Lea wipes away her tears.

"We shook him up. Did you see how he was totally defenseless when we were all crying? How he let us go before he changed his mind? That's a process. It proves he has a good heart."

Rashida shakes her head, this time crying tears of rage.

"No, he doesn't. No one with a good heart would put us through hell."

Lea leans against the wall behind her, pulling her legs closer to her body.

"I'm not saying he has a big heart. I'm saying he has a good one. It's just a matter of knowing how to crack it."

NINETEEN

Serge sits on a bench in his favourite park and revels in the beautiful day. He has long since stopped paying attention to the disapproving looks he gets from people passing by and mothers who drag their children away from him, as if he were planning to hurt them. His long, shaggy beard and his rags don't instill confidence, he admits. But he is no monster. Behind his vulgar attire hides a good man.

Broken, but good.

When he closes his eyes, he can turn into what he used to be. He can almost see himself back in the same place, thirty-five years earlier, wearing a suit and tie and eating his ham and cheese sandwich like he did every day at lunch, when he worked around here. Back when people admired and were jealous of him. He takes a deep breath as he listens to two robins chatting in a tree behind him. He always fancied the freedom of animals, even when they were domesticated. As a child, he wished he could switch places with his cat, who would watch him leave for school, basking in the sunshine on the living room floor. Today, he would give up his life to be a bird and be free to fly wherever and whenever he wanted. To feed on what the Earth provides. To fly away and never to return. To be free in his movements, but especially free of his body. To fly over the city slowly without the slanderous gaze of humans. He watches people come and go, most of the time slaves of their smart phones, or their "mind-numbing phones" as he calls them. Further on, an imposing guy drops groceries in an old grey van. He thinks it's Viateur Demers, a guy everyone in his inner circle dreads, but who, thank God, was picked up by a charity and is now renting a room in a vast building. Everyone on the street sleeps more peacefully now. They feared him because he was tall, massive, and dumb. An explosive combination. So, everyone kept their distance, never contradicting him or infuriating him. Serge was no exception. He knew better than that. Except there's something wrong with this. There are about ten bags of food filled to the brim in his shopping cart. Serge quickly works out that there must be four hundred dollars of food in there. There is no way Demers can afford a grocery bill of this magnitude, especially since he lives alone. Unless the house is having a party and mandated him to do the shopping. After all, he certainly doesn't own a van.

Serge gets up and walks quietly towards Demers. He slows down when he gets about fifty meters from the vehicle. His curiosity outweighs the danger of being seen, even though he is hiding in the trees. He watches stealthily as Demers ends up putting the bags in boxes in the back of the truck. He looks nervous, glancing around a little too often for someone who has nothing to worry about. Serge thinks he must be up to something fishy. He's a perfect catch for criminal gangs who need someone powerful and scary, but easily swayed. Serge tries to get a clue from the van, a distinctive sign, a logo, or something that would lead him in the right direction, but nothing. It looks like someone has repainted it with a paint roller to hide any previously visible artwork. Really weird. Once Demers gets behind the wheel and hits the gas, Serge tries to write the license plate number down, but the van has sped off, and oncoming traffic obstructs his view. He resolves to walk over to the rooming house Viateur lived in, to find out what it might be all about. It's not too far, a few blocks from the park. However, there is no sign of Demers' vehicle once he arrives. Serge waits for several minutes, in case Demers has to do some more shopping on the way back. Then, he enters the building and asks some questions. He approaches a lady who seems to work there. She looks at him suspiciously.

"We have no more rooms," she says.

"I don't want a room. Can you tell me if Viateur Demers still lives here?"

With suspicion in her eyes, the woman scans him from head to toe, trying to figure out what a bum could possibly want from one occupant.

"Maybe," she answers.

"Which room?"

The woman stiffens.

"I don't give any information about our tenants, let alone provide any personal data about them. I'm sorry."

"Are you having a party or some kind of activity?"

The lady who went back to her book looks at him with a squint.

"A party?"

"Yes, did you ask Viateur to do the shopping for any activity?"

Obviously, the woman has no idea what he is talking about.

"Look at this place. Do you really think we have time to party? People are trying to survive here, sir. This is not a summer camp. Now, if you don't mind, I have work to do."

She goes back to her document, sighing deeply. Serge looks around for a clue. What were you doing with all that food, Viateur? he says to himself. A noise behind draws his attention. An older man in a shadowy area of the lobby signals him to approach.

"You look for the big tool?"

The guy looks nervous, arms crossed, wearing a Montreal Canadiens jersey with shorts that haven't been washed in a while. A little smell of sulphur wafts from his clothes.

"It depends on what tool you're referring to," Serge replies.

The man sighs and looks around, as if to make sure no one

can hear them. Serge almost feels like he's in a James Bond movie. A Dollar store James Bond, but James Bond, nonetheless.

"Demers. Searching for Demers' room?"

"Yes, I am."

He holds out his hand, obviously expecting to be paid for the information. Serge searches his pockets, but finds only a five-dollar bill, which is huge for him. But it takes what it takes.

"This is all I have, buddy."

The man pouts with disappointment but stuffs the five-dollar bill in his pocket, anyway.

"Room 116, down the hallway."

He approaches Serge and whispers.

"But you didn't get that from me. All right?"

"I don't even know who you are."

"My name is—"

Serge raises his hand to interrupt him.

"No, you idiot. If I don't know your name, I can't rat you out."

The guy smiles and tips his index finger to his temple, showing that it's very ingenious.

"You're not as dumb as you look," the informant says with a sneer.

Serge frowns.

"OK then, what's your name?"

The man stops smiling.

"You told me not to tell you."

"Get lost," Serge says, laughing and waving him off.

He walks quietly towards the rooms looking for Demers's door. It's there, second from the left. Serge presses his ear to the door but hears nothing. He knocks timidly with two knuckles, still no answer. He turns the door handle, but it is locked. Serge goes around the building. There must be a window with a view of the room. Indeed, they all have a window. He looks at the second one from the right and presses his hands against the windowpane to hide from the sun and buries his face in looking inside. It is difficult to see inside the window because of the backdrop of the curtain. He comes to smash the window but stops his momentum. The noise will attract attention. He can give the information to Phil, who will investigate further. Or he can wait for Demers to be back and ask him questions himself. This is a bad idea. If Demers were unpredictable before, nothing proves he's changed now that he lives here.

Unless.

Serge has nothing to lose in trying. He plunges his fingers under a small protrusion at the base of the frame and tries to open it by pulling upwards. Nothing moves. He forces, shakes a little, and then a satisfying click draws a smile on his face. He opens the window and enters the room. There is a musty smell, proving that the place has not been ventilated in a long time, or backing up the thesis of an extended absence. Where could he be? Serge looks for clues, but finds nothing but 1988 pornographic magazines, presumably stolen from an old family collection, many colouring books, and an ambitious collection of chewed-up crayons. Serge looks through the pages of one sketchbook, and it feels as if a ten-year-old has spent hours clumsily colouring in between the lines. He knew that Demers was stupid, but this much? Probably elementary school IQ. Even if he finds nothing tangible, he'll follow the big guy the next time he sees him. To find out what he's up to.

"Curiosity will kill me one day," he thinks.

But he can't help it. Before leaving, he notices a glass jar with some cash in it. He takes five one-dollar coins and stuffs them in his pockets. At least he has not lost everything.

TWENTY

After an unsuccessful stint looking around, Marcel Lafleur feels it's time to take a break. He has set aside some of his agency's less urgent files to focus on Lauriane's case but has reached the point where he questions his relevance. After all, could he really bring something to the table? He wants to help Martin Lafs, because he admires him. He envies his style and his wit. He thinks he's a perfect complement to him and his office, but is it worth the effort? At a nearby convenience store, he looks for something to cool down. A beer lover, he rarely drinks at work. And since he's a bit of a hop elitist, he won't settle for a commercial brand. He heads to the cash register to pay for his soda water bottle and cake when his attention is drawn to the front page of a newspaper: "Lauriane Derome's disappearance: Police are amid a mystery." The convenience store clerk looks at him, waiting for his payment. Marcel smiles at him and puts his things on the counter.

"Nasty story, huh?"

"What?" says the young man, laconically.

"Lauriane Derome's case."

The clerk's eyes brighten.

"Yeah, I know her. We both go to the same high school."

"You do? What's she like?"

"Super pretty. Everyone likes her."

Marcel takes out his notebook.

"Does she have many friends?"

"Yes, she is very popular."

"Any names?"

The clerk scratches his head, thinking.

"I'm a loner, you know. She's surrounded by beautiful girls and douchebags, but I don't really know them."

Marcel hears a sigh from behind. A woman taps her foot, her arms full of groceries.

"Tangerine, I'm sorry," says Marcel while moving a step aside.

He allows the chubby woman to pass as she glares at him.

She lingers at the cash register, asking to check out an impressive quantity of lottery tickets, to Lafleur's dismay. He hates those people who appear to buy lottery tickets for the entire city. Do they really think they will one day draw the right number? Haven't they figured out that it's a bad plan to put all their hopes and a significant portion of their savings into this crap? That they're more likely to get struck twice by lightning than win the jackpot? Finally, the clerk is done with the line of people, who were waiting, and comes back to Marcel.

"By the way, I had a weird conversation with a guy the other day. I was chatting with a customer about this and a man behind him said something really strange."

"The customer?"

"No, the man behind him."

"What did he say?"

"It was last Tuesday, no Wednesday. No Tuesday. No, Wednesday because I just talked to my sister who—"

"Lemon, nobody cares. What did he say?"

"He said the girls are safe."

"The girls?"

"Yeah, that's what he said. It was Tuesday though."

Lafleur rolls his eyes.

"But why "the girls"? You were talking about Lauriane, right?"

"Yes, we were. And he said that the girls are safe and sound. The other customer and I looked at each other and wondered what he was talking about. He seemed to talk about something else, or he was trying to be interesting."

"Maybe he misunderstood."

"Or maybe he didn't," the clerk says, smirking like Inspector Columbo after breaking a deadlock.

"Green Lime. We don't know, indeed."

"What's with the citrus?"

"Never mind. Do you have the footage from that day?"

"No, they wiped the recordings after a week in here. It's been at least ten days since."

Lafleur sighs.

"Can you describe him?"

"Yes, I can."

"..."

"..."

"So?"

"Ho, you mean now? He was tall and bald. A strong man, though, and his eyes were not too sharp."

"Your way of saying he looked like an idiot?"

"Yeah, you could say that."

"What did he buy?"

"Bread."

"Do you notice if he was driving a car?"

"No, I didn't. Why, you think he had something to do with it?"

Lafleur shrugged.

"We can't rule anything out."

The clerk looked at him, realizing that he was not a casual observer.

"Who are you?"

"Lemon, yes, excuse me." Lafleur takes a business card out of his jacket." Marcel Lafleur, private investigator. The mother hired us to search for her daughter."

"Lauriane's mother?"

Lafleur nods proudly.

The clerk analyzes the business card with a concerned look.

"You don't think she ran away, do you?"

"For the moment, we don't know. It's unclear. But if your big guy is right, and there's more than one girl, we're probably dealing with human trafficking or a pedophile ring."

"Those bastards hang out in a ring?"

"What? No, it's like the Farmers' Circle, it's an organization."

"Why a circle then?"

Lafleur looks for a sensible answer for a few seconds before shaking his head.

"Grapefruit, who gives a fuck? That's not the point."

Lafleur thanks him and leaves the convenience store. As he drives towards his agency, he thinks about all the tall bald people he knows. He takes a detour to Lafs office.

TWENTY-ONE

I am tucked between two buildings to eat an ice cream sandwich with no worries. Phil, and especially Nicole, lecture me on my poor diet, consisting of just junk food and sugar. Since I'm thin and have a body to make your old aunt drool, I tell them to fuck off. Nevertheless, my pants are getting tight. I never had a weight problem before, but one of my uncles had the kind of waistline where you couldn't tell if he's facing front or back. He had a waitress's ass both front and back, as if he was perpetually sitting in a balloon. Not to sound unnecessarily alarmist, but there's a genetic thing going on. Except that right now, it's hot, and I need to eat something cold, and I won't give these two morons the chance to lecture me again. Phil has a way of spotting me, no matter where I am. Like the son of a bitch is spying on me. I know I'm lovely, but having my employee follow me around is a bit of a stretch. Of course, when I ask him about it, he denies it all.

"Why would I follow you, Lafs? I've got better things to do with my life, and you don't interest me enough to bother."

Nicole giggles like a turkey, despite my rude look.

I'm near the Lotus massage parlour where I used to go in another life, but since Kassandra, my beloved masseuse, left, I don't feel like going there anymore, except to piss off Sandra, the owner of the place. Sandra and I have a love-hate relationship. I love her, and she hates me with a passion. I watch all these women with their long, tanned and toned legs while stuffing this crap down my throat. I involuntarily smear ice cream around the edges of my mouth like a child suffering from Parkinson's. This is not how I will attract one of these beauties. Then I decide to walk back to the office. A fifteen-minute walk will allow me to stretch my legs and wash down the ice cream that I already regret eating. I walk through the Lotus parking lot instead of going around it, in order to save a few meters in the process. When I hear a door open, I jump back to hide behind the building wall. Who do I see? The Big O heading towards a black car. He obviously has a driver because he rushes into the back seat. I just have time to take a picture of him before he slips into the car. I've got him by the balls now, that idiot. I laugh out loud as I close my eyes. I pull myself together and walk towards the locked service door. I burst through the main entrance with a bang.

"Sandra, my darling," I say, yelling at the top of my lungs.

She looks up from the document she was drafting, and her eyes darken. "What in the world did I do, for God's sake?"

"You hit the jackpot, Sandra. You crossed my path, a pleasure few mortals will ever experience in their lives."

"I would gladly trade places with them."

I approach her with a smile as wide as my ears.

"Come on, don't be so stiff."

"The stiff could kick you in the dick."

"No, thank you."

"What do you want, Lafs, so you could get the fuck out, and I can go back to a world where you don't exist?"

"Kassandra didn't come back, did she?"

Sandra sighs with an annoyed pout.

"For the thousandth time, Kassandra is working in an accounting firm, and she's never coming back. At least not to take care of morons like you. I'd introduce you to one of the new girls if I hadn't banned you for life."

"Oh, that's right," I say, slapping my forehead with an open hand. "I keep forgetting that you arbitrarily kicked me out."

"Arbitrarily? Lafs. I had a million reasons to do it, like because you're a dumbass. And since it's a private business, I can do whatever I want."

"A private business flirting with prostitution, yes."

Sandra widens her eyes and plays dumb.

"What are you talking about? We are a very respectable salon here. I even have my permit. Do you want to see it?"

I giggle.

"Yes, of course. And the Hells Angels are just a humble motorcycle club."

"I don't know about that. I hate motorcycles almost as much as I hate you."

I put my hand on my heart. "Ouch, that hurts Sandra," I say in a falsely wounded voice, "but otherwise, always so happy-go-lucky?"

"Until ninety seconds ago, yes. And it's going to get even better when you stop being a jerk and get your fat ass out of my lobby."

Fat ass? Is it that obvious? Shit, I shouldn't have eaten that damn ice cream sandwich. I walk up to the counter. "Tell me, Sandy—"

"It's Sandra for you, Lafs. And you know what? It's Madame Sandra."

"Madame Sandra. That sounds like a brothel owner, no?"

She clenches her lips. I have a point.

"So, tell me, Sandy, was it the Big O I saw coming out of your building, by any chance?"

Sandra seems nervous suddenly. "The Big O?"

"Yes, don't play dumb. You know who the Big O is."

"The Olympic Stadium?" she says with a shit-eating grin.

"Mayor Ouellet."

"Oh yeah," she says, as if she finally realized who I was talking about. "No, I didn't see him."

I smile wickedly.

"He literally just walked out the back door."

"Well, colour me surprised."

"Kiss my ass."

"No way," she says.

"Does he come here often?"

"Who does?"

OK. Enough now. She needs to quit fooling around.

"Imagine the scandal if his wife ever found out that he hangs out at this dump."

"Stay polite, buddy. We can give crap to each other all we want, but this is a no-no."

I look sheepish.

"Noted. What about a vermin pit?"

She glowers at me.

"Stop messing around, Sandy. I want to talk to the girl who jerked him off."

"Like I said, I've never seen him around. But come to think of it, there is someone I'd like you to meet."

"Really? Finally, some good news."

She chuckles.

"Depends on whom."

She picks up the phone and asks for someone to join us. She looks at me strangely.

"You'll be very surprised, I'm sure."

Heavy footsteps come from the passage, suggesting that King Kong is approaching. I understand now that I will be disappointed. You're right, I should have known when that bitch's face came to life. So much so that I see an enormous mountain of a man turn the corner of the hallway and walk towards me, lowering his head so as not to hit it on the ceiling's wooden beam. That's how big he is. He's bald, wears a leather jacket worn to the bone, tattooed up to his neck, and he growls a bit like Chewbacca in Star Wars.

"Bam Bam, meet Martin Lafs, the guy I told you about the other day, remember?"

Bam Bam? Are you kidding? What a stupid nickname! He nods as he approaches and stares at me like I'm a tuna tartare.

"Hi Bam Squared," I say in a weak voice, taking a step back each time he takes one toward me.

He grunts again. I take a step sideways to look at Sandra.

"Can he talk?"

She smiles.

"Let's just say he has his own way of communicating."

"I hope he doesn't shit in the house," I say like an asshole.

"Oh, I wouldn't say that if I were you, Lafs," Sandra says with a falsely sorry look.

The orangutan grabs me by the collar and lifts me off the ground. Our two faces are facing each other now, except mine is turning blue as he strangles me with his huge paws. I try to kick him with my feet, but I might as well be banging against a brick wall. I feel like I'm going to pass out when I hear Sandra's distant voice ordering him to let go of me. I crash to the floor, rubbing my throat.

"Any more sarcastic comments, Lafs?"

I would like to answer, but no sound comes out of my mouth. I keep massaging my throat and wave her off. The huge twit is still standing there, staring at me like a horny gorilla.

"Can I borrow him?" I say in a hushed voice. "I'd like to introduce him to some of my enemies."

Sandra looks perplexed.

"Why would I harm people who share the same disgust I have for you?"

"Good point," I reply, getting up.

I look at the hulk who could kill me with a snap of his fingers, then at Sandra. Both of them observe me like blood-thirsty beasts, ready to pounce.

"Listen, I don't want to disturb you any longer," I say while backing up blindly towards the exit door.

I was taught never to turn my back on a bear. I open the door with a bang and get the hell out. Sandra has finally got herself a bouncer, like I advised her to do a few years ago, given the suspicious customers that come in and out of this shithole. I didn't think I would be at the receiving end of this one day.

TWENTY-TWO

Phil is in his office assembling an IKEA shelf. Lafs told him to take the money out of the petty cash box with a clear warning that he would not help him. He kept his word until now, meaning that he hadn't lifted a finger to assist him. Nicole observes him snickering from the reception desk.

"Help me instead of giggling," Phil says, irritated.

"I'm no good at this. Back home, Gilles is taking care of that, and I'm watching him. I'm better at watching people getting angry, assembling furniture with a crappy little key made for children's fingers."

She giggles again.

"You're right, if there was a trophy for the most judgy and less contributing person, you'd win it," Phil says with a smile.

"My favourite thing. Why do you think I work here if it's not only to judge all the crap Martin does?"

"You get your money's worth out of this, right?"

They laugh. Martin Lafs is their preferred target.

"Gilles wouldn't mind taking fifteen minutes of his time to help me with that, would he?" Phil asks, a few seconds later.

Nicole shakes her head with great intensity.

"He's playing golf with his retiring friends. And afterwards, he'll probably shove another box of Oreo cookies down his throat."

Philip sighs. He listens distractedly to the television mounted on his office wall, scratching his head. He can't figure out how to put the shelf together, with all those dotted lines and arrows. He can't believe that nowadays, manufacturers aren't providing how-to videos instead of those useless paper instructions. It would save trees, and besides, they are easy to produce. Any neophyte with a cell phone camera can make a quality video and post it online in minutes.

The TV news shows the same old bullshit; a politician says something to gain political mileage, or he says he will do something even though he knows he won't keep his word. Someone broke into a shoe store. It's supposed to rain over the weekend and FC Montreal lost again. Montreal's mayor pops up on the screen, surrounded by reporters discussing a local story that Phil listens distractedly to, cursing at the tiny Allen key that has hovered in the room's corner. He watches the mayor thinking back to what Lafs told him about their unexpected meeting a few days ago. Normally, officials don't care if a private investigator gets involved in solving a crime or not, as long as he doesn't interfere. Except for some zealous police officers, no one would refuse their help since the goal is to collect evidence and find the culprits, especially for missing persons, and even more so when it comes to teenagers. Mayor Ouellet is addressing a mundane situation in one of the city's boroughs, but there's one thing that bothers Phil about the way he talks. He says some words strangely. It sounds like there's something wrong with the city's chief magistrate. Is the Big O on drugs or something? If not, stumbling over words is one of the warning signs of a stroke. At least, that's what he read somewhere. He asks Nicole to come into his office. She approaches after taking a long time getting up from her seat.

"Listen to this and tell me if you notice anything weird."

He plays the scene he has paused on his TV receiver, and Nicole complies. Phil looks at her, analyzing her every reaction, but she doesn't budge.

"I don't see it," she says, almost embarrassed she can't help.

Phil rewinds the footage. His receiver allowed him to pause a live broadcast, and even rewind it.

"Listen to how he pronounces certain words."

In the clip, the mayor talks about how the lack of housing in this borough is something that needs to be addressed, how difficult it is for the residents. Phil again notices that Nicole cannot grasp what he is getting at. She apologizes that she can't help and goes back to her desk, looking defeated. Phil watches the mayor speak to reporters with confidence, then realizes that Nicole is upset with herself.

"No worries, Nicole," he shouts from his office. I guess I was imagining things.

Nicole mumbles something Phil doesn't catch, but he guesses she's saying it's okay. Phil knows how to cheer her up when she's feeling blue. He asks her about a tv show she listens to daily, and she instantly forgets all her troubles. He doesn't get how anyone can be so passionate about these crappy, overly dramatic shows with zany, unrealistic storylines. But if it allows them to escape from their boring lives for a bit, why not? He replays the footage again and sees that he's not delusional. It's unequivocal: the mayor is saying the word "difficult" oddly. He substitutes cult for cole, he says the situation is "difficole." He didn't want to sway Nicole and give her too many clues about what he wished to confirm, especially since she has a habit of telling him what he wants to hear. She doesn't like dispute. Maybe the mayor has always had this speech impediment, and Phil never noticed it before? When you're not looking for lice, you don't dig deep in your nephew's head. He looks at the fragmented shelf on the floor, then at the plan in his hands and shakes his head. He's not stupid. He just has to focus, and he will get it done. Millions of people around the world assemble IKEA furniture. There's no reason he can't do it. He grabs the small Allen key lying on the carpet and looks at the instructions again. He joins boards A and D together and takes one of the F1 screws. He turns it three times before the Allen key slips through his fingers again and makes one more glide to the corner of the wall, this time to his right. He feels an immense surge of rage coming on but controls his temper. He nearly throws the two pieces of wood through his office window. Why are these damn Allen keys so tiny? Like they were designed to challenge customers' patience. He sighs deeply. There's no point in getting pissed off at a crappy fucking shelf. He pulls himself together and figures he'll take it one piece at a time. But it will undeniably be an extreme display of self-control. The goal of the afternoon is not only to successfully assemble the cabinet, but to limit the amount of punching the wall and screaming in despair.

TWENTY-THREE

Lafleur tells me about his convenience store story, and I honestly wish I was interested, but God knows I'm not. After all, didn't he just spend the last five minutes explaining to me why he chose one sparkling water flavour over another? Why the hell should I give a shit? You can drink turpentine for all I care. All of this, interspersed with screaming citrus names all the time, nothing to help my indifference.

"Flower, get to the point!"

Lafleur hates this nickname. To him, Flower is Guy Lafleur. There's no way he'd rob him of his nickname. Guy is an ice hockey icon. Obviously, the day Lafleur mentions this to me, is the day I start calling him Flower as much as humanly possible. You know my mythical kindness, don't you? As he rambles on, describing the details of what happened, I massage my temples and shake my head in despair. A convenience store clerk, that's the big story? Lafleur seems surprised by my lack of enthusiasm. I'm really surrounded by jerks who give themselves more credit than they deserve. In the meantime, Phil slips into my office to listen to Flower's account. This day had been off to such a good start.

"What do you mean by "the girls," the fat man asks.

"Who cares, Phil? Don't give credit to his whims."

All too happy to find an attentive ear, Lafleur resumes his

story, jumping up and down in his seat like a little girl who has just learned she won a trip to Disneyland. I bury my face in my hands as Nicole approaches, wearing her typical "what's going on here?" smile. She plants herself in my door frame. The more I listen to Lafleur's story, the more disheartened I become. Our cause rests on the shoulders of a convenience store clerk with too much imagination. I have never felt further away from solving a case than I do right now. I've looked hard, but I don't see how anyone can drop a pro bono case without looking like a total asshole. Although that's not something that would normally faze me, as you can guess.

"So, if there are multiple girls, it's an organization that's bigger than us. Organ trafficking maybe?" Phil says, rubbing his chin.

He thinks it makes him look more intellectual.

"We should call the RCMP and get out of the way," I say laconically.

"Maybe," Lafleur says after giving it a few seconds of thought.

I explode.

"No, you dumbass. I was shitting with you. We won't hand over everything we've got to the police when they've done all they can to block our way from the start," I say. "Think about it."

"Lafs," Phil says softly, "I don't think this is the time to have a pissing contest. The goal is to rescue Lauriane, and the other girls, if there are any. The "how" is irrelevant."

"The goal is to get you out of my office. There too, the "how" is irrelevant," I reply furiously.

But these morons stay put and keep talking to each other. I watch them, unable to grasp their stupid logic. Tell the police? About what? That a convenience store clerk saw a man talking about some girls?

"There's more," Phil says as I throw my arms in the air, meaning finally something tangible. "Come into my office."

This is a really crappy day. Why can't he tell us in my office for the love of shit? Upon arriving at his door, I get it. There's a half-assembled wooden shelf lying on the floor. It would have deserved a better fate than to end up in Phil's clumsy hands.

"We don't have time for this. Come on, Phil."

He looks at me quizzically, not quite sure what I'm talking about. Then he spots the boards on the floor and connects the dots.

"Not this. I want to show you something on TV."

"Who gave you permission to get that shelf?"

"You did."

"I literally never—"

Phil grabs a portable tape recorder from his desk and presses "Play" while watching me with a placid look on his face. A man with a voice that sounds like mine says that yes, he can buy a shelf, that he doesn't give a shit, and to ask Nicole to use petty cash to pay.

"Nothing proves it was me on that tap—"

He interrupts me by waving me off for a moment. A few seconds later, he starts the tape again: "So you, Martin Lafs, authorize me to buy a shelf at IKEA from the petty cash box and put it in my office?" The voice that sounds like mine says, "yes, you asshole, you can buy the damn shelf and stop making a big deal out of it."

Phil looks at me, a smirk on his face. I give him a stern glare and sigh.

"OK, what did you want to show us?"

He puts down his tape recorder and turns on the TV, then navigates the remote for a few seconds. He shows us a mayor's press briefing from earlier at noon. Then he pauses the video and looks at us, his eyes sparkling as if he's just walked into a bakery. I watch Lafleur to see if I'm the only one who doesn't get it. From the look on his face, I am not. We watch Phil hoping he'll enlighten us, but there he is, with his dickhead, staring at us with an "I told you so" look.

"What are we supposed to see, Phil, for the love of God Almighty?"

He's got a way of getting me on my nerve, this guy.

He plays the excerpt again and asks us to pay attention to the pronunciation of certain words. Yes, it's true that he seems to say difficole instead of difficult, but maybe he always did? I see him digging through his recordings and I hate his way of having an answer for everything. He shows us a passage from six months ago. It looks like he's pronouncing difficult correctly. Phil looks at us with a smug look that makes me want to shove his shelf up his ass. Doesn't he realize how anecdotal this is? Maybe he made a mistake that day, maybe he was tired? Holy shit, he's looking for another recording. I rub my eyes as Lafleur seems genuinely interested. What a jerk. Phil shows us two more tapes where the Big O is still titillating on the word difficult.

"Checkmate," says Phil with all the pride in the world.

"Checkmate what?" I say, bursting. "Checkmate nothing. You have absolutely nothing solid. What do you expect us to do with that, Kasparov?"

Phil scratches his head. He does not know. I look at the tape recorder on his desk.

"Are you sure you don't have the answer on your tape?"

I look at him and Lafleur.

"You guys are a bunch of losers. I hope that while you were wasting your time with your fads, another girl wasn't abducted."

I turn around, and there's Nicole with her glorious air. "So, you're admitting that there's more than one girl and that someone kidnapped them?"

I look at her reproachfully. "Let it go, poor man's Columbo."

I walk back to my desk and feel a lump in my stomach. Holy shit, I hope they are wrong, and this is not an organization trafficking girls. The more it goes, the more this pro bono is bullshit.

And the more it scares the bejesus out of me.

TWENTY-FOUR

There is a crowd next to an old disused building near the old Champlain Bridge. Serge moves closer to inquire about the situation. Joe, a well-known homeless man from the area, is sitting on a concrete block, trying to regain his composure. One man in the background sees Serge out of the corner of his eye and beckons him to come closer.

"Joe is a hero," he says.

"What do you mean?" Serge asks.

"Tell him, Joe."

Joe is gasping for air. Serge hands him a bottle of water he just bought, and the poor guy chugs it in one gulp. He tells them that he was walking in a park to get some shade, and then he saw a man coming from the other side of the clearing. It was a big man. He came up to a girl from behind like a cheetah stalking its prey and grabbed her, lifting her off the ground, and crushing a hand over her mouth.

"I didn't think twice and told him to leave her alone. He squeezed the girl in his arms, and she went limp like a rag. I grabbed the iron bar from my backpack and walked over slowly. "Let go of her," I said again. But he just looked at me, holding the kid close to him. He instructed me to get lost if I didn't want any trouble, so I raised my iron bar, telling him repeatedly to leave the girl alone, and kept moving in his direction. I got the fright of my life. I think I even pissed myself."

Joe runs his hand through his hair, as if telling the story gives him an adrenaline rush, as if he's searching for the best words so that everyone sees the magnitude of what he's been through.

"Then voices came from further away, at which point the giant dropped the girl in the grass and left quickly. I went over to her, but she was unconscious, so I asked for help. One of the kids who came to see what I was shouting about called 9-1-1 and the girl eventually woke up. She wasn't in any pain, just a little dazed and unhinged. I told the cops what I saw, but they didn't believe me, as usual. A tramp like me, you know? They thought I'd probably had too much to drink and made the story up."

Serge shakes his head. The police really don't give them much credibility. Probably they even thought Joe was the assailant. He looks at the man, convinced he is telling the truth. While some of them have a bad habit of making up stories to be more interesting, Joe is far too dazed to have come up with any of this.

"Did you see the guy's face?"

Joe signals no with a shake of his head. "He had a ski mask and a deep voice. He was huge, like six foot six or something like that. I'm six foot one, and he was towering over me."

"Did you notice anything else? Anything distinctive about the way he moved?"

"Here we go. Serge is playing detective again. You okay, Hercule Poirot?" sneers one man further back.

Serge has a reputation for asking a lot of questions and trying to know everything that happens around, but he embraces that reputation without qualms and smiles. If he only knew why he does this.

Joe stands up to stretch out. "Not really anything to catch the eye. Except maybe that he was walking funny."

Serge gets excited. That's what he wanted to hear. He asks him to elaborate.

"It looked like he was limping slightly," Joe says.

"On his right leg?" says Serge.

Joe widens his eyes. "Exactly. Do you know him?"

Serge waves off the question. He guessed it. After all, he had a fifty per cent chance of being right.

Once everyone has left, Serge goes over the information Joe has given him, but he already knows that his instincts are right. A gigantic man with a hollow voice and a limp in his right leg— it could only be him.

Back outside Martin Lafs's office, Serge is impatient, wishing Phil would take his cigarette break soon, or that he would see Marcel Lafleur or, at the very least, Martin Lafs if he has to. After about fifteen minutes, he sees Lafleur and Lafs approaching. Lafs rolls his eyes as he listens to what Lafleur is saying. Serge stops them and explains his theory. Joe's story, coupled with the grey van, the big grocery store and the abandoned room, for him there is only one possibility:

"I suspect someone I know."

Martin Lafs chuckles and says that of course they will follow all the leads made up by alcoholics in need of a thrill. But Lafleur is more sympathetic. He asks questions even though Serge would not disclose his suspect's name. His concerns stem from Viateur Demers' being an ex-itinerant, and Lafs tendencies to jump to conclusions.

"Serge has nothing to lose by working on this lead, boss," Lafleur says.

"Besides his own time, no," Lafs says, chuckling as he heads back to the office. Serge watches him rush into the building and wonders how this man can run a private detective agency with such a narrow mind. And why do so many people keep helping him? Why do Phil and Nicole remain loyal to him? Why does Lafleur call him boss? He has to admit, he too is still here.

He shakes his head. He doesn't give a damn about Martin Lafs. What really matters is this beginning of a lead, and he already knows his attention will be on Demers from now on.

He'll be watching him to see where it leads. Who knows, maybe
to Lauriane Derome.

And the other girls, if any.

TWENTY-FIVE

For the first time, Lea sees Rashida looking totally lifeless, extinct. As if she has lost all hope. Lauriane also stares at her with a concerned expression. Then, she goes to Lea's bed to talk her into keeping up her charm operation towards Blondi. She believes he will eventually cave in, so they must never give up. Anyway, they don't have any other options.

"It won't work," Rashida says in a weak voice, staring straight ahead.

"I will fight until the end," Lauriane replies in a dry tone. "We will find a solution."

Rashida laughs. "Good luck with that."

Then, she lies down and wraps her head in her blanket.

Lauriane goes back to her bed, annoyed by her friend's attitude. The last thing they need is a ball and chain to drag along. They need to rebuild Rashida's confidence if they're to have any chance of getting out. The problem is she's been unresponsive since their failed escape attempt earlier. The door opens heavily, startling Lea at the same time.

"Hello, girls," Blondi says with his low voice, pushing his tray on wheels.

Lauriane looks at Lea, surprised; he is cheerful as if he has already forgotten about his previous rage. Rashida doesn't move a muscle. Blondi watches her for a few seconds with a quizzical look.

"What's wrong with this one?"

"She is tired," Lea says with a tense smile.

He approaches Lea by holding out his plate, and she wants to speak to him. He obediently sits down on her bed and listens as she says how much she misses her mother. How much she misses her life. Blondi gazes at her tenderly, just nodding.

"You would like my mother. She is such a pleasant woman. Would you like to meet her sometime?"

"Of course," he says.

Rashida uncovers her head and glances quickly at Lauriane, who listens attentively, biting her thumbnail. She likes the way Lea leads the discussion around family. She asks questions about Blondi's family, but as usual, he is not very outspoken about his private life. Lea explains what she plans to do when she gets out, how nice she thinks he is, and how she would like to introduce him to her folks. Blondi is hooked.

"You're so strong," Lea says, stroking his forearm, "I like real men like you. You would protect me."

She lowers her head, embarrassed, and twists her hands.

"I'm uncomfortable asking, but—"

She remains silent to assess how he will react. He urges her to carry on like a child, begging his parents to open his Christmas presents.

"Would you like to be with me in the real life?" He puts his enormous hand on hers, causing her to shiver with disgust.

"I'd like that more than anything in the world, Lea. I never told you, but I think you're beautiful."

He looks away at once, dubious of his audacity. He asks her to forgive him. It was inappropriate. She has a reassuring smile. She finds him charming, too. There is no harm in that.

Lauriane would have eaten popcorn if she could have. Lea's talents as an actress impresses her.

Rashida keeps listening, pretending to sleep.

"But it's impossible as long as we're here," Lea says in a

sorrowful tone. "Can't you get us out? I'm tired of them too," she said, pointing to the other two teenagers with her chin. "As long as they're here, we can't live our romance."

Blondi glares at the other two girls, then turns back to Lea. "I know, but I can't."

"Why not?" she asks, careful not to put too much pressure on him.

Blondi stiffens. He doesn't like the way things are going

Lea reverts to her initial pitch. "Would you like to get married one day?"

He relaxes instantly. "Of course, wouldn't you?"

Lea lowers her eyes. "Yes, it's every little girl's dream, you know? A day just for them, a fairy tale."

"And the honeymoon," Blondi says, then blushes and apologizes.

"No, you're right," Lea says, putting her hand on his. "So is the honeymoon."

The idea of being with this monster makes her nauseous, but she conceals it.

She asks him to let the other two girls go, so they can finally be alone and find out where this could all lead. They would go to her mother's house for dinner, formally introduce him.

"I'd love to, but I can't."

Lea's eyes fill with tears. "But why? You don't like me, is that it?"

"Of course not, come on, I just told you how beautiful I think you are."

"So, what's stopping you? A man must do everything for the one he loves, right?"

Blondi is disturbed. It's the first time Lauriane sees a sign of doubt, as if he were looking for a way to indulge. Her heart is pounding.

"I'll talk to him."

Lea glances furtively at her friends.

"Him? Who, him? I thought it was only us?"

"The boss."

"What is his name? Why haven't I seen him yet?"

"I don't know. I do as he says. But he doesn't mean you any harm. You'll like what he has in mind for you, I swear."

Lea ponders for a few seconds, then grabs Blondi's hand again.

"I only want to be with you. I want nothing from him. You get that?"

He nods.

"I would want that too, believe me."

"Is he stronger than you?"

"No, he's not."

"So, you can do whatever you want, right?"

"It's complicated."

"Do it for me. We deserve to delve into our interest for each other, to see where it will take us, don't you think?"

He looks at her with affection.

"Oh, yes!"

"Then make it happen."

He stands up, then promises to see what he can do.

"Don't tell him about what we talked about. We need to keep this between us because I'm sure he'll think I'm manipulating you. But look at me."

He stares into her eyes.

"Do you think I could fake a true love like this?"

He wavers a little, then signals that he doesn't.

"So don't tell him. We'll talk to him when you figure out a way to get us out of here. And one more thing, can you leave the door unlocked? It's cramped in here, and I need to stretch my legs. I'd like to walk down the hall. I'm not leaving here without you, anyway."

He smiles and hands the trays to the other two girls. He massages his right thigh, which is sore from his injury a few weeks ago. He glances at Lea and closes the door, except that they don't hear the usual click of the lock. After about ten minutes, Lea gets up and pulls the door open. Rashida jumps up.

"Holy shit, Lea, you're a genius."

Lea ventures into the dark corridor and explores in silence. Her two partners follow her lead, tiptoeing up to the stairs leading to the ceiling hatch. They step back when they hear a door close loudly. Then another man's voice.

They don't quite understand what it's all about, because the words are muffled, but the discussion escalates. Then the other man yells, and this time it is crystal clear: "If you're not the man for the job, I'll find someone else."

Then heavy footsteps above their heads approach in their direction. They sneak back into their room. Rashida gets excited.

"That's exactly what we needed to do, but who is this other guy? I thought we were just supposed to get past Blondi, but there's the other jerk too? Why do we never see him?"

Lauriane goes over what they've learned: something's coming up. Blondi says they'll be thrilled with it, and there's this other man Blondi calls "the boss" who yelled at him and said he'd find someone else if he didn't do what he told him to do.

"One thing is for sure; keep the seduction going until the end, but don't rush him. It must look real," Rashida says. "Lea, you absolutely have to slouch. After what the other guy said, it's clear that Blondi will be wary the next time he gets down here. The good news is that he trusts us enough to leave the door unlocked. So, as soon as we hear him coming down, we need to get back here. If he catches us in the hallway, he'll get scared and lock the door again."

The three girls see a small light at the end of the tunnel. They have a chance to trick Blondi, but they must be patient and cunning. How to get past the other line of defense remains to be seen.

How could they overcome the unknown that seems to be at the root of their misfortune?

TWENTY-SIX

Hiding behind a tree, Serge Côté has never felt more like playing detective as he does now. It's not the first time he's followed someone, but this time he feels the danger. No one is paying attention to him, as usual. He is all alone in an abstract and busy surrounding, which is perfect for patrolling. No one suspects him, no one cares he exists. His homelessness is not all bad, and he has an unquenchable need to be left the hell alone. He didn't drink alcohol this morning, contrary to his habit. He wants to be in control of all his senses. Normally, he helps Lafs's team to catch cheating husbands or insurance fraudsters, ordinary cases. But this time, the lives of teenage girls may be at stake. Who knows what's up with all those missing girls who strangely vanish and are never heard from again? If he can do his part, maybe his life will change forever? Maybe he'll recover his former groove? Or at least enough of it to make his life slightly more bearable? No time to fantasize. He needs to focus on the task at hand. He sees Viateur Demers enter a pharmacy and waits for him to come out, still hidden behind the huge oak tree standing in front of the store.

"What are you doing?"

Serge is startled. He turns back and sees a man nicknamed Ti-Mousse, a homeless man he knows well. Shit, what is he doing here, for heaven's sake? He will screw everything up.

"Now is not the time, Mousse," he says, waving him away.

"What are you doing?" Ti-Mousse asks again with a large toothless smile.

"I told you I can't talk to you. Go away."

Ti-Mousse loses his cheerfulness, and his eyes darken. He stares at the ground silently. Serge feels guilty.

"That's okay, Mousse. I'll see you later. I'll explain to you. But you really must go now."

He shoves his hand in one of his rag pockets and hands him a few dollars.

"Here, have a cup of coffee on me, OK?"

Ti-Mousse's face brightens, and he thanks Serge, who heads back to his lookout. Just as his fellow bum is walking away, Serge finally spots Demers coming out of the facility and heading to his right. It's now or never, Serge thinks. He must follow him quietly, far enough away to go unnoticed, but close enough to keep him in sight. Demers will probably overlook him like everyone else, but one can never be too careful. The giant takes a right turn past a huge red brick building that is no longer inhabited. Serge goes in the same direction as him, about thirty seconds later. Demers is still too far away for his liking. He will have to get closer. If Demers notices him, he will pretend to be drunk and meander. Where is he going? It's a long way from his place. What can he be doing? Serge focuses his attention on Demers' unsteady gait. He still has a chronic limp. He doesn't remember ever having seen him walk normally. It is one of his distinctive signs. Intellectually limited, not much money or support, he lives in the same shabby room Serge broke into earlier. He too has a penchant for alcohol and drugs, which could make him unable to pay for his room and return to the streets to sleep under the stars and terrorize others. Serge always hated the expression "sleeping under the stars". If people knew how ugly the stars can be sometimes. He feigns a stagger as he approaches his target, who doesn't suspect his presence. Demers has a lethal combination: he is big and strong, but he is also very gullible. Under the wrong influence, he could do a lot of damage, and that's what Serge fears most. That someone with bad intentions would take advantage of his intellectual flaws to get him to do things he wouldn't normally do, for the lure of gain, to improve his life.

Serge gets it. No one likes to be miserable. No one wants to be looked down upon and ignored by society. No one fantasizes about begging for money, while sitting in their own dried urine. For many, it's a matter of life and death. So, Demers probably figured it was better to do something slightly illegal than to play by society's rules and lose every time the sun rises. Viateur Demers never looks back to see if he is being followed. He goes ahead, suspecting nothing, which makes Serge doubt his theory. What if he has nothing to do with this? What if Serge is just making up scenarios that exist only in his mind? It wouldn't be the first time, and certainly not the last. Lost in his doubts, Serge slows down unintentionally. Nothing makes sense anymore. Demers is frivolous, but not to the point of walking like that, freely, without looking around continuously if he has something to be sorry about. Still, Serge speeds up to get even closer to him. Even if the giant is not involved, Serge needs to know for sure. He has to take him out of the equation, with no doubt.

Serge turns right into the alley Demers has just taken a few seconds before, except that he no longer sees him. He stops and looks around. Did he turn in the right place? He rages against circumstances. How could he have lost him? He takes two more steps forward, still scanning his surroundings, when a figure emerges in front of him.

Demers.

Serge freezes, so surprised that he forgets to pretend to be drunk. The two look at each other blankly. Demers stares at him, his eyes dark with rage.

"I—I think I took a wrong turn," Serge says in a faint, unconvincing voice.

Demers answers by smashing his fist on the old man's face.

TWENTY-SEVEN

Since I decided to walk more rather than drive, I look like I don't own a car. I always judge people who walk, looking exhausted, from my full-blown air-conditioned car. Especially those bussers waiting in a row as if their life depended on it. I know, you think they do it to save the planet, that they are better humans than me driving my car by myself, that I should be hanged from the Greenpeace scaffold. To which I would reply first, screw you with your medieval executions, and second, I call bullshit. No one loves the earth enough to willingly ride an ass-breaking bus. However, I'm not getting any younger, and since I started my agency, I've been physically inactive. I'm sitting at my desk or in my car trailing a candy thief. So, when I get a chance, I take a walk and listen to music. It helps me maintain my godlike body and avoid looking like Phil, the chubby one. Although he too has a God body. After all, Buddha is a god, right?

I move to the rhythm of The Doors' songs. I am on my way to meet Anne-Marie, who agreed to see me again after what I could describe as the "contract fiasco". I want her to realize that my intentions were good. You just can never be too careful nowadays. But she's right, if you don't act like a jerk, there's no reason to be concerned. I am a well-known name in town, after all. There are far too many people who would like to blackmail me. I don't hold back on judging cheating spouses aloud when I catch them in the act. I remember storming into a hotel room to nail one of my clients' husbands. Her cheating spouse was with another woman. They closed the curtains and stayed there for hours. I was tired of waiting for them to come out, so I could take a revealing picture. I forced fate. I only do this when I'm sure the guy is not a physical threat to me, in the sense that I would never do this with a guy who can beat me up. I knocked on the motel room door insistently, and gone in and pushed the guy in, then photographed them still oozing with sex. A round of insults followed, you guessed it. We went from "your mother must be proud of the job you're doing, scumbag" to "fucking parasite". But see, I have no problem getting called names by a jerk who is riding a woman who isn't his wife, much to the chagrin of the one who is. "Wifey isn't as dumb as you thought she was, eh, motherfucker?" I tell them every time. After a while, as the asshole took off, leaving his girlfriend behind, I looked at the splendid woman sitting on the bed, who hadn't even bothered to cover her wonderful breasts. She looked at me furiously, which made me horny. I won't lie to you. I checked my watch and since I had some free time, I took a shot.

"What should we do?" I asked with a smirk on my face.

"Get lost, dumbass. That's what you should do."

She didn't know, but the madder she was, the hornier I got.

"Come on, the jerk paid for the room. You're hot. I'm handsome as fuck. Why waste this moment?"

She stared at me with a look that meant "who is this idiot" and hissed a wicked laugh between her perfect teeth.

"That's right, he paid me, you didn't. So, get out, asshole."

"Come on," I said as I got closer. "You're ready, and so am I. Look." I pointed at my pants, exhibiting a blister of the Martinator.

Anyway, I'll spare you the details, but it ended in insults and screams. The Martinator went back to his shell, and we got even with calling each other a jerk and a whore. But now, with Anne-Marie, it's different. I will join her at our coffee shop (yes, we made it our own) to explain ourselves. I mean, to explain myself.

She has nothing to explain. Everything is clear on her side. I hope to find the right words because frankly, I would love to do her so much. It's not even funny. The more I see her, the more I like her, and the more I like her, the more I want us to be together. And the more she pushes me away, the more I want her. It's like I'm a girl who can't get out of a toxic relationship with a man who wants nothing to do with her except to fuck her once in a while.

There's a gathering to my right, and although I know I shouldn't interfere, even though I'm sure I'll regret it, I can't help it. I'm going to go and see what's going on. I'm a private investigator, remember? By definition, that means that I get involved in things that are none of my business. So don't think I don't interfere in everyday life. I hear a lot of commotion, so definitely I'm going to stick my nose in. Don't go snowflake on me now! There are about ten semi-dumb people standing in front of a huge waste container, giggling like girls watching a boy's band. I stretch my neck to figure out what is so funny but can't see anything from where I stand.

"What's up?" I ask, looking at my watch to make sure I have enough time before I'm late for my date. One guy looks at me blankly, looking annoyed.

"You want me to really annoy you, you little prick?" I say to myself, clenching my fists.

"Get lost, Grandpa," another asshole says to me.

Okay, that'll do. I walk toward him looking menacing when I hear another voice say, "Hey, guys, he's moving."

He moves? Who does? I lost interest in the ageist moron and moved closer to the container. What the hell is he doing here? I wave my badge quickly to make it look like I have some authority, so they get out of the way. The container reeks with rottenness. What the fuck is Serge doing sleeping in there? I mean, I know he pisses himself sometimes, but lying in a smelly dumpster is the last straw. I aggressively push away everyone between me and him and notice that his face is bluish. Fuck, he looks worse than usual, and I swear that's no small thing. I squint to fight the scent of urine and waste abusing my nostrils, and I shake his foot to wake him up.

"Hey Serge, what the hell are you doing in there?"

He is not responsive. He moves quietly, but like someone sleeping. He must be dead drunk.

"Do you know this old retard?" says an obnoxious voice behind me.

"Shut the fuck up, you bastard. I'm the only one who can call him a retard."

He replies something that I would have a huge trouble giving a shit about, and I keep trying to wake Serge up. His face is smashed, as if an army had beaten him up. I call for help with my iPhone, keeping my eyes on him. The other idiots eventually lose interest in an unconscious wanderer on garbage bags and leave one by one to go to some equally unproductive occupation. I go with Serge in the ambulance, even if the smell is unbearable. I stare at the medic who is sitting in the back with us and jealously look at the mask on his face.

"Wouldn't it bust your balls to throw me one, too?"

He looks at me, puzzled.

"A mask," I say. "The old chap stinks."

He looks in his bag and hands me a tiny jar of Vicks. What on earth does he want me to do with that? Noting my incomprehension, he sighs and makes me spread some under my nose. Goddamn it, it's strong. My eyes fill with tears as if I've just received a jab in the face. I look at the paramedic, pissed. This guy is fucking with me. Shit, it works. Once I inhale through my mouth, I can't smell anything. I tried to breathe in through my mouth earlier, but the smell was still getting to my nostrils. Now nothing. I give the medic a thumbs up, but he couldn't care less.

I must have spent two hours at the hospital with Serge still unconscious. Those jerks gave him a powerful sedative. They didn't care to tell me instead of having me stand there waiting for him to open his eyes. It looks like he's going to be out all night. I contact Phil to come and take over, if he wants to. I have plans for the evening, but I can't remember what they are.

Holy shit. Anne-Marie.

I look at my iPhone and I have twenty-one text messages. I don't need to look at them to know what they are about. Actually, I only read the last one, which reads, "Fuck you, moron. Don't ever contact me again."

I look at Serge furiously. If he didn't already have a broken nose, I would handle it myself. Then I calm down, seeing him dozing off. I figure he's entitled to rest from time to time. It must be decades since he's slept so deeply, with a trickle of drool dripping down his repulsive beard.

You've earned it, old fella.

TWENTY-EIGHT

Back at the hospital the next day, I look at Serge's swollen face, feeling no particular emotion. Am I a psychopath, or do I have selective empathy? Whatever the reason, there is a vast difference between Phil's resolutely worried look and my impassiveness.

"How much longer will you play dumb like this?" I say to an unconscious Serge.

Phil looks at me with an angry and disconcerted look. I tighten my lips as I meet his gaze and check my watch, sighing heavily. I have other things to do and—

I throw myself at Serge.

"Why? Why does it always happen to the best of us? My God Serge, not you (I look up to the ceiling with my arms stretched to the sky). Take me instead, God. Take me instead."

Phil is confused, but when he hears footsteps behind him and looks at the beautiful nurse who is watching me with concern, he gets it, and his face hardens.

"Nice use of people's misfortune, asshole," he says, whispering in my ear before sitting down on the big green armchair in the room's corner.

I'm still lying on top of Serge, trying as hard as I can to get some tears out, but nothing happens. I hoped that the smell would help, but it looks like they showered him. Or at least they sprayed him with some kind of scent neutralizing agent. Holy crap, do I have to stick a finger in my eye socket for this? My lack of acting skills will be my downfall one day.

"You know, your friend is fine. He just needs to rest," the beauty says, smiling.

Her voice is like an angel stroking strings on a divine harp. My groin twitches.

"Are you sure? He's in a coma, I don't understand."

She has an even more charming giggle than her voice.

"He isn't in a coma at all. We sedated him. Didn't you know that?"

"Yeah, Lafs, didn't you know that?" says that scumbag Phil from his shitty chair.

I get up and give him a devastating look, then I come back to the beautiful nurse.

"Sorry, emotions are running high. I can't believe Serge is in such a state. Poor Serge, so fragile, so vulnerable."

Damn it, give me an Oscar right now.

"We didn't find any paperwork on him. Do you have any information about his identity? For example, his last name?"

I look at Phil, who looks back at me with a mocking smile I'll wipe off his face in a hurry.

"Yes, it's Serge... I want to say Martel, but... I have a blank, it seems. It rhymes with that anyway."

Phil sighs.

"Serge Côté."

"That's it, Côté."

"Crazy how it rhymes with Martel, right, Lafs?"

I wave him off with a quick movement of my hand. She's now addressing Phil, and I try to get in her line of sight, so she'll come back to me.

"Any idea what year he was born?" she says, moving around a bit more to maintain eye contact with the puffy dough boy. I go with an educated guess.

"1934."

Phil laughs loudly, like a donkey giving birth. "1957."

"I know, I was joking."

I'm not convincing anyone. I think the pretty girl sees right through me. I must clean up my act.

"It's a good thing we've got a bunch of care attendant like you who—"

Her face hardens, and I hear Phil chuckle.

"What did I say?"

"For your information, sir, no one has called us care attendant since at least the late seventies. The correct term is nurse."

I'm trying to figure out why care attendant is insulting, but I'll play along.

"I know, honey, that—"

This time, it is pure astonishment I see on the face of the less and less courteous woman.

"Honey? Get out of the way."

She hustles me, and I realize this is the only physical interaction I will have with her in my life. Phil grabs his face with both hands, shaking his head. I'm thinking I've lost my touch with women. And it fills me with a bitterness that would make Colombian coffee beans jealous. To tell you how dispirited I feel right now, especially looking at the perfect curves of the care atten— what the fuck is wrong with me? I motion for Phil to get up so I can sit down, but he doesn't flinch. I will have to stand by the wall like an asshole, not knowing what to do with my hands, and more importantly, not knowing how I can redeem myself to the nurse from this.

She's done with Serge, I approach:

"Thanks again for taking care of our elderly, without you folks—"

I stop talking as she disappears into the hallway, ignoring me. I look at Serge, whom I suddenly hate with renewed anger. Relax, I am not a monster. I am worried about him. But I am especially eager for him to wake up and tell us his attacker's name. I can still hear Phil laughing.

"Get over it, asshole."

He nods and goes on for a good five minutes, which I use to evaluate how I might rip his stupid head off.

"I found this in his coat pockets."

He hands me a paper that I snatch from his hands furiously. The paper twirls gently in the air, but I don't even come close to catching it despite many efforts. It lies on the ground, and I am overwhelmed by an intense melancholy. I just want to move to Costa Rica with Roger Zadinar's ex-wife. I bend down to pick up the piece of paper and feel a sharp pain in my lower back. I wince as I lean against the wall. I need to get these vertebrae checked out soon.

It feels like everything is suddenly going wrong. I get up with difficulty and read the name. "Viateur ? Did he forget an A in aviator?"

"It's a first name," Phil says. "I have an uncle with the same name."

"Are you kidding?"

"No, I'm not."

"Do you know who it is?"

"I told you, he's my uncle."

"Serge's Viateur, you idiot. Not yours."

"Ha. No, I don't."

The nurse comes back with a document in her hands, ignoring our presence.

"But of course, Phil, we will find the sick bastard who did this to him. We have to find what happened to our friend Serge Côté, born in... March 1957."

"October."

Fucking hell.

TWENTY-NINE

No matter how much she flips the situation around, Lauriane Derome can't see how they can escape this rat hole unscathed. She has seen stories of girls freed years later, and still alive, but cops did not find most of the girls, and when they did, it was too late. The damage was done. She goes over the sequence of events leading up to her abduction. She wonders what she could have done differently to prevent this. If she had not stayed longer at school, more people would have been on the road with her, if she had not passed through the park, she would have been less vulnerable, if she had not worn her headphones, she would have heard her assailant's footsteps and could have reacted faster. Then she shakes her head. It's not her fault. She was living her teenage life like millions of others. Her scumbag kidnapper is to blame for all this. She looks at Rashida and Lea but doesn't get the comfort she is looking for. They are as helpless as she is. Whenever she thinks of her mother, tears come to her eyes. If she could at least tell her she is alive, reassure her she is relatively healthy. The two are like the fingers of a hand. Lauriane is a single child and Josiane is a solo mother. A thud from far away brings her back to reality. Blondi is coming, but something seems to differ from the previous times. What changed? Lauriane has a strange feeling right before Rashida and Lea get up. She follows their lead, but her legs are limp.

The door opens and Blondi appears first, followed by a second man with a stern and worrying look. He is smaller than Blondi, but still imposing and neatly dressed. He looks at them with a devious smile, then turns to the big man with an amazed pout.

"I must say, you chose them perfectly, buddy. This is exactly what I was looking for."

Lauriane glares at the man. This? As if they were objects found at an auction. And the confirmation that Blondi actually abducted them infuriates her even more; he's not just the passive jailer he pretends to be.

"What do you want from us?" Rashida says in a shaky voice.

The wickedness that emanates from this man is so intense that they are totally petrified. They do not perceive any goodness in him.

"That's an excellent question, uh—"

He turns to Blondi, who whispers something in his ear.

"Rashida. That's precisely why I'm here. But first, I'm sure you've recognized me by now. Although, by the looks on your faces, I'm not really sure you did."

The teens look at each other to see if someone recognizes him, but none of the girls dares a guess. The man has a mocking chuckle.

"The navel-gazing youth of our society. No idea what goes on outside their circle of friends, so glued to their damn smart phones."

He laughed at the word "smart".

"Since you guys are too dumb to know who I am, I won't say more. It's not really important, anyway. What is damn important, though, is that you pay attention to what I'm about to tell you. I don't want to hear any yelling or whining. I have a major headache, and no patience. Is that clear?"

The girls are completely stoic.

"Perfect. So, here's the plan. I've bought a beautiful piece of land in the Eastern Townships, a ranch of sorts where we will settle down. You know, the kind of place where there's no phone or Wi-Fi. Just nature and silence. I need silence, and I will have it. And if I have to kill one of you to get it, then I will. I've got acres and acres of land. I've got plenty of places to bury half the population of the province."

The man looks at them defiantly.

"I've killed before, you know. And believe me, I won't give a second thought to doing it again if you disobey me. Don't test me."

He tucks the collar of his shirt back in.

"Okay, so we'll move to this beautiful commune where you'll first be detoxed from your addiction to materials that mess with your mind. Your clothes, your electronic devices, the damn television that destroys your neurons, and everything else. We will be self-sufficient and get the balance of what we need from the internet. You will live as any person should, that is, in harmony with nature. Then we will have perfect children. Kids who will combine my power and intelligence with your beauty. Superior children who will lead society, and set it on the right path, bring back the good old values. Make Canada Great Again."

It devastates the girls. Not only is this man insane, but he intends to rape them and force them to bear his children. Lauriane shakes her head. "Over my dead body," she says, "I won't do it." She'll fight until she gets out of there, or she'll die trying. Blondi glances at Lea, but she ignores him. He's not smart, but he's clever enough to realize that the boss won't allow them to live their romance like he promised. He will have to talk to him again later, try to get some guarantees. Although he towers over him by a head and a half, Blondi is terrified by what the boss can do to him.

The boss smiles as he looks at the girls standing silently in front of him.

"I'm glad to see that you have a good grip on your emotions already."

He pulls a gun out of his jacket.

"I thought I might have to use this, but that won't be necessary. Will it?"

No reaction.

"Look, I'm sympathetic, and I understand that you're in shock, so I'll bear with your lack of interaction. But sooner rather than later, you will not only answer me when I speak to you but also respect me, or else die. Ultimately, it's your choice."

After another rant about the virtues of living together, the man announces that he will be back with more specifics shortly, but they should get ready to leave soon. And by "soon" he means a few days, at most.

He nods to Blondi to show that the discussion is over, and he leaves. The giant looks at Lea one more time, but she still ignores him. He sighs and closes the door behind him. As soon as the men have left, Lea collapses in tears on her bed. Lauriane and Rashida look at each other. They are on the same page; they won't comply with whatever this evil man suggests. They would rather die.

"Who is this monster? He talked as if we were supposed to know who he was," Rashida says after a few minutes.

Lauriane looks down. Lea whispers something inaudible. Rashida feels like Lauriane has something to say.

"I know who he is," Lauriane says quietly.

The girls stop breathing.

"So, tell us." Rashida says.

Lauriane looks at them, disheartened. "I can only tell you we're screwed. No one will rescue us."

THIRTY

I pretend to be excited hearing that Serge has woken up. The hot nurse told us the news. Yes, the same hot nurse whose pants I tried to get into the other day, unsuccessfully. I blame Phil for this. I look at him with contempt as he drives us to the hospital.

"I hope he remembers something," he says, looking straight ahead with both hands on the wheel, as he was taught in his driving classes some twenty years ago. Give it to Philou, he plays by the rules. The thing is, in our business, it's more of a flaw than a quality.

"I don't think he will," I say, "considering he reeked of alcohol when I found him in the garbage bin."

"Speaking of which, how did you know he was there?" he asks me, almost in a suspicious tone. This discussion could go south very quickly.

"What are you implying?"

"Nothing. Only that you were there by accident, right?"

I laugh harshly.

"Of course, I was there by accident. There was a crowd, and it caught my eye. I went to check it out, and I saw this jerk lying on a pile of garbage. There is no conspiracy or plot, Philippe. It's merely a coincidence."

He tells me in a high-pitched voice that he didn't mean to imply anything. When Phil lies, he switches from baritone to soprano. We pull into the hospital parking lot, so I cut short this pointless discussion.

I get to Serge's room, deceptively out of breath, as if I had climbed the stairs two at a time, too eager to see him to wait for the elevator. Of course, I took the elevator. I'm only playing along in case the sexy nurse is in the room. Since she's not, I stop panting like a stray dog.

"You look better than in that damn container," I say, giggling with far too much enthusiasm.

Serge sighs and rolls his eyes.

"They didn't drug me enough to put up with you, Martin."

After all I did for him, this is how he thanks me? Asshole. I was about to put him back in his place when the nurse enters the room with her libidinous curves.

"My God, Serge, we thought we'd lost you. Thank you, Lord. Thank you," I say in a loud voice, arms outstretched to the sky.

If Serge didn't have his arm in a sling, he'd stick his middle finger in my face.

"You again, huh?" the nurse says with a smile.

"You better believe I came running as soon as I knew my precious friend regained consciousness. Thanks for the call, by the way. You obviously care about your patients, and that—"

"Yeah, yeah, yeah." she says, interrupting me with a lively wave of her hand as she approaches an entertained Serge, who looks at me with a malignant grimace on his swollen face. I look at him and strongly suggest that he cooperate with me on the nurse's case, or else...

Well, or else nothing. I won't pick on him directly on his hospital bed. I have manners.

"How long will it take to get our Sergio back in shape?" I ask, my voice still trembling with crocodile tears.

"He must rest. We'll keep him for a few more days," she says, not looking at me.

"Don't worry," Serge says, "he normally ignores me completely. He's putting on this act to lure you into bed."

What a jerk. I widen my eyes and shake my head. She looks

at me and smiles. But not a complicit smile or a smile of someone moved, but a mocking, borderline sarcastic smile.

"Nah. He's good-looking, but not really my type."

Good-looking? Hello!

"So, you're saying there's a chance?" I say casually.

"No, I'm saying the exact opposite."

And she walks out, wiggling her booty. I would have sold my mother just to have her for myself at least one night. I glance furiously at Serge.

"Thanks, jerk."

He shrugs.

"My pleasure."

"I should have left you in that fucking container."

He smiles.

"There's my good old Lafs. He just can't stop his true colours from shining through."

"No," I correct him, "drive the beautiful nurse away, and lose an ally."

The bearded man's bluish face gets suspicious.

"You didn't think you had a chance with her, did you?"

"Of course, I did."

"Oh, Martin," he says with a deceptively distressed look.

"Oh, Martin, what? She just said that I'm good-looking."

"Yeah, that's her courteous way of bracing you for bad news like "you're not my type". She told me I was good-looking too just before the doctor performed a rectal exam on me."

Phil giggles like an idiot. I wave my arm at him to shut him down. But he regards it as an opportunity to speak up.

"Do you remember what happened?" he asks, presumably to Serge.

"Well, if you must know, the doctor turned me on my side, put on a latex glove and—"

"Not the rectal exam, silly. How did you end up in the garbage dump?"

I laugh out loud.

"I was following someone I thought was suspicious, hoping

he would lead me to Lauriane Derome, but I lost him, and when I turned the corner, there he was, looking scared and angry at the same time. Then it got blurry."

"Why did you think he was a suspect?"

"He's a guy I knew from the streets, who later went through a government rehabilitation program and got a subsidized room. Except one day I saw him driving a truck full of grocery bags, enough to feed a tribe."

"Maybe it was related to his job," I say, a little too curious about his story.

"I doubt it. He never could hold a job for long. He has serious psychiatric issues and is not socially adept."

"He's got a good right hook though," I say, neither good nor bad.

"Martin, for the love of God," Phil says in an angry tone.

I look at him with fury, reminding him of his rank in the company, and especially mine. But he doesn't care. He always has and always will not care. And you know what? He's right. He could get a job somewhere else, no problem. What saves me is his reluctance to change. He hates the unknown. So, he stays put. Lafleur has repeatedly threatened that one day he would snatch him from me. This is perhaps the single reason I have to partner with this citrus lover. Serge says that his assailant's name is Viateur Demers, and that he rents a room at Chez Lise. Just as he finishes telling us all this, the nurse comes back.

"Don't worry Serge," I say in a sharp tone, "we'll find the son of a bitch who did this to you, I promise."

I look at the gorgeous woman glancing at me with an impassive face.

"Still no?"

"No."

THIRTY-ONE

I tap on the Chez Lise reception desk, waiting for someone to finally greet us. I am close to skipping this useless step and knocking on every door like a madman. I am confident that, by magic, someone will somehow show up to deal with us. Meanwhile, Phil is sitting quietly in one of the reception chairs.

"How can you be so relaxed?" I ask with extreme annoyance. It sounds more like a reproach than a proper question. He says something inaudible back to me tersely, but I don't care. It was rhetorical. I ring the bell again so aggressively that it bounces from the force of my blow, spins around and ends up on the floor behind the desk.

"Well done," Phil says, laughing.

"It was useless anyway. As you can see, no one could hear it."

Of course, just as I say that, an old man shows up. I look angrily at Phil, daring him to make a comment. He wisely keeps his mouth shut. I stare at the man as I wait for him to settle down behind his desk. He looks just like the old clerk in the madhouse in The Twelve Tasks of Asterix. I take this as a sign that the day promises to be tough.

"Did I wake you up, Grandpa?" I say in an acrimonious tone. He takes forever to bend down and pick up his damn bell before answering me.

"I beg your pardon?"

Goddamn it. This really is a madhouse. I rub my eyes out of frustration and take a deep breath. I make introductions, reducing Phil's role to that of my assistant, which highly pisses him off. Behind us, two men are arguing about the temperature.

"Who are those two jokers?" I ask the old man, pointing at them with my chin.

"Matt and Matty."

"That can't be their real names."

"That's what we call them."

"Do they live here?"

"Yes, they do."

"How can you tell them apart?"

"I'm sorry, what?"

I swear to God, this day is going to be very long.

"How do you know which one is Matt and which one is Matty?"

"Easy. The one on the left is Matt, and the one on the right—"

I wave him off since I don't really give a shit.

"Does either of them have Demers as a last name?"

"I have no idea."

I look at him and think that if he weren't so old and stunted, I'd give him a well-executed uppercut on the chin. I look back at the two clowns.

"Hey, Laurel and Hardy. What are your last names?"

I'm quite proud of this line because they do look like Laurel and Hardy. Even Phil chuckled. The first guy is dark-haired, overweight and has a Hitler-like moustache. The second is taller, skinnier, and has a permanent sorrowful face.

"Leave us alone, asshole," says the latter.

I'll give you a reason to feel sorrow, pal. I approach him threateningly. I often do this when I know I'll have the upper hand physically over someone. If I feel uncertain, I'm much less confident, as you can imagine. You guys do the same thing, don't tell me otherwise. You are always braver with one type of person than another. I've got you pegged; you're not fooling anyone.

"What did you say to me, you bastard?"

He looks at me with his cocker spaniel's eyes.

"I said beat it, asshole."

I have to hand it to him; he's brave. Unless he's reckless. This is when I reach the limit of what I can do to intimidate someone. Because if I want to keep going, I either shut up or I grapple them by the throat and manhandle them. And it's inconvenient with witnesses around. You look at somebody the wrong way these days, and you get charged with assault. I look serious now.

"Listen to me, you fake crybaby; either you tell me your names, or I'll put you in jail. Is that clear?"

"You a cop?"

"Detective Sergeant indeed, so you want to play?"

"Lafs," Phil says, his tone of voice shows he doesn't agree that I'm impersonating a police officer, a violation of the criminal code.

I wave at him to shut his mouth. Laurel sighs, and after checking with Hardy, who shrugs, he tells me that his name is Jean Fortin and that the fat guy is Marius Ricard. I watch them laughing.

"Thank you. But you know what?"

"What?"

"I'm not a cop."

I leave them hanging, giggling, and head back to the reception desk amidst verbal abuse from these two jerks. Phil looks at me with a disapproving pout I couldn't care less about. I walk back to the half-assed derelict.

"Listen, buddy, we're looking for a guy named Viateur Demers who lives here. Hurry, we have other things to do." I tap on the desk impatiently.

The old man refuses to budge.

"It doesn't ring a bell."

"Look in your book, you probably don't know everyone in this dump. You couldn't give me these two freaks' names."

"I can't do that. Talk to the manager."

"Call him then."

Several minutes later, a failed pseudo-artist comes striding toward us. The kind you know is leaving before he gets here because he's so "overwhelmed". I say "pseudo-artist" because he looks like one. Brown corduroy pants and a scarf around his neck, giving him a cursed poet look with his round glasses.

"Yes, what is it?"

"We're a private investigators working on a case. I need to see your tenant's records, pronto."

"Do you have a warrant?" he asks, pursing his lips.

"Why would I need a warrant? This isn't the Pentagon, for heaven's sake. I'm looking for Viateur Demers. Do you know him?"

"You know, there are so many people here."

I'm really sick of this. I mean, it's easy to figure out. Look in the damn rental records, I don't know, but there's got to be a record somewhere.

"The privacy of our residents is paramount, mister—"

"Lafs."

"For real?" he says with a smirk.

"For real what?"

"Lafs, is your last name?"

"Yes, it's an acronym for Legendre-Auger-Fort... shut the fuck up. It's not important. We are looking for Demers. Do I have to ask each of your tenants one by one? Because—"

"Yes, let's do that," the talentless poet says, sneering.

"I've already asked Laurel and Hardy here and—"

He laughs even louder.

"They do look like them."

Proudly, I mellow out.

"Come on, man. It's taking too long."

"Philippe Lavoie?" the manager says, looking at Phil.

"Hi, Robert," he says, still sitting comfortably in his chair.

"You're with that idiot?"

"Yup."

That idiot? Are you kidding me? I look at Phil angrily. He

gets up with the gusto of a teenager who must empty a dishwasher. After some polite exchanges with this Robert, I step in.

"Okay, ladies, you're happy to meet each other again, and stuff. Can we get down to business now?"

"Who is this jackass?" the manager asks Phil, not looking at me.

I walk over to him.

"You know what the jackass is going to do to you?" You guessed it; I think I can take him in a street fight. Enjoy my random bravery. But Phil steps in. He introduces me as his assistant, and I laugh out loud.

Well played, Phil.

The manager finally agrees to search his records to see if there's a Viateur Demers in this shithole. I stand back. For once Phil is taking the initiative, I won't get in his way, you know?

Bingo! Viateur Demers. Room 116.

"Well, let's go," I say, heading for the rooms.

The asshole manager stands between me and the hallway. As if he could stop me. I watch him from head to toe, a condescending smile on my face.

"What do you think you're doing, Bob?"

"You won't bother my people, I guarantee you."

The tension is building up dangerously, so much so that I'm not so sure anymore that I would prevail in a fight. For all I know, he may have a black belt in jiu-jitsu and will humiliate me in front of the elderly and the two jokers. I look over at Phil, urging him to say something to his buddy, or whatever. I don't want to know the nature of their relationship. I've always suspected Phil of having a shady past. I don't want to lose whatever respect I still have for him.

Phil sighs and says,

"Listen Robert, someone assaulted a homeless man a few days ago to the point that he ended up in the hospital, and he told us that this Viateur Demers would know what happened to him. We would be very grateful if you would allow us to talk to him for a few minutes. We swear we don't want to bother him."

Robert what's-his-name looks at me as if he's waiting for me to confirm, which I do with the zest of a child compromising with his school principal, and he agrees to walk us to Demers' room. Phil has found the right words to help us reach our goal. I look at him approvingly, but he doesn't appear to give a damn. Robert knocks on the door, and I can't help but wonder how humans can live in this dump. Then I think about my apartment and get depressed. It is not much more appealing than this. After three tries, the doorknob finally turns, and the door slowly opens. A giant appears, causing me to take a step back. He seems very nervous and only opens the door a few inches. The manager introduces us and when he hears the word "detective", Demers tries to close the door, but like the excellent investigator that I am, I have previously positioned my foot between the door and the door frame. I smile at him, he smiles at me. We're already good friends. Then he opens the door wider and slams it shut on my foot. I can't describe the pain I felt from my foot to my right testicle. I fall down holding my shoe as Demers steps over me to run away. I order Phil to go after him, but he runs like he's carrying a refrigerator on his back. Hence his nickname "Refrigerator Phil" which I gave him in honour of William Perry, the huge former Chicago Bears offensive lineman who was appropriately nicknamed "Refrigerator Perry". He won't catch up to him. I instruct him to stop being a jerk and get back. The bedroom door is open. If we can't talk to that scumbag Demers, we can look around in his room.

"You can't enter," Robert says.

"You've done enough damage, Bob. Beat it and leave us alone," I say, moaning like a cow.

He looks confused. I point to my foot, which is probably broken. But he is adamant; the answer is no. He insists on waiting for Demers to show up. God in heaven, my foot hurts, except that I won't wait until he returns while reading an old copy of Reader's Digest with Dalida on the front page. I figure he'll go around the back, so I hop on my good foot and head for the emergency exit door. Robert tries to talk me out of it, says it's risky to confront him alone, but I ignore him like I should have since he showed up with his ugly face. Outside, I'm on the verge of tears every time I put weight on my damn foot. I'm craving murder right now, and Demers is at the other end of my appetite. I see him turn the corner and walk towards me, unaware that I'm hiding in the shadows. I am behind an overhang of the building and grab a wooden board that's lying around. "Yes, that's right, come to me, asshole," I say to myself, licking my chops. My arms are shaking with anticipation, my teeth clench like every time I'm about to swing. Just as he appears in my field of vision, I take a backward swing and hear "No Lafs" as I bring my wooden board down behind his head.

No effect.

I'm standing there like an idiot with what's left of the plank in my hands and Demers, towering over me by four and a half heads, scrutinizes me with his dark eyes. I smile shyly. Demers makes a dash to smash my face and I close my eyes, waiting for the blow. I hear someone to my right yell "Viateur" in a powerful voice. I open one eye and see Demers' colossal fist inches from my nose. And by fist, I mean Thor's hammer. It's fucking huge. I slowly turn my head to my right to see the man who just saved my life and notice a third guy, along with the pair of morons. He seems to have a special grip on Demers, because he is looking at him, still holding his fist close to my face. So close that I can smell Cheetos on his orange-stained fingers. The third guy comes up to us with a commanding look and a chin beard.

"Leave the man alone. We've already talked about this. This is how you get in trouble. Back off."

Demers lowers his fist and looks at me with a sorry look on his face. If I didn't contain myself, I would run to the man and wrap my arms around his neck, calling him my hero. But since I'm not a frail princess in the tower of a video game castle, I refrain. The guy controls Demers with the deftness of Chris Pratt with the Jurassic Park dinosaurs.

He whispers questions to me about what's going on between Andre the Giant and me.

"Are you asking me?"

"Of course, not him. Dummy."

See, I already like him a bit less.

"I'm a private investigator and I need to ask him a few questions. What's your deal? You a Jedi or something?"

"Psychiatrist."

"Same thing," I say, laughing. "Both are fictional, with a
fondness for fluorescent phallic objects."

He looks at me, reminding me he's the only reason I'm still
alive right now. I look down. I need him.

"Sorry, you are—"

"Psychiatrist Aleksander Gniazdowskinovich."

"What's that?"

"Call me Doc Alex, like everyone else around here."

"Your name is worth a lot of points at Scrabble," I say,
giggling like an orangutan.

"Hey, you're the first one to tell that joke," he says, with a
look that deserves a slap on the face.

I have a shit-eating grin, and he asks us to follow him,
Demers and the other two jerks into his office. I admit I wouldn't
mind sitting down, because of my foot, you know? Goddamn it,
I'd crawl into a corner and cry.

Phil stares at me while holding the door as everyone else has
ducked inside the building.

"So, are you coming?" he asks with a cocky smile hanging on
his face. He can see that I'm limping along like a turtle with my
shitty foot.

"Fuck you, asshole."

He shrugs.

"All right."

He then lets the heavy door close behind him just before I
arrive.

I have a hard time opening it since I can only put weight on
one of my feet.

Didn't I tell you this would be a shitty day?

THIRTY-TWO

They are all there. Robert and his failed painter look, the shrink and that big jerk Viateur. Oh yes, and Phil, who is watching me, a bright spark of laughter in his eyes. If my foot didn't hurt so much, I'd put him back in his place right away.

"Here you are at last," says that bastard Robert.

"No thanks to you anyway," I say, irritated.

The big idiot stares at the floor, like a dog that chewed his master's slippers. Doc Alex grabs a file and quickly speaks up, even though no one asked him to.

"What can I do for you?"

I chuckle as I look around at the others. Is he stupid or what? Where did this smart ass come from? But no one laughs back.

"We know that Viateur seriously injured a homeless man a few days ago," Phil says. "A homeless man who is still in the hospital, by the way."

"And what makes you think that?"

"First, the homeless man himself when he recovered consciousness. Oh, and that he answered Viateur Demers to the who did this to you? question."

I love when Phil is condescending. With others, that is. I could kill him when he does that to me. Doc Alex looks at Demers, who is staring at the floor. I'll spare you all the "Is it true, Viateur?" and the multiple shrugs.

"What we told you is true. Let's stop beating around the bushes," I say, wincing with pain. "The question is why?"

Demers mumbles something that no one understands. Doc Alex asks him to repeat.

"He was following me."

"Well then, case closed. You beat the crap out of people when you think they're following you. Come on, Phil, let's get out of here," I say, throwing my arms in the air.

Doc Alex shouts at me to shut up with a highly irritated look on his face. Doesn't this moron know who he's dealing with, or what? Robert asks the gigantic idiot for more details, but he just keeps repeating that Serge was following him. And you know what? Given his obvious lack of brains, I wouldn't be surprised if that's what happened. So, let's move on. That's not why we're here, anyway. Phil is about to say something when I gracefully interrupted him.

"Demers, what were you doing at the grocery store with all those bags?"

He looks at me quizzically. I repeat my question, and I can feel him getting nervous.

"What exactly are you talking about?" the shrink asks.

You know I signal him to shut up with an irritated look. How enjoyable that one is.

"What was all that food for? Demers? And for whom? Will you answer me, or should I call the cops?"

He gets agitated and slams his head with his hands, screaming. Doc Alex grabs him by the shoulders and whispers things while glaring at me. I retort with a pout, suggesting that he can go fuck himself.

"It was for Blondi," Demers says, calming down.

"Blondi? Who's Blondi?" I ask.

Demers cradles on his axle, still cuddled by his doctor. I look at the others.

"Is this a joke? Blondi, really?"

Nobody reacts.

"Did you bring the food to his bunker in 1944, or did you see him recently? Was it before or after the Blitzkrieg? Was Eva Braun there or not?"

No one gets it, since everyone is looking at me, wondering what I'm talking about. I sigh deeply.

"No one knows Blondi was Hitler's German shepherd's name?"

Doc Alex smiles, enjoying my culture. He didn't put it quite that way, but that's what his approval smile means.

"Blondi is also one of our tenants' pseudonyms," Robert says with a dispassionate look.

"Because he's blond?" I say, a touch too interested.

"No, he's bald."

"Was he blond before?" I say, despite my urge to stop talking about it.

"What? I don't know— who cares?" Robert answers, annoyed.

I have to admit, we really don't care. I let it go.

"Where do you take the groceries?"

"In a house."

"Blondi's?"

Demers shrugs. I roll my eyes, which fill with tears as the pain in my foot grows worse. Before long, I will have to go to the emergency room to get some painkillers. I ask Robert if he has seen Blondi lurking around. His bewildered gaze tells me he couldn't care less about the comings and goings of his residents. As long as they pay their rent, he doesn't give a shit. I ask him if he has paid his rent on time. Again, he doesn't know.

"Tell me about it. Administrators managing their businesses like pros," I say in a deadpan voice.

"Kiss my ass, man. I've got employees to take care of that."

"Yeah, sure," I say before looking at the big dingo. "Do you have the address of the house?"

He says he does, but that Blondi made him swear not to tell anyone. I ask him if he would go to jail to keep his word. Doc Alex, who has sat down, approaches Demers again in order to prevent another hysterical crisis, which won't happen.

"No, I wouldn't."

I soften my tone.

"Listen, Vibrator—"

"Viateur."

"That's right, Viateur, I don't want to get you in trouble. If you give us the address, we'll go there and pretend we're city inspectors, or something like that. Blondi won't suspect you. How's that sound? Plus, we can treat him to a can of Dr. Ballard."

I look around at the others and smile, proud of my dog food joke, but no one is laughing. I'm telling you; these freaks aren't the light of the party. Viateur finally agrees to provide us with the address, and I wince in pain as I hop on my foot to follow them to his room. I am on the verge of tears as I see the heavy door, the cause of my mishap. Demers can't find the address, though. Either he's lying or he's a complete idiot. And seeing him act from the beginning, I know the answer. He tells us it is on Clark Street. He goes there by sight, recognizing the house. He obviously refuses to take us there, too scared of what might happen to him. I tell him that the next time he goes back to pick up groceries, if he can write the door number, but he says that he hasn't heard from Blondi in a while. He stares at the floor, then at me as I lean on Phil to keep my balance.

"Sorry about your foot."

"That's okay, big guy," I say half-heartedly.

Better to have those big ninnies with Herculean strength on our side than the other way around.

THIRTY-THREE

I realize that the last thing you want is to hear me complain about my foot for several more chapters, but you don't know what it's like to be in pain until you've had a limb crushed by a heavy door shoved shut by an idiot with Hercules-like strength. Enough to keep you crying for months. I take all the esoteric concoctions prescribed by my doctor, who is as reliable as a bankrupt man in front of an open safe full of cash, but nothing helps. I look at my foot after taking my stocking off. There are fifty shades of purple. Then someone knocks on my door. I don't expect or want to see anyone. Probably one of those damn hucksters again. The bastard knocks again.

"Go away."

"Martin?"

A female voice? I don't recognize it right away. What if it's the enticing nurse who has come to her senses and now would like to provide me with first and hopefully second and third aid? I shudder with excitement, though a doubt nags at the back of my mind: could she be a peddler? It smells like an ambush, and the distance between the door and me isn't worth the effort. No way will I suffer just to find out she's an encyclopedia saleswoman. Haven't they heard of Wikipedia? Who needs encyclopedias when you have a more or less reliable source at your fingertips? Holy shit, another knock.

"Who is it?"

"Anne-Marie."

I need about ten seconds to figure out who Anne-Marie is, but as soon as I do, I jump up with a grimace and hop to the door. There she is, resplendent, dressed in a long navy-blue raincoat, her hair pulled up in a toque behind her head and a smug grin on her face. She is a hundred times more beautiful than the nurse.

"What are you doing here?"

"Nice way to greet me," she says with a naughty smile.

"I just thought that after the failed date, you would be the last person to—"

"What could have made you believe that?"

"Your twenty-one texts, and the time you said never to contact you again?"

"Will you let me in or not?"

I'm such an idiot.

"Of course," I say, opening the door and hopping on the only intact foot I have left.

"Are you okay?" she asks, looking worried as she notices my injury.

Time to make up a story to make me look good.

"Yes, I ran after a burglar who stole a granny's purse and bruised my foot."

"Sweet Jesus, did you at least catch him?"

I chuckle as I think back to that semi-dead prick crawling along, dragging his shattered leg on his back like a backpack.

"Oh my God, did I ever."

"I don't get it."

"Never mind, sit down."

I signal her to move to the sofa where everything went wrong last time. She approaches the furniture as I am patting myself on the back for mixing two true stories to make up a false one. She then stops and looks at me with a teasing look.

"What's going on?" I ask, intrigued.

For her only retort, she opens her raincoat that she lets it fall at her feet to expose her splendid body wearing only delicate lingerie. Let me tell you that the Martinator is already responding. What? You, too, are irritated that I call my penis the Martinator? You are such a killjoy! I jump up and down on the sofa.

"I'm speechless, Anne-Marie. What makes you suddenly want to—"

"I got riled up the other night," she says, interrupting me. "I get your contract idea, the #metoo movement. You can never be too careful. I can buy into your argument, but trust me, you have nothing to worry about from me."

That's exactly what someone from whom I should fear the worst would say, isn't it? Besides, didn't Yvonne tell me the same thing? If you don't know who I'm talking about, just read Don't Find Roger, that's all. Available at all good bookstores. It smells like I'm about to be fucked, no pun intended. I get disillusioned as my brain works its way through a series of wacky scenarios. Why the sudden change of course-again? When it's too good to be true, it's usually too good to be true.

"Why don't you say something?" she asks as she picks her raincoat up in her hands.

Anne-Marie is not stupid. She can feel that if I haven't thrown myself at her goddess body yet, there's something rotten in the kingdom of Denmark.

"What are you really doing here?" I say, a hint of reproach in my voice.

"I don't understand."

"Why this sudden turnaround? Who sent you?"

Her face could not convey confusion any better than it does at this moment. "Martin, I don't understand what you're saying."

"It's quite simple. You stormed out of my house, swearing never to see me again. Then you texted me never to contact you again. And suddenly, you're back with your stunning good looks—"

"Thank you."

"—in very nice lingerie—"

"Too kind."

"—but it doesn't make sense that you're here. I stood you up the other day, too, and you were even angrier than the first time."

"Yes, but I heard it was to take your friend to the hospital. I get it."

I almost burst out laughing when she refers to Serge as "my friend." Let's keep it real, kiddo.

"Who sent you? Who are you working for?"

"Martin, you're scaring me."

"Did Yvonne send you to torture me?"

"Who?"

"Read Don't Find Roger, you'll understand."

"Don't find who?"

I signal to her to drop it. She looks at me dubiously and quietly slips on her raincoat.

"I think it was a bad idea."

"Do you? Did you think you would play me like a schoolboy again?"

Anne-Marie goes around me to the door.

"That's it. Walk away, you and your sublime body. I already gave in the matter. I won't fall for it again."

She comes back to me, looking furious.

"Martin?"

"Yes?"

She savagely stomps on my aching foot, and I fall to the floor.

"Fuck you," she says, slamming the door.

I bawl. Tears are literally streaming down my cheeks. It hurts more than anything. It hurts more than a kick in the nuts, more than your period pains, because that too, ladies, like childbirth pains—get over it.

I cry like a child as I get up and sit on my cozy sofa.

"Pull yourself together for God's sake," I say to myself.

I barely manage to calm down when I realize not only that Anne-Marie surely didn't have bad motives, but also that I'm not enjoying her exquisite body. Instead, I'm squealing like a kid who just dropped his ice cream in the sand. I imagine all the positions I would do right now with this goddess if I hadn't been such a jerk. Yvonne has screwed me up for life. I will never trust a woman again.

"Anne-Marie," I yell from my couch, like Marlon Brando in *A Streetcar Named Desire* summoning Stella. "Anne-Marie, come back."

"Shut up," my neighbour on the left yells.

I cry like a Dalmatian. How stupid I am.

I whisper "Anne-Marie", swallowing my salty tears.

THIRTY-FOUR

Josiane Delorme cries, holding a frame with Lauriane's picture in her hands. Where the hell is she? She never felt so alone in her life, nobody to help her. Is it because she doesn't have a lot of money? Or because Lauriane and she carry little weight in the social arena? "The police would be much more pressing if Lauriane were the daughter of a politician, or a star," she thinks. This simple thought brings her face to face with her doubts and setbacks, increasing her sense of incompetence. Everyone told her how brave she was to raise her baby by herself, with no help. Her husband died while she was pregnant. He was her rock, and the sole provider for the family. She never felt lonelier than when she held the frail Lauriane in her arms, alone in her hospital room, in the agony of silence.

Occasionally, a distant old aunt would visit, the last remnants of a family she never had. Her family is Lauriane. She and her daughter, hand in hand, against all odds. It is her greatest achievement, the best she has ever done. Lauriane is so much better than her, so much smarter, braver and more determined. If Josiane leaves any legacy to society, it will be that marvelous girl full of promise. But that was before disaster struck. Josiane couldn't protect Lauriane from the horrors of life. She knows she didn't run away. That is not her style, and anyway, Josiane gives her everything she wants. If Lauriane would have wanted to go somewhere, her mother wouldn't have stopped her. No wonder she is angry when the police imply she ran off. This is a great misunderstanding of her daughter, a great misunderstanding of their dynamic, of the extent of their relationship, of how they are like two fingers on the same hand. To think that she would have left giving no news is ridiculous. Even when they had the biggest fight of their lives, when Lauriane took refuge at a friend's house, she called her an hour later to apologize for the words she used. When she stayed over with friends, Josiane almost had a complete plan of the evening's, even if she didn't ask Lauriane to account for it. She has full confidence in her daughter and does not need to babysit her. Lauriane is a serious and responsible young woman. For Josiane, losing Lauriane would be worse than death. She could no longer go through life without her daughter. Lauriane's disappearance confirms what she already knew: that she only lives for Lauriane, through her. She wouldn't be capable of surviving her. She howls, the step just before sinking into insanity, as if the body and the head are trying to discharge the pain in an ultimate self-protection. She has just spoken to the police, and it felt the same as every time. That lack of urgency in their voice and tone, their condescending justifications, as if they know Lauriane better than she does. She screamed, cried, begged them to take it seriously, to prioritize the case, but they simply said that they were taking care of it, and that there are murders happening to other families who are just as grieving as she is. Who also need answers.

"So, once she's dead, you guys will worry about her? Is that what you're saying?"

They didn't answer, only sighing. These people are disgusting.

Then there's the mayor who promised her the world, who promised that everything would be put in place to find Lauriane, and who didn't keep his word like all the goddamned politicians on Earth. So, she feels so alone now, so neglected. Then the image of Martin Lafs comes to mind. Surely, he, too, has forsaken her. She doesn't have the guts to call him after she sought to keep him out of the investigation, so she reaches out to Melanie amidst her nervous breakdown. Her friend swears that her boyfriend and his boss are still looking for Lauriane, that they are currently following a lead.

Later, Philippe Lavoie calls her and reassures her they have made some progress in the investigation. They have targeted a sketchy individual. He tells Josiane about the conversation they had with him. He says that it may have nothing to do with Lauriane, but that they will explore every lead they come across. The man attacked a homeless man, so he may have bumped into Lauriane. He may know where she is, although he fiercely denies it. Philippe tells her that Lafs probably broke his foot confronting the man, showing that he would do anything to track down Josiane's daughter. Philippe also says that he requested the police interview the man to make sure that he had nothing to do with this, but they declined, claiming that they have no grounds to question him other than hearsay. Phil also tells her about this fellow Blondi that they are trying to track down at the moment. As he hangs up, Philippe swears to her he will follow up with her regularly, that Lafs will also keep her posted, and that they will do everything possible to find Lauriane alive. The call brings Josiane to tears. Although the discussion with Philippe is meant to reassure her, she doesn't enjoy hearing about the man assaulting another. What if Lauriane has fallen prey to a violent lunatic who would do God knows what to her? What she feels, this mixture of hope and fear, is worse than the anxiety she felt at the beginning. Something will have to happen soon.

Her last line of defense is that silly looking private investigator and his team.

That's all she has left.

THIRTY-FIVE

Phil is mad at me, and again I don't know why. Dealing with this guy is like dealing with an emotional bomb twenty-four hours a day. He could explode at any moment for any reason outside of my control. I won't lie to you; I've had enough. I've had his half-filled-out termination papers for years in a drawer in my desk. A kind of blank check, so I can get rid of him with a stroke of the pen. I smile at the thought of it. Whenever I can't remember what we are fighting about, it means it was trivial, and he has no reason to be emotionally psychotic about it. Haven't we had enough problems at the office without creating them for ourselves on top of it? Not to mention that damn messed up foot. The doctor says it's not broken, it's just a bruise. I felt like bruising his nose, but, hey, I'm civilized. It's killing me, so between you and me, I could do without Philippe's existential crises. As one bad thing never comes alone, Nicole approaches with her goddamn Tupperware container full of muffins. Nicole regularly bakes big scoops of muffin when she feels tension in the air. She grants me one as she opens the lid, and the sweet smell turns my initial "no" into a playful, "fuck yes".

Her muffins are fantastic. She sits down in front of me. Shit, she's in talk mode.

"You know, Martin, you should apologize to Phil."

"Hmouatt? Hmmfufoukoi yhmmfa—"

I pause as I realize that, first, I can't say an intelligible word when I have a mouthful of muffin, and second, I'm spitting a bunch all over my beautiful cherry wood desk. I motion to her to wait as I try to finish my bite. Seeing her dumbfounded look, I repeat,

"I did nothing. What should I apologize for? He lost his mind again, not me."

"Do you remember at least what the argument was about?" she asks, intrigued.

"I don't, which proves that it wasn't that big of a deal."

She's like, "yeah, you're wrong," which makes me want to fill out her termination papers too. "You were talking about a guy named Blondi."

"Yeah, we need to track down a guy with that nickname."

"Then you asked him if Blondi was the name he gave Melanie."

Yeah, I remember that. Nicole doesn't have to continue. She does anyway, since she's as savvy at detecting people's non-verbals as a priest behind his partition in the confessional.

"And you wanted to know if the curtains matched the—"

I raise my hand.

"Yes, I remember that," I said, rolling my eyes. "But I was just kidding."

"Even when you shrugged off his request to take it back and said—"

"... she must be hairless," I say.

Nicole purses her lips, hoping I'll get it this time. I take another bite of her luscious muffin and reach for a second one, but the silly woman pulls the container away with a glare. Like a struggling heroin addict, my hand is shaking, and my eyes are pleading. And like a coked-up junkie in need of a fix, I tell her what she wants to hear to get my shot.

"OK, I'll talk to him. Give me more muffins for the love of God Almighty."

My hand grabs two super soft muffins that make me drool.

After a few seconds of watching me gorge myself like Phil at a Chinese buffet, Nicole clears her throat to get my attention.

"Hmmi hmmmeesss. Hmmving."

Which could be translated as "Yes, I'm going."

I arrive at Phil's desk. He has both feet up on it, listening to the TV. As I snatched the muffin container from Nicole's hands to present an offering, like one of the Three Kings, I hold out my arms to give him one, which he refuses.

"Nicole already gave me plenty."

I confess it hurts me to come second, and I look at Nicole with the eyes of a broken lover. She looks down. I turn back to Phil.

"Listen, sport—"

I enjoy talking to him like a ten-year-old. He waves me off and tells me to sit down, turning up the sound on the TV in the corner of his office. It shows a crowd of media in front of an empty podium full of microphones, and a mention that Mayor Jean Ouellet will make an announcement to the public in a few minutes.

"Jesus, what in the world would he—"

Phil shushes me again with a wave of his hand.

"But he's not even there yet."

Phil looks at me sternly. Okay, I'll keep quiet. I cross my arms like a sulky teenager as Jean Ouellet approaches the microphone. He will probably talk about the upcoming election as the rumour mill has it. It's a good time to call for the election. I hate him so much with his porky face, his exaggeratedly swarthy complexion, and his fluorescent white teeth. It's not just his personality that's fake. Yet, I used to like him. When I would run into him at a charity event, he would shake my hand with the same abandon that he used with the rest of the crowd. But for a while now, he's had it out for me. I figure he is just adding to the long list of people who dislike me. Nevertheless, if I'm being totally honest, I feel bad about it. I am going to say one more thing, but Phil glares at me. I grab another muffin and gobble it down in one go. I stand up, annoyed, seeing that I can't stop eating these damn sumptuous pastries, and take the container back to Nicole.

"You know, you can have some more, Martin."

I look at her, eyes pleading with full cheeks like a squirrel stocking up for the winter. I contemplate the muffins left over, but in a superhuman effort, I return to Phil's office, leaving the delights of the gods behind. Jean Ouellet is about to speak, looking stern. My God, will they report that they have found Lauriane dead? I look at Phil, who seems as worried as I am. Ouellet quickly discards that worry by announcing that he will not seek another term. We breathe a sigh of relief, as much for Lauriane as for his departure. Let's face it, his fixation on me and the agency is getting old. Ouellet tells us it is difficult for him and his wife, that he wants to do something else in life, that it is time to pass the torch to a new generation. He emotionlessly recounts his journey and how proud he is to have represented Montrealers so well over the past fourteen years, and some other unworthy nonsense. Phil is as relieved as I am. After Ouellet takes questions from reporters and leaves the podium, Phil lowers the volume and looks at me with a stare that I can't quite define. Is it hate with a hint of disgust, or is it disgust with a hint of hope?

I speak up despite myself.

"Phil, I apologize for my bad joke. I thought I was being funny, but if I put myself in your position—"

"It's okay, I know you. Look, I—"

"No, it's important that I finish. When I asked you if the curtains—"

"Shut up, Martin."

I shut up. He sighs. I smile. He purses his lips. I shrug. He widens his eyes.

"What?" he says.

"What do you think of Ouellet's decision?"

Phil accepts my change of subject like a bishop, a leper.

"It's a good thing, he's been unbearable lately. Probably the reason he left. You could tell he didn't have the passion anymore."

"Indeed, but I must agree with you," I say in a serene voice.

"Martin, I swear to God, if you talk about Melanie's hair colour again."

Many splendid jokes cross my mind in a few milliseconds, but I refrain. I'm getting a little wiser with age, you see.

"No, I'm talking about Ouellet. You were right about him."

"I don't understand what you're getting at."

"His speech impediment. In particular, his trouble with the word difficult."

"It's true that he says "diffcole,"right? I'm not imagining it."

"No, you're not, Phil. It's very subtle, but your powers of observation have served you well again."

I talk a bit like Yoda, don't you think?

I go all in with Philippe, and he notices it, since he looks at me like someone who wants to tell me not to overdo it.

"Lemon, your muffins are so good, Nicole. You're a match made in heaven," says Marcel Lafleur who came in a few seconds earlier.

Nicole giggles like a mare giving birth. I look at Phil with a mocking look.

"Talking about speech impediment."

THIRTY-SIX

The three teenage girls look at each other, dumbfounded. Blondi has just left, and for a moment, they think he is agreeing to help them get out of this mess. It all starts with voices coming from upstairs. Normally, the girls don't decipher what the conversation is about, except this time it is loudly spoken. And since Blondi's boss often picks on him, they can hear the whole thing. They have figured out that if they put their ear to the wall in the hallway, they can pick up most of what is being said through the vibrations when the people above speak up. They can then use some of the information they gather here and there to shape their speech towards Blondi and influence him so that he turns against their abuser and helps them get out of this place. Blondi comes down after another argument, Lea looks at the big guy with gentle eyes, making him believe she is worried about him. The worst part is that it's not entirely fake. She doesn't like the man who is manipulating Blondi, and she feels that as long as Blondi acts as a buffer between the girls and him, they are protected. Lea is confident that Blondi won't allow anything bad to happen to them. Rashida jumps in, reminding Blondi of how the man threatened him about what would happen if he doesn't do everything he is told. She reminds him of how the other man told him that he is stupid to think the girls like him, that he has been lulled by their sweet talk, and that if Blondi doesn't obey him, he will hire someone else.

"He will kill you," Rashida tells him.

Blondi shakes his head. "No, he wouldn't kill me. Come on."

Lauriane speaks up here. "Of course, he would. Didn't you notice the look in his eyes? Cold as a snake's. He'll swallow you whole, and he won't even blink. You know snakes don't have eyelids, right?"

Blondi shrugs, but Lauriane sees that her speech has had an effect. For a rare time, she senses fright in the man's eyes.

"I don't want anything bad to happen to you," Lea says.

The three girls are working him over.

"Nothing will happen to me," he replies with a lack of conviction, as if he realizes he may not get out of this alive.

Lea buries her face in her hands, hammering it home that if he isn't careful enough, something bad will happen. Then she plants her gaze right into his, and tells him he is their only hope of getting out of this, and that afterwards, he and Lea will run away together. They can finally live their lives together. Blondi smiles as he gazes at her fondly. But he refuses to promise to help. He just listens to them, and that makes Rashida mad. How can he not recognize how dangerous his boss is? How can they not close the sale, find the clincher to get him to agree? To make him see things their way? He is obviously intellectually challenged. He probably has the brain age of a ten-year-old. So why can't they deal with him more easily?

"Are you afraid of him?" Lauriane asks, taking advantage of a moment of silence.

Blondi shrugs again.

"But you're twice as big as him. You can handle him easily," Rashida says. "You could even lock him up somewhere, and he couldn't do shit. What are you afraid of? Is it just because of the money?"

He nods.

"A lot?"

He nods again.

"How much?"

He stares at the floor before confessing that he doesn't know the exact amount, but he thinks it's around a hundred dollars a day.

Rashida chuckles.

"I could double that only with my allowance. Frankly, my folks are rich. If all you're worried about is money, don't worry. They'll greatly reward the man who saved their daughter."

The other two can see the idea making its way into the giant's narrow brain. Lauriane is jumping up and down inside, excited about the turn of events.

"My mother will do the same. I'm the apple of her eye, and—"

"You're the what now?" Blondi asks, frowning.

He doesn't know what the apple of her eye means.

"She cares about me a lot and would do anything to bring me home," Lauriane says more simply.

Rashida widens her eyes at Lea, inviting her to hit the same nail on the head.

"And my parents would pay for our apartment," she says. "They've already offered. We could live together, you and I. Begin our life together. You know, like we've wanted to do all along?"

She puts her hand in the giant's huge palm. His gaze softens as he looks at her.

"This is what I want most in the world," he says.

She smiles.

"So, help us. Let's get out of here together, the four of us. Let's leave this jerk behind and get on with our lives."

"What the hell are you doing, for Christ's sake?"

The voice comes from the other end of the corridor. Shivers run down the three girls' spines. Blondi frowns, and he stands up promptly.

"Sorry, I have to go."

"Please think about what we said," Lea says, begging him. "Think about us."

Blondi just looks at her, pursing his lips, and leaves. But he smiles at her before closing the door.

"I think this can work," Rashida says, whispering to the girls. "For the first time since this shit started, I'm actually hopeful that we can convince this jerk to help us."

"Are your parents that rich?" Lauriane asks.

Rashida smirks. "They don't have a dime to save their lives. We live in a slum. They may not even notice I'm gone," she chuckles.

But it's a sad chuckle. Lauriane feels it and pities her. "This big dummy will help us, I'm sure of it. We can make him believe whatever we want. The end justifies the means. Do you think Lea really loves him? Come on."

Granted, it's not literally love, or even physical attraction that Lea feels for Blondi, but she can't help but feel a certain connection to the big dude. She doesn't know if it's because she's playing her part so well that she's convincing herself, or if it's real feelings, but even though he's to blame for bringing them to this damned place, she sees good in Blondi's eyes, a great vulnerability. She develops an affection similar to the one you have for a little cousin who keeps disappointing you, but who you would like to salvage. So that he will eventually learn, and be happy, too, one day. Almost a maternal affection.

But Lea will never admit it openly.

THIRTY-SEVEN

Since my foot feels better, I've been walking at an almost normal pace again. I went back to the rooming house, to find out more about this goddamn Blondi, to find out who I'm dealing with. If I'm to go into the lion's den, I might as well be prepared. Now, every time I think about his nickname, instead of the German Shepherd, I hear "Call me" from the band of the same name. An unbearable ear worm. Just for that, he deserves the death penalty. As I look around, there's only one conclusion to be made: it's a shitty neighbourhood. I don't know if the city planners made it a shithole on purpose, but past this street, it's already more middle class. Of course, everything along the waterfront is for the city's rich and thugs. The neighbourhood is dilapidated. Not attractive to anyone, not even to me, and I've seen my share of crapper. Let's just say that my family wasn't exactly flush with cash. We lived in a mobile home for a long time, which was threatening to collapse at any moment, and which left much to be desired in the hygiene department. I made a point of naming the roaches who shared my room. I could hear them crawling around on the floor next to my bed with quick, sly, brief clicks. Sometimes I would wake up swinging my arms around as if to chase away whatever had just touched my face. As we didn't have a pet, it could only be Micheline, a thick and slightly obese cockroach who always stared at me with a grumpy look. The last to flee when the lights turned on. As if she was challenging me. For a long time, I thought she was planning my murder, but ultimately, she couldn't do it for the simple reason that she was a goddamn cockroach. But if she had been a boa constrictor or a tiger, I wouldn't be here to tell you about my legend.

At school, my engaging personality saved me from solitude, and I had just enough decent clothes to fake like I was middle class. But I had to use all my tricks to explain why I invited no one over to my place. Fake it 'till you make it, right? Except that dwelling on my shitty childhood won't help me right here, right now, even if the surroundings and the human misery I see around me in this dreary area remind me of my modest origins. Maybe that's why I'm so hard on Serge. I can't fathom why a smart guy like him, who had a dream life before, can get up every morning and accept his grim life as a bum. I've done so much to get out of the poverty trap that I don't understand how someone can wallow in it like a cow in a pasture. Anyway, fuck it. And no, I don't want to know where you came from and how you suffered when you were a young brat, barely able to keep from shitting your underpants. This whole damn thing is about me, yes, or no? If you want to be talked about, write your own whiny tale.

I approach a group of toothless idiots with a casual demeanour. I must look like someone who doesn't give a shit and is here by accident. They talk about God knows what between two muffled hisses characteristic of people lacking incisors and molars. There are two jerks, their backs against the wall of the building, engaged in reinventing the world. I'll start with them. I must be careful in case Laurel and Hardy show up. They will jeopardize my plan.

"Good evening, gentlemen," I say right off the bat. My originality has knocked your socks off, hasn't it?

The two stupefied men look at me as if I wanted to sell them a boy scout calendar. I get over it and get to the heart of the matter.

"Have you seen Blondi? He was supposed to meet me here."

"That asshole Blondi? What the hell do you want with that creep?"

"I have a job for him."

Both men's eyes brighten.

"You do? What kind of job? We sure can use a little money."

OK, failed strategy. As my GPS would say, "Recalculating."

"It's pro bono. As you pointed out, he's not very bright," I say, chuckling.

They go back to their disabused looks, visibly disappointed. I'm surprised they don't ask THE question. I can't help it.

"You know what I mean by pro bono, right?"

They both nod, but I'm not content with that.

"What does that mean?"

"You don't know?" one of them says, with an inquisitive eye.

"Of course, I do, but I don't think you do."

The two of them look at each other, giggling.

"You speak as if it is complicated," says the other with an equally inquisitive eye. "Everyone knows that means you're volunteering."

There are days when you feel like the ultimate ignoramus, aren't there? Well, that's how I feel, right now, in front of these two fools who look at me as if the real riddle is coming.

It's not coming.

"Getting back to our buddy Blondi, do you know where the fuck he is?"

Both shrug.

"Do you know his real name? He told me, but I forgot."

They shrug again.

"Well, do you know who his close friends are around here?"

They shrug once again.

"What the hell, are you practicing the Thriller choreography?"

They both squint, not getting the reference. I blow up.

"You know what pro bono means, but you don't know what I mean by choreography, you hicks?"

The guy on the right smiles with his filthy lips, sporting a huge cold sore.

"Of course, we've all seen Michael Jackson's legendary choreography, we just don't get the—"

He stops, realizing what I meant.

"Eureka. He just figured it out," I say, crossing my arms and putting a wide grin on my beautiful face.

I leave them hanging and ask around among the other people. I finally find someone who can help me. It's about time. I was starting to think Blondi was a ghost.

"But we haven't seen him in a while. If you talk to him, tell him I'm still waiting for my five dollars."

I roll my eyes. Of course, I won't tell him, you silly bugger.

"Pfff, Blondi, huh? Quicker to bum you some cash than give it back, ain't I right?" I say, acting like I know him well.

"You said it, chubs."

I play the Columbo game, which comprises leaving, stopping and coming back to the person for an ultimate question. It always has a significant effect. At least in my head.

"One last question, ma'am."

"Ma'am?" says the guy, who suddenly has no idea what I mean.

"Do you know Blondi's real name? He told me once, but I don't remember."

He searches far too long to know.

"I know his first name is James, but I'm not sure about his last name."

"And what about his room number? Do you remember that?"

"Yes, 113."

"Not superstitious."

"Obviously not."

"Thank you, my good man," I say, ignoring the question of why I want to know his real name.

I nod to the old man at the front desk, who obviously doesn't give a shit. Getting in here is like walking into a barn. I go to room 113 and knock a few times on the door, calling Blondi sometimes by his nickname, sometimes by his first name. In both cases, no answer. I turn the door handle; It is locked. According to my assessment, the latch will be difficult to break, and I don't have my tools with me, anyway. I notice that there are two doors leading to two other rooms on my left. When I'm in the back-yard, I'll see if I can get to the window of the big nerd's room. When the giant jerk crushed my foot and nearly murdered me, I looked at the window frames in rows. Going around the build-ing, I end up in front of the third window from the right, which, according to my educated calculations, would give access to Blondi's room. Of course, it is locked, but it appears to be in terrible shape, ready to give way at any moment. Robert, the manager, can act like a poor man's intellectual all day, but he is a mediocre building manager. I shake the frame a bit to get it to give way, and you know what?

It gives in.

I slip inside the room, and Jesus Mary Joseph, it looks like someone took a dump on the carpet. It reeks of sewer-bottom in this room. It needs to be aired out at once. I inhale through my mouth, but I still taste that shitty smell. Kind of like when you go to the country in the middle of manure season. You may only breathe through your mouth, but it still tastes like you're sucking on a cow's anus. I'm looking for anything that will give me a lead. I won't be here long, as you can imagine. There are lots of clothes lying around on the backs of chairs, and on an old, stunted couch. I grab one pair of pants, and, by God, whoever is wearing them must be as big as Viateur Demers. How come they only house giants here? I don't want to turn on a light and attract attention, but it's hard to see ahead. My eyes will get used to the darkness in a few minutes. I focus on the larger objects, but I see nothing that is worth my consideration. I notice envelopes containing what looks like unpaid bills and I finally get the name of this dirtbag: James Romano. I take one and stuff it in my inside jacket pocket because I could forget his name in the next five minutes. You know, me and my caterpillar memory. I tap on a computer keyboard that turns on the antiquated screen, but it requires a password. However, the screen lights up enough to see a snapshot on a corkboard on the wall to my right. There is a man and a woman, and since the man towers over the woman by at least a foot, I assume it is Blondi. I take the picture and put it in my pocket too. Well, there's nothing else interesting here. I am about to walk away to prevent from asphyxiating myself when I see a piece of paper on the corner of the desk. A scribbled address in childlike calligraphy: 54 Clark Street in Montreal. Bingo, that must be where this moron is hiding. I take it with me, too. I have to get out of this shithole before I pass out and die. I step outside by the window, and I run into Hardy, from the duo I met the other day. He looks at me; I look at him; he looks at me; I look at him.

"Do you live here?" he asks in a harmless voice.

I raise my eyebrows, not sure if he's bullshitting me or if he's serious. Given the collective IQ of the residents of this complex, I play along.

"Yes. You never saw me before?"

"You look familiar. Do I know you?"

"Sure, you're Matt?" I took a chance. It's either Matt or Matty. I have a 50% chance of getting it.

"No, I'm Matty."

No luck, as always. "That's what I meant."

"And what's your name?"

"Laurel Hardy," I say, struggling to keep from laughing.

"Nice to meet you, Laurel."

He extends a solicitous hand to me. I almost feel attached. The protruding belly, the short moustache, the round kettle-shaped face. I want to pinch his cheeks.

"Nice to meet you, Matty."

I leave him hanging, giggling like a turkey. Matty really has a goldfish memory, which is worse than my caterpillar memory, if you know the mnemonic rank of the bug kingdom. I say that, but deep down, I do not know.

What I'll find at 54 Clark Street remains to be seen.

THIRTY-EIGHT

Blondi enters the room, followed by his boss. All three girls are sleeping deeply. The boss smiles.

"Perfect. I told you what you added to their grape juice was enough to incapacitate them. I parked the van in the garage, so you can carry them in."

He leaves Blondi to his task and goes back to pick up the rest of his things. He didn't know that Blondi hadn't a driver's license when he hired him. It hurts the operation a bit. But since Blondi found someone as dumb as him to help with the shopping, it was okay, even if it wasn't ideal. The other idiot won't make the connection between the missing girls and Blondi. Anyway, they never allowed him in the house, only in the garage, to pull out the many grocery bags away from the neighbours' prying eyes. The initial intention was to find five blonde girls, but it turned out to be more difficult than expected. In any case, they can find more once they are at the ranch. There are five cottages to accommodate them with all the amenities including a chain anchored to the middle of the floor which will be secured to their ankles, allowing them to move anywhere they need to in the house and on the small porch outside to get some fresh air and socialize. When they are needed to work in the garden, he will switch the chain for one linking their feet together at a sufficient distance so that they can walk slowly, but not run. Just like prisoner's shackles when they stand trial.

They, too, are prisoners, in a way, even if he would rather believe the opposite. He is confident that the girls will eventually adapt to their new life, succumb to his undeniable charm, and especially to bear his children. He must repopulate the earth with humans who will be dominant like himself and gorgeous like the girls. The perfect marriage of intelligence and beauty. Of courage and elegance. With the education he plans to provide them, they will seize control of society, and be a positive influence on the country and the world at large. If, by some misfortune, one girl turns out to be infertile, then she will suffer the same fate as any other who refuses to cooperate: death. No one will leave this ranch alive. Neither the big guy nor the girls. They'll sustain themselves with everything on the ranch. With satellite internet, solar power, animals, and immense gardens, they barely will need to go out. He has set aside a business address in his name in the city nearby where he can get his mail and packages. He has thought about it thoroughly. He can't fail.

He will finally live the life he has always dreamed of. The life he envisioned the entire time he was locked up. When he was looking at palm trees dancing in the wind from afar. When he would hear the guards' voices in a foreign language that he mastered over time. He deserved it, after all. He has achieved his revenge on the person who betrayed him, and now he can leave with peace of mind, doing what he aspired to do when he was a kid. Everything he was told he could never do, that his dream was not only inhuman, but illegal and unrealistic. He realized long ago that some people are merely objects to be used and discarded when they have served their purpose. They're like animals, although he has more respect for animals than for his own species. It hurts him more to slit an ox's or a rabbit's throat, to break a chicken's neck, than to slaughter a human. Humans are inherently evil anyway, whereas animals have no malice. He rubs his hands together in excitement. Only a few more hours, and they'll be there. He went to the ranch yesterday to make sure everything was ready in the remote area. He puts aside the question of what he'll do with his dumb assistant once he gets there, but that's not important right now. He'll decide later, one thing at a time. He hasn't been this excited since he broke out of his dingy prison with two other fellow inmates by tunnelling under their cell. He knew there would be no problem once he was out of that third world country. He could move into the developed world without hiding. His jailers weren't the type to ask for help from Interpol, anyway.

In the garage, Blondi has already moved the drowsy bodies of two of the three girls. Then he gently picks up Lea in his arms and brings her into the van. She is so pretty, so sweet. Her sleeping angel's face brings emotions unknown to him. He is madly in love with her. He has never felt so intimate with anyone in his life. And that this feeling is reciprocal troubles him a lot. He doesn't know how to behave, torn between the boss's instructions and his wish to run away with his darling. He carefully places her in her place and buckles her seat belt. All three are sound asleep, securely fastened and perfectly safe. The boss indicated they will sleep until nightfall, so they have plenty of time to get their things, get to their destination and get them into their cabins before they wake up. He asked the boss if he can live with Lea, but the boss didn't seem too keen on the idea. He stubbornly replied he would think about it. Blondi hopes he will agree. He doesn't get why the boss wouldn't want them to live their love. After all, they will all live together. That leaves the two other girls to the boss. They are just as pretty as Lea, although Lea has a little something extra to him. But maybe not to the boss. James Romano, his real name, doesn't fear many people in life, but the boss scares the crap out of him. He says his name is Rock, but James doesn't trust that it's true. He thinks he is referring to the actor Dwayne Johnson, nicknamed The Rock. No matter what his name is, the boss is capable of the most horrible atrocities imaginable and feels no compunction whatsoever. Rarely has he seen the devil more incarnate than in the boss's eyes. When he raises his voice, as he often does, James shivers and freezes completely. He is powerless to confront him, even if he knows he would physically dominate him with great ease. Except that the boss has a grip on him, an unhealthy magnetism. As if he has hypnotized him. But if the boss refuses to allow him to pursue his romance with Lea, he will have to do something about it. He will have to stand up to him, find an unsuspected strength in him to get what he wants.

He watches Lea's face, slumped on the side, and pats her hair with his big thick hand.

"We'll be together soon, my love. Just like we wanted. I'll make it happen, I swear. I love you so much."

"What the hell are you doing, Romano?"

The boss's voice startles him. He jumps to his feet, banging his head against the top of the car. He rubs the crown of his head, grimacing to keep the pain at bay.

"The girls are in the van," he says in a loud voice that echoes through the garage.

"Then help me with the rest."

"Yes, boss."

He gives Lea one last tender look, then rushes through the doorway to join the boss.

THIRTY-NINE

Everyone is on high alert, except for me, of course. Who gives a shit that no one has seen crazy Jean Ouellet in days? After all, with the way he has treated me lately, he could have drowned, admiring his reflection in the ocean for all I care. But the news reports are freaking out. No response at the mayor's home, no sign of him at work. Even his wife, who rarely shies away from the cameras, has vanished. It's been a long time since she made a public appearance, contrary to her usual way. Still, it's odd that the two most attention seeking people in town have disappeared unnoticed. But as I mentioned, and believe me, I can't stress this enough; I don't give a damn.

"The funniest part is seeing these asshole cops stammering in front of the TV cameras, unable to explain where they are," I say to Phil, who is talking to a semi-psychologically distressed Nicole.

"Nothing funny about that, Martin," she says in a reproachful, grumpy way.

"Of course, there is," I reply.

"Absolutely not," she says, daringly

Is she confronting me? Really? I will tear you apart, dummy. I look at Phil, who is watching me like a bishop, a layman. I give him a condescending look.

"I suppose you—"

"It is indeed not funny."

"Of course," I hiss between my teeth.

A bell rings announcing a visitor coming, who I guess is Marcel Lafleur. Who else would climb the stairs shouting all the citrus fruits in the book? He emerges in front of us, scarlet-faced, out of breath as if he has just completed the Boston Marathon.

"Someone needs to work on his cardio, eh, Lafleur?" I say, snickering.

I look at Nicole. She's still not laughing. I'm getting a bit irritated with her. Maybe a few days of forced leave would put her mind at ease? Although when it comes to cardio, I can't lecture anybody.

"I've never been known for my fitness," Lafleur says, trying to catch his breath, which won't be back for a few minutes.

"No shit, Sherlock."

He turns to Phil and Nicole.

"What's up?"

"Did you hear about the mayor?" she says, on the verge of tears.

She's always liked him. She volunteered for him in both of the last two elections. This suddenly comes to mind, and I'm upset. First, because I see why she's crying like someone stole her lottery tickets. Second, because I could have used that against the mayor when he pissed me off right before he disappeared.

Lafleur approaches her, massaging her shoulders.

"There, there, sweet Nicole. I hope nothing serious has happened to him."

"Martin thinks his disappearance is funny," she says, looking at me as if I were the worst possible monster.

Rage grips me by the throat.

"No, you idiot, I am not amused by the disappearance. I am pleased that the police are totally helpless. Don't put words in my mouth, you know I hate that."

"Still, it's not funny," Lafleur says, massaging the shoulders of the grieving woman.

"Shut up, Lafleur. Besides, you're probably about to scream out a citrus name or two, right?"

Phil and Nicole look at me with their mouths wide open, as if I have just committed a cardinal sin. Man, they are a handful today! They're barely tolerable under normal circumstances, so what is their deal today for the love of Christ?

"Pff, mandarin," Lafleur simply says.

I smile. But the shitty atmosphere turns me into an obnoxious mess. So, I head off to my office. Lafleur follows me in. He is not very good at reading a room. Usually, he shows up exactly when I least want to see him. I pretend to read a document as he describes how much it hurts him that I don't care about his lemon Tourette's syndrome, and I nod like I care.

"Still nothing about the mayor?" I ask, without a shred of interest.

Anything to change the subject.

"My sources have seen nothing. And yours?"

I don't really have any sources. In fact, my most reliable one is currently lying in a hospital bed. But other than Serge, I have little. Lafleur's network is stronger and more developed than mine, I'll be the first to admit. I'm more of a gut feeling kind of guy. But sometimes I would like to use his contact network. You know I would never admit that to him. You know me more and more now. I appreciate it. You are more perceptive than the average person. That's always a plus. Saves you and me a lot of time.

"Honestly, I didn't ask," I say in a disinterested tone. "Let's just say that I haven't seen the mayor in a good light lately."

"I understand perfectly."

I glance at him. Does he know about my issues with the city's chief magistrate? And then I realize how he got it.

Philippe.

In the least likely to keep a secret category, Phil wins every time. I give him an acidic glance from afar that doesn't faze him in the least.

I turn back to Lafleur.

"Do you really want to find out what happened to him?"

"I do."

"I don't," I say, turning back to my document.

"Not even to crack the case before Bouchard and the other asshole cops?"

I sigh. That argument never fails. And everyone is using it a little too much for my taste.

FORTY

As they sit on their veranda, Lauriane Derome has been watching Rashida Lafleur for several minutes now. Out of the two girls, she is most concerned about Rashida. She hasn't spoken a word since their arrival at what looks like a ranch. The land stretches as far as the eye can see, and there seems to be no civilization for miles around. There is no sound or sign of life. Until they got there, Rashida was confident they could get away from it all, that they would find a way. But not anymore. Rashida was already losing motivation as the days went by while they were trapped in their dungeon, but Lauriane never saw her so desperate, as if she had no fight left in her. As if she was accepting her fate as a surrogate for this moron. On her right, Lea Briand displays a perpetual fake smile. She's chatting with Lauriane, but she's as resigned as Rashida, even though she's doing everything she can to prove otherwise. Not Lauriane. She will fight until her last breath. This madman that insists on being called Rock Mercier will never touch her. Better to die. If only she wasn't the only one willing to stand up for herself. She watches Rock's and Blondi's comings and goings, looking for loopholes in their modus operandi, identifying opportunities to escape.

The three girls woke up in an unfamiliar place a few days ago, but instead of being together again as before, they are secluded in small houses. They have a full view of their living space from their bed; a kitchenette and a dining table, further on, a sofa overlooking a turned-off flat-screen TV. Lauriane has turned it on, but they have access to nothing but streaming services like Netflix, Disney+ and HBO Max. No access to more traditional stations or news. No way to know if people are talking about them, if anyone is looking for them, or if anyone else cares but their parents. A thick metal collar secures their left ankle to a chain welded to the middle of the floor. It is long enough for them to access every corner of the house and to go outside on the veranda they share. They each have a rocking chair to pass the time and chat with each other. That's where they are right now. Rashida rocks gently in her chair, staring straight ahead, expressionless. Lea answers Lauriane's questions laconically, a sad smile hanging on her face, but she does not contribute to the conversation. Lauriane feels like she is lonely. The last one to have a fire in her belly and the desire to break free. She seriously doubts that anyone will ever join her in an escape plan.

Blondi prowls near the houses, keeping his eyes on Lea. He also looks worried about her. Lauriane is scared for her friend. With everything she told Blondi about the fake love, he is buying into the whole charade. It can only end badly for her. When he comes closer to talk to her, Lea smiles blissfully, but doesn't pretend anymore. She no longer asks him for help. She has taken refuge in a quasi-mutism which is not helpful. Lauriane knows Blondi is the only chance they have to thwart the maniac's schemes. She tries to convince Lea to play the role one more time, but she doesn't want to. Like Rashida, she has given up. If Lauriane hears them say, "What's the point?" one more time, she will get really mad. She hates fatalism, even more so when it negatively impacts her life. She loves her two partners. They've developed a strong bond, typical of those who experience the same drama, but she cannot stand their surrender. The only time she feels depressed is when she thinks of her mother. This is when she feels like she is losing her drive. This is when she is at her lowest. She knows her mother, that she must be in a state of shock. Her husband's death changed her forever, but she survived. But she won't make it this time. Lauriane shuts out these thoughts as best she can. She cannot allow herself to be in this state of mind. It weakens her, and she needs all the strength she can muster to get out of this ordeal. She keeps on trying to coax Lea to use her charm, but it is difficult. She thought she found the right words the day before to win her over. For the first time since arriving in this hellhole, she noticed a flash in the young blonde's eyes. She needed to keep working on it until Lea agrees to play the part, the role of her life. Lea swore she never took acting classes, never acted in anything. Lauriane said that she therefore had a natural talent, that she should make use of it when she gets back to her normal life. She hoped that by giving her a glimpse of an interesting life away from here, she would inspire her. Lauriane talks to Rashida constantly so that she doesn't fall into a catatonic state. That she is at least functional the moment they run away. Thus, Rashida must maintain a minimal level of consciousness to obey instructions when the time comes. Therefore, Lauriane compels her to interact, even if her answers are monosyllabic. She tries to make her laugh, which she does at times. In fact, she never really laughs, but she has a slight smile that is worth any laugh from a normal person.

Mercier told them he will soon put them to work on the farm. They will need to contribute for their food and shelter. Lauriane said they didn't ask for it and refused to work even for a minute for him. She expected a violent response, but he just smiled and said that they will see soon enough how it'll go. She is convinced that this man is the very definition of evil. She has never seen evil represented more distinctly than in this monster. He lives in an alternate world in which it's okay to kidnap girls and turn them into his slaves. His lack of concern for the consequences if he fails is disarming. Does he really believe no one is looking for them? Does he really think he is safe on this ranch? Doesn't he know helicopters can fly overhead at any time, and that their parents well search high and low to find them? How can he be so oblivious? So sure of himself? Yet, he is a public figure. Lauriane often saw him on TV, but he went by another name. She doesn't care about politics, but it's hard not to recognize him. She is astonished that her two girlfriends never saw him. Besides listening to videos on TikTok and YouTube, they aren't really into TV, but still. Lauriane can't conceive that one can be so ignorant of their surroundings. When she revealed who he was, they were doubtful. Why would this man do all this if he already had a fulfilling and successful life? When they got to the ranch, Lauriane confronted him about his public life, which he vehemently denied. He rebuked her, ordering her to stop putting misguided ideas in the other two minds. His gaze went mad to the point where she stopped insisting, fearing he would do something rash. She notes, however, that the topic throws him off. All she wishes deep in her soul is to have a flash of genius that will reveal how they can get out of this mess. She frequently asks her father for support. She asks him for advice to find a way out of this mayhem, to put her on the right path. Because although she looks strong and confident, deep inside, she is totally helpless.

FORTY-ONE

I'm parked in front of 54 Clark Street, and I scan the area. It's a very cushy neighbourhood, but the small house looks nothing extravagant either. It has old-fashioned brown brick walls, an ivory tin front with two gigantic windows giving it the look of an owl, and a garage with a white door embedded in the house. Nothing to write home about. Two immense oak trees guard the entrance, showing a gloomy look. I might as well check out what I can find there. I cross the street galloping like a lover too happy to meet his mistress, then I knock discreetly at the main door, so as not to look like a policeman or a bailiff. I wait a few seconds, then I knock again, this time with force. After a few minutes of this merry-go-round where I increase the intensity of the impact of my knuckles on the door, I fall back on Plan B: the doorbell. But it is defective. Anyway, that's what the total absence of sound inside tells me. I try to see through the window to my left, but the daylight glare prevents me from seeing a thing. I am too far away to lean with my hands on the window. I will walk around. My first thought is that this house was left to decay a long time ago. My second thought is that I should get out of here promptly. I don't have a good feeling about it. It looks like a scary movie opening scene, and that's bad. Because you know what happens to the first character in a horror movie, right? He dies. But hey, I've long since accepted I'm too curious and reckless to live to be old; I know I will die on the job. I've come close a few times. So, it might as well be today. Why keep the suspense going? There's plenty of dog poop in the backyard, which is just a muddy field that stinks of a dalmatian's ass. It has never been taken care of in the first place. No one ever bothered to do a lawn job. Even for a maintenance-averse guy like me, it's troubling. There's a metal door behind, I knock energetically.

"Open up," I say, shouting as if my life depended on it. Nothing.

What are you doing here, Blondi? What's with this house? Are you squatting here with the rest of your sort? I understand that your room reeks a monkey's ass, but this place isn't much better, and I don't think it's going to get any better once I get inside.

"Can I help you?" says a voice to my left that makes me jump forty feet in the air. And I'm hardly exaggerating.

A jerk on his balcony looks at me with all the concern in the world. His residence has a window overlooking the muddy yard of the house.

"Yes, do you know who lives here?" I say, trying to regain my senses.

"It used to be René," he says, as if everyone knew that asshole René, "but he sold it two years ago."

"Thank you. That helps me to know who lived here two years ago. My real question, and sorry if I wasn't clear enough before, was who is staying here now?" I say that sentence with all the condescension I could muster.

"No idea. There's a bit of coming and going, but I've never seen the owner. Sometimes there are vehicles that come down to the garage, but they leave right away. I have seen no one in the yard. You're the first one in ages."

"In other words, you can't help me."

He realizes that indeed, there is nothing he can do for me other than waste my time.

I sigh and press my hands on the small upper window of the old-fashioned door. It looks vacant. You can tell when there is activity in a house and when there isn't, and right here, I swear there isn't. The idiot keeps looking at me like he is watching a play, and I am the main character. I look at him with a scowl showing all the contempt I have for him, and then suddenly, just like that, his face brightens up.

"Wait, I have some information that might help you."

I know this scheme. That jerk will ask me to pay for the info. I've seen it several times before.

"I've seen the mayor around here a few times. He wouldn't stay long, but he'd come in and go."

He tells me this without asking for money, the bastard. I would have easily paid a few hundred dollars for that intel.

"The mayor? What mayor?" I ask, even though I know exactly who he is referring to.

"The mayor of Marseilles, asshole," he says, laughing like a pig. "Montreal's mayor, of course. Jean Ouellet."

What the hell would the Big O be doing in this shithole, and why isn't that the first thing this jerk told me? It's not a trivial piece of information. It should have come up long before that idiot René. It can't be the fortieth thing that comes to mind when you think of this decrepit shack.

"It suddenly came to me," he says, justifying himself when I point it out.

"Are you sure it was Ouellet? Maybe it was someone who looked like him."

"Maybe," he says, "but it would still be quite a coincidence."

"What would?"

"That the mayor's look-alike also has a chauffeur."

I know the mayor's chauffeur well, so I ask him to describe him to me. He says he didn't get a good look at him, but that he was tall, chubby, and bald.

Holy shit, it was that motherfucker Jean Ouellet. I am careful not to show my excitement to the nosy neighbour, and I thank him timidly as my heart races as if I have just done a long sprint. Then I calm down. It doesn't make sense. Why would Ouellet waste his time in this shitty place? A lover maybe? That would be surprising since his wife is permanently clinging to his arm, but it's not impossible. I have seen more twisted things. But then again, unlikely. Why would Blondi live with them? Is he gay? Does he come here to have an orgy with this guy Blondi? Why would the mayor pick him? You know what? I don't care who people fuck. Maybe the big guy has unsuspected talents in the sack. And given the change in the mayor's personality over the past few weeks, that would be the reason. It's never too late to live your life, to get out of the closet and experiment with your most secret fantasies. I realize I am staring at the door, alternating between thinking, smiling, and frowning. The neighbour must think I'm schizophrenic or something. I wave goodbye to him and go back to the office, telling no one about this. Because obviously, I will come back alone in the evening, like an idiot, and expose myself to any danger that could arise in this shithole instead of having some colleagues with me. Like in the creepy detective movies where a sleuth ventures by himself to a ruined house, in the middle of a storm. You would shout: "Why didn't you call for backup, you moron?"

Several hours later, as it is getting dark, I park in front of that gloomy house again, this time wearing a black toque, a long black sweater and, you guessed it, black pants. Ha, and I put on work boots and brought my gun. One can never be too careful. There are limits to being a jerk. There's still no life in this house, and that worries me more and more. Fortunately, it's not raining. I gather up my courage and go for it. I go to the side of the house, stealthily walking along the cedar hedge that has seen more glorious days. Arriving at the corner of the residence overlooking the courtyard, I hear footsteps behind me. With a quick movement, I jump at the shadow chasing me, grabbing my gun, which slips out of my hand and falls somewhere under the cedar hedges.

Damn, I'm clumsy.

I will have to play it old timer, swinging with my fists, arms, feet, and anything else I can use to subdue this asshole who is neither the mayor, nor Romano since the assailant is a little shorter than me. But the bastard is strong. He turns on me and gets the upper hand by grabbing me by the throat. I reach out to the ground, trying to pick up something I can smash on his skull. My hand finds a rock and I crush it on his temple. He promptly lets go of me, screaming. Strangely enough, the voice is familiar, but I don't have time to think, and I jump on him like a leopard on a baby wildebeest.

"Lemon, boss, let go of me!"

Lafleur? I look at him and yes, it's that motherfucker Lafleur, who has smeared mud on his face and wears exactly the same clothes as me. I'm not lying to you, the same toque, the same black long-sleeved shirt. What the hell is he doing here?

"Phil told me about the house—"

"Will you shut up," I whisper to him with authority, "we mustn't be spotted."

"Sorry, boss, but can I ask you a favour?"

"Of course."

"Can you get off of me? You're crushing my balls."

I stand up and allow him to do the same.

"What are you doing here, you moron? Did you follow me?" I ask him, incredulous.

"Yes, and no. Phil told me you had spoken to Demers, and that he mentioned a house on Clark Street. Then one of my contacts gave me the address of that house."

"You mean this crapper?"

"Grapefruit, that's ugly, huh?"

"Grapefruit indeed."

Lafleur's story seems implausible to me. Normally, he would have rushed to my office to give me information about his contact, but this time, he was working alone? You might say that I did the same thing, it's true, and shut up. But I always work solo. I never involve this freak unless I have to. I don't have the time to grill him any more than I have to, because time is running out. We must get into this house. I'll deal with Lafleur later.

"Hey, boss."

Again, I direct Lafleur to shut the fuck up. Are we on a top-secret mission or what? But there he is, with his muddy face revealing only his huge smile while he holds the back door open.

"It wasn't locked."

You know when I said that his abrupt apparition is suspicious? Scratch that, it's downright questionable. There's something not right about this citrus lover.

But first things first. For now, let's check out what we can find in this dump.

FORTY-TWO

It's exactly what you would have imagined: a creepy house to make you shiver. Nooks and crannies littered with well-woven spider webs, the work of a bug a bit too safe not to be bothered by humans, dark rooms because the electricity is out, God knows why. In short, Lafleur and I walk along with our flashlights illuminating our every step, while all we want to do is to run away from this stupid house. My curiosity will get the better of me one day, and maybe that day has come. You'll enjoy it, it will fulfil your appetite for the morbid, won't it? At least, you will have had your money's worth. Witnessing firsthand the death of the famous private detective Martin Lafs, you will tell your grandchildren about it to impress them. You will have known a legend. You'll get bragging rights for having met me at my prime. We advance in muffled steps on this parquet floor, which saw better days. If our plan was to be furtive, we failed. This damn floor cracks under our feet. It's an old shack, probably built in the days when the muddy streets of the city were still full of horses. As I am not one half of an idiot, I let this oblivious Lafleur walk in front of me as we explore the surroundings. I think of him as a serial killer's spotter. He'll get killed while I'll do a quick one hundred and eighty degree turn on myself and flee the scene by the time Jason and his seventies goalie mask finish him with a machete. I chuckle as I imagine Lafleur screaming citrus names while the jackass butchers him. Shit, I'd pay to see that. But let's focus. I obviously didn't notify the cops about my stunt. They'll find out about it at the same time as the media. They wanted to hinder us? Then they can kiss my cute little hairy ass.

"Lemon, Lafs, I can't see a thing around here."

I instruct him to go on. Lafleur sighs and continues. I'm sure that if I told him to jump off a bridge, he would. I don't know why he's so intrigued by me, and why he treats me as if I were from the French monarchy. After all, his agency is as successful if not more so than mine, but one man's beauty and charm can lead another to put him on a pedestal, just to reap the low-hanging fruit. And by fruit, I mean women. If you didn't already figure it out, you're slow. We went around each room, not finding anything interesting or to give us any clue. I'm getting slightly impatient. Is anyone messing with us? This is the kind of BS Lafleur draws with his kid party entertainer vibe. I was counting on this lead, but admittedly, there are no traces of Romano or anything that would suggest the Big O was here. The neighbour was clearly imagining things.

"There's nothing here," I say, sharing my intuition with Lafleur.

"Let's continue," he replies, as if he were commanding me.

Who does he think he is? I feel like dropping him in this horror museum and get out without warning, to see how long it will take for him to understand I dumped him like a cheap sock oozing foot juice. I rant and rave as I watch us walk hesitantly through this filthy shack. This can't be the key to the puzzle. I barely resist bawling because it's so ugly. It looks like my uncle Raymond's house, that morbidly obese man who made as many bad choices in decoration as in nutrition. This is the only place I've seen a velvet wallpaper on the wall. I swear it's true, and not only that, but it was burgundy. I've seen nothing so hideous besides the back of Lafleur's bald head that I'm staring at as I keep in his footsteps like a puppy, the nipples of his mother. He took off his toque, arguing that it was too hot in here. He looks like a mild moron with his face smeared with dried mud and his crown of hair soaked with sweat. He has a protrusion on the back of his head that makes him look like a Martian who got lost in a godforsaken suburb. If you told me that this guy was indeed an alien, I would believe you. Not only that, but it would explain a lot. I see a carpet underneath the dining room table with one corner folded down, revealing a division on the floor, like a hidden section. I push the table and the carpet aside. I turn a handle embedded in the floor and a panel slowly drops to a cellar that didn't exist until now that we know of. Stairs materialize on the wall as it falls forty-five degrees downward. I must admit that it is well designed. And surprisingly clever for an otherwise crappy house. I look around for Lafleur, because honestly, I'm not keen on venturing into this opaque black basement by myself. I'd much rather Lafleur did it. I hear him walking further away over the creaking of the floor, but he doesn't respond to my calling. I am more curious than irritated to know what he is up to. I shine my flashlight down the staircase and see a passageway that leads further down to the far end of the house. The floor is in better condition downstairs than upstairs, as if someone renovated the basement long after the original construction. I call Lafleur again and he is still incommunicado, even though I can still hear him walking around. Perhaps Jason is following him. This thought etches the first hint of a chuckle on my face. Screw that, I head down to the basement. I know I shouldn't. I know that's where idiots die in horror movies, but what can I say? The whole thing bores me to tears, and the sooner we circle this shithole, the sooner we'll get out of here and wipe these few unproductive minutes from our memories.

"Where are you going, Lafs?" says the nutcase, who suddenly gives a sign of life.

"To the strip club."

Asshole.

I swear there's something wrong with this lunatic. He doesn't respond for several minutes even though I'm screaming like a madman, and then he's suddenly worried to see me going down the stairs? Why wouldn't he want any of us to go downstairs? What is he hiding? I hear him laughing and snorting like a piglet, and I roll my eyes. A machete slash across my throat would be nice, after all. Put me out of my misery, for God's sake. I step down and walk nonchalantly toward a whirring, thumping room that sounds like a heating room about to break down. Fine, I'm going in. I told you; I don't care. I don't know why I try to turn on a light with a switch that refuses to obey, making a haughty little snapping noise, as if it were telling me to fuck off. What did you expect, asshole? For the lights to switch on even though the power is obviously out? Once at the door, I take two steps back and rush to open it with a shoulder blow. The door hardly moves, but the crack of my shoulder and the pain that ensues do not lie. I just dislocated it again. It hurts like hell. I crumple to the ground screaming in pain, and I'm on the verge of despair as I see my flashlight roll off to the wall beyond. I am immersed in total darkness. I'm crying because it hurts so much. I don't know about you, but I'm getting the feeling that I'm hurting myself a little too often in this complete wreck. My foot, and now my shoulder; is this a goddamn joke? Since it never rains but it pours, Lafleur walks up to me quickly and points his light directly at my face, making me squint.

"Stop blinding me with your fucking flashlight!" I say, crying.

"Lemon, sorry, boss. What's wrong with you? I heard a high-pitched noise, like a goat giving birth."

"It was me, yelling in agony, you prick!"

Lafleur sneers. I tell him to give me my flashlight back rather than acting like a fool. I get up slowly. It's not the first time I've dislocated my shoulder, so I gauge the distance between the wall and me. It's going to hurt, but then I'll feel better. Whatever it takes.

"What are you doing, boss?"

I step back a little and take a deep breath. If I knock my shoulder the right way against the wall, I'll put it back in place myself. There's no way in hell I would ask Lafleur to help me. He'd do more harm than good, and that is assuming he understands what he needs to do. I won't take that chance.

"Lafs, not a good idea."

"What the hell do you know about that, you moron? Are you a doctor all of a sudden?"

I take three practice swings before I go in for the coup de grâce.

"Tangerine, no boss."

And then, holy shit right there. The worst pain of my life. My foot injury is nothing compared to what I'm feeling right now, flat on my back after my knees gave out under the intensity of the pain going through my body. I'm crying my eyes out in a fetal position. I don't care anymore. I have no pride. I cry. I just cry. It was the worst idea in the world. I worsened my shoulder instead of fixing it. I'm at the end of my rope. The pro bono, and now this? I'm so sick and tired of this. Because I couldn't say no to Phil and his silly Melanie. Because I wanted to be nice. My mother always told me, "Martin, you're too nice. It will be your downfall."

Wipe that smile off your face right now. It's a true story.

I feel Lafleur grab me by the shoulder with his filthy hands and before I have time to object; he screws the joint off my shoulder with a sharp quarter turn, and I scream like, yes, a goat that has breeched. Then, about three seconds later, it doesn't hurt anymore. It's like none of this happened. Nothing but a slight warmth on my shoulder. I stand up, wiping away my tears and realizing that I owe Lafleur an apology and a thank you. I point the beam at his face and see him smile. He stands there before me with his face plastered with dirt and his pristine teeth. I would take him in my arms and kiss him on his bald forehead. I hold back and express my gratitude with empty words. He shrugs and pushes the huge door open for us to enter. This time I let him go ahead of me because you know? Jason? He may have rescued my shoulder, but if I had to choose, I'd still rather have his throat slit than mine. Why should I always be the one suffering? What we see is unusual. There are five metal beds, one next to the other, leaning against a concrete wall. At the base of each bed, there is a chain with one end attached to the floor and the other to an open latch. People were held prisoner here, and it doesn't take me three hours to figure out that if Lauriane didn't run away, this is probably where she was. So that means there are four more girls?

"Two of the bunks were left undone," Lafleur says.

"True. Maybe not all the beds were taken."

"Do you think Lauriane was here?" he asks.

"Yes, I can smell her perfume."

"For real?"

"No, you idiot. How should I know if she was here or not?"

I see I hurt him. I try to redeem myself by telling him it's a strong possibility, that he's probably right. That doesn't seem to comfort him, so I move on.

"Let's keep looking," I say, walking away.

I hadn't noticed, but as I walk back to the stairs leading to the first floor, an unpleasant smell strikes my nostrils. I open one room of the corridor and it stinks. I enter, and a pungent smell grabs me by the throat. It smells like Mariette, my childhood nanny. A mixture of dirt, dampness, and salmon sauce that I always thought was the smell of her vagina. I distinguish a white crate through the gloom that I assume is a freezer. With the lack of power, everything in there must be rotten. I don't even dare to think of the nauseating blast I'll get in the face if—fuck no. I won't—like the dumbass that I am, I'll open it. I know I am about to open the damn lid. What the hell do I expect? What kind of crappy decision is this? Immediately, I cringe as I open the freezer. The smell, I can't tell you. Holy shit, I don't think I've smelled such a foul smell since a friend of mine in high school was spraying himself with Brut 33. What the hell is this?

"Lafleur," I shout, trying not to puke my guts out.

He doesn't answer. Didn't he follow me? What the hell is he up to now? Did Jason kill him already?

"LAFLEUR," I say, insisting.

"What?"

"Come here!"

He's coming along so fast you'd assume he has some athletic ability. He doesn't.

"What, that—OH TANGERINE!"

"Tangerine indeed. It reeks of the worst."

"What the hell is this?"

"Rotten food. What do you think? There's no power, and there's a freezer. Do a simple rule of three. You'll figure it out."

He makes a hollow sound like a cat about to throw a hairball up, a kind of thumping sound coming from the chest.

"Don't you dare throw up!"

"Green Lime, I will."

"No, you won't."

"Tangerine."

"No, not tangerine."

"Yes."

"I'm telling you, you won't puke."

"I won't?"

"No. Now see what's in there."

After making sure that his dinner stays in his stomach, he goes forward. I told you, he'll do anything I ask. Bad idea, I'm the kind of guy who would test his limits. One day, he will have to say no to me. He pops the lid of the freezer open and immediately closes it.

"What is it?"

"Go see for yourself," he says as he quickly exits the room.

I hear him vomit further away.

"Goddamn it, Lafleur. I mean, isn't it stinky enough as it is?"

He throws up like a tsunami, and hearing people throw up makes me want to do the same. But I hold it in. I breathe through my mouth and hold my breath. I open the lid and... God damn it.

I take three steps back. My heart wants to jump out of my chest to join the other moron.

A vision of horror.

There, buried under a sea of dead haggard looking fish, are the half-putrefied heads of the Big O and his wife.

FORTY-THREE

Lea watches her friends with a smile as wide as the moon. Lauriane stares at Rashida to see if she knows what's going on, but she is just as numb as ever.

"What's the matter with you?" Lauriane asks Lea.

"He'll do it."

Lauriane frowns.

"Who will do what?"

Lea looks towards Rashida, who is suddenly curious. She gets it.

"Blondi, he will get us out of here."

"What? But how?"

"I made it clear that nothing will happen between us as long as we are in this shithole. That the other lunatic wants to compel us to give birth to his freaks. At first, he didn't believe me, but the more I told him, the more he connected the dots."

"Wait a minute, honey," Lauriane says, interrupting her. "Are you telling me that this big dummy has thought things through and made deductions of his own?"

Lea nods energetically.

"Go on," Rashida says in a weak voice.

"So tonight, he will do his usual routine. He will check on us to make sure we have everything we need and are ready for bed, but instead, he will free us from our chains and help us run away."

"Does he have a car?"

"No, but he knows the way to the road. And from there, we could stop a car and beg them to drive us to the nearest police station, or at least call 9-1-1."

Lauriane clenches her lips, pondering. Lea asks what's bothering her.

"I'm not feeling it, Lea. The creep is a hundred times smarter than Blondi. He will see through it. Come on. Blondi wouldn't fool one chicken in that damn henhouse," Lauriane says, pointing to the small, fenced buildings beyond.

Lea throws her arms in the air.

"Do you have a better idea? Because that's pretty much the only option we have."

Lauriane concedes she doesn't. She turns to Rashida, who smiles shyly at her. The young girl's pale complexion suggests nothing good to her. It's as if her soul has gradually escaped from her body shell.

"We have nothing to lose," Rashida says, mumbling.

"Except to be badly tortured for trying to escape. Not to mention what he might do to Blondi," Lauriane replies.

Rashida shrugs. Seeing her friend so helpless and frail, Lauriane is sure she won't survive another week here. "This girl is about to do something drastic, that's obvious," Lauriane thinks. She sighs, figuring that even if she doesn't buy it, there's a better chance of escaping this way than there is by doing nothing at all.

"Okay, she says," resigned.

Lea claps in excitement. She'll tell Blondi that they are all on board and to put the plan in motion.

Lauriane thinks about her mother, and how much she wants to be with her. How she would like to tell her to hold on until she gets out of this mess. She doubts Blondi's ability to lead them to safety, so she thinks of a Plan B. What will she do if Mercier screws up their plan? They'll go tonight, so she'll use the darkness to sneak away, but she won't get very far since she doesn't know how to get to the road. She will see where Blondi leads them, and she will keep walking in the same direction. As she goes along, she will eventually get somewhere. Then, at some point, the day will come, and she will see more clearly. She will adjust her course. Then there's Rashida, who can barely pronounce two three-syllable words in a row. How will she cope? How will she react if the plan fails? That will probably be the final nail in her coffin. Because let's face it, Rock Mercier won't just escort them back to their house as if nothing happened. He'll be furious. And if he takes his anger out on them, Rashida won't survive. Lauriane is certain of it. Yet she tried everything to bring Rashida back to her former self, the one who welcomed her with such aplomb when she first arrived. Where is that girl, where is that grit? Now would be a good time for her to make a comeback. But Rashida doesn't react to her stimuli, or she reacts so slightly. It is as if Lauriane is talking to an elderly aunt with advanced Alzheimer's disease. She is there, material before her eyes, but her mind is off. Everything that used to define her has vanished, leaving behind an empty shell of what she once was. Lea, on the other hand, has a carefree optimism. There is always a solution to everything, always a way out. Humans are all good, somehow. It's just a matter of scratching the surface long enough for it to come out. Her mindlessness is her weakness, but Lauriane much prefers that to Rashida's mutism. So, she doesn't mention the hazards of the operation to Lea. She's got enough to deal with, helping Rashida.

Lauriane is at the center of these two poles. Not necessarily disillusioned, not necessarily hopeful. She is cautious by nature. Life took her father away from her before she even saw the light of day. So, she has a latent wound that keeps her from getting excited when things go well and from despairing when things go badly. She has the fatalism typical of people with the misfortune gene. That's what makes her so fearful and cautious about Lea and Blondi's plan. She wonders if her rational mind is setting off all the alarms in her head, making her feel like it will never work. Except that there is no other way, and doing what Rashida does and giving in to her fate is out of the question. She's said it several times: she would rather die than to serve as an object to this sick man's pleasure, and to have his semen inside her. She is a virgin and won't allow her first mate to be this old creep. She would rather die. She means it. She watches the sun's location and figures it must be around 4:00 pm. Another five or six hours, and the die will be cast. They'll put all their chips in the centre of the table without good cards in hand.

A die-hard bluff.

FORTY-FOUR

The image of Mayor Ouellet's half-open eyes looking at me through a sea of fish still haunts me. I can't stop thinking about it. It makes me gag constantly. Yet this is not the first dead body I've seen; however, it is my first severed head. And since it is a two-for-one, of course I am shaken. It shakes me so much that I suspect everyone. The Big O didn't just make friends over the past few months. He destroyed relationships that took him years to build. He behaved like a pasha, a cad, a king in front of his subjects. This change of heart was as surprising as it was difficult to understand. Of course, he could be a bit aggressive with his high-pitched voice, his haughty demeanour, and the hackneyed expressions he would throw at us like an old cassette, but he was pleasant in general. I say that because when he didn't like you; you were in the doghouse for a long time. I don't know how to deal with everything that's happening. I won't lie to you; I think about giving it all up. But at the same time, I'm curious to see this through. What is the link between Demers, Blondi, the Big O, his wife, and the crumbling house? Were the five beds in the scabrous basement used to detain hostages, or was it just a gloomy room for deviant sex games? As I stood next to the beds, I wondered if Lauriane Derome was there a few days before. The overly tanned mayor called it quits, but probably didn't expect it to turn out this way when he stated he had "other fish to fry".

Why did his wife have to go as well? Was she a collateral victim? Was she part of something shady that cost her husband his life, or was she just an inconvenient witness? Granted, she had a nasal tone comparable to a crow's lament, but why chop off her head too?

I walk in the night, feeling fuzzy. I don't know where to turn. When I try to put the pieces back together, to assess if there is a link or a common thread, I can't put my finger on it. The pro bono, Phil and Melanie insisting that I take the case, the mayor interfering, the police making no effort to track her down, Lafleur taunting me with his harmonica, Viateur Demers, Laurel and Hardy, and then this shitty house. No, I don't see it. I'm confiding in you. I'm open like I've never been open with anyone before, so shut up, okay? Don't tell anybody I said that. What I've failed to tell you is that I've had a bit of an argument with Marcel Lafleur. Needless to say, he shouted grapefruit and lemon until he couldn't take it anymore. The angrier he gets, the more he hurls citrus fruits at you like a nutritionist enjoying acidic food a little too much. All this is to say is that we won't join forces. I must trust someone completely to work with them. I sometimes criticize Phil and Nicole, but if there's one thing, I trust them with my life. Of course, Philippe tested the waters by insidiously shoving a pro bono down my throat, but I would put my life in their hands any day. I can't say the same for the grapefruit enthusiast.

Lafleur always comes up with solid information, which he swears he got in such an implausible way that I figure he's either blessed by the gods—which is obviously not the case, judging by his corpse-like face and his speech impediment—or he's somehow involved in some not-so-clean racket. When I challenge him, he gets on his high horse. But I think that when you have nothing to blame yourself for, you have no reason to get upset, am I right? So, I have trouble believing his story about the gas station guy claiming to be Lauriane's classmate, and him suddenly showing up at the slum on Clark Street when I was the only one who had the information, only to have me believe he got it from some obscure resource. If you've been paying attention, you'll remember that I stuffed the note with the house address in my coat pocket before I left Blondi's dirty room, so I'm the only one who knew about it. And Phil told me he only gave Lafleur the street name, so how did he know? That's what I grilled him about, and that's when he started screaming citrus names while wiggling his fingers.

"A source told me he saw Romano in this house."

"He did? Who exactly?"

"You know I don't rat out my sources."

"Handy answer."

"The word you're looking for, boss, is logic."

I moved towards him with a resolute face.

"There's something wrong with you, Lafleur."

"Lemon, boss, what the hell are you talking about? There's no one more transparent than me."

"Lemon me all you want. It won't change my mind. Too many strange coincidences."

"They are not coincidences. I just told you. That said, I don't really like your tone and your innuendo, Lafs."

"You don't? You don't like my innuendo, do you?"

"No, I don't."

"You don't, huh?"

"Not one bit."

"..."

"..."

"I have nothing." I was bummed, because I thought I had something clever to throw at him, but nothing came to mind. That's when it got a little, shall we say, out of hand.

"Lafleur, did you order the Code Red?"

"The code what?"

"I want the truth!"

"You can't handle the truth, son."

"Ha ha, I got you!"

"You got me to what?"

"..."

"..."

"Fuck me."

I don't know what was wrong with me, but I was like Phil in a dating lounge: unable to close the deal. Lafleur left in a huff, telling me to shove a lot of weird citrus up my ass. I threw a few juicy retorts at him while bemoaning my inability to come up with the right words to get to him, or at least make him look bad. The result is that I am once again alone with Phil to solve this morbid case. Phil is, as usual, furious that I'm taking Lafleur off the case without asking him, arguing that there are never too many people working on finding his friend's teenage daughter, and other such nonsense. I don't give a damn about Lafleur and Phil, except that now I don't know where to take it all, and I wonder if I will go on.

This whole thing is starting to give me the creeps.

FORTY-FIVE

I won't lie to you. For a rare time in my career, I am scared to death. The horrors I uncovered in the ghastly Clark Street house keep me awake at night. I finally told the cops about our findings, and they took over the case. I know I've criticized the Big O more often than not in the last few months, but I would never entertain the idea of chopping off his and his wife's heads. It takes a real lunatic to do that. And even then, you need to be a fucking psychopath, a Rocco Magnotta of politics. The whole thing stinks, and I'm not just talking about the fumes from the freezer. Everything about this case smells like skunk. Whether it's the mayor getting in my way, the cops doing everything to get out of this mess, the pro bono shit, Lafleur and my suspicions about him.

You guessed it; the double murder is the only thing on the news. Who murdered the mayor and his wife? And why? Questions we don't know the answers to as we speak. I can kind of get it for Ouellet, but his wife? Had she become too much of a witness? Was she in the wrong place at the wrong time? One thing is certain, I don't want to deal with this case anymore. I'm sorry, but I won't put my life in danger for a job I do for free. Fuck Josiane. She wanted to get rid of me anyway, and let the police handle it? So be it. Let them take care of it. She'd better get over it, though. No one will care about these missing girls now that the police's attention is focused on nailing whoever killed the mayor, even if it seems related to the missing girls. After all, the five-bed basement dungeon was within a few feet of where we discovered the two royal heads. Assuming that Lauriane Derome was sleeping in one of those beds, of course. One thing I don't understand, though: why stuff the freezer with piranhas? What was the underlying message? Here I am again, trying to make sense of this when I already told you about a thousand times that I am quitting. You have reason to roll your eyes all the way to the back of your skull.

You know that Guy Lefebvre questioned our presence at the house. He was not about to miss an opportunity to implicate us in one way or another. He wanted to know where we got the address of the house. I referred him to Viateur Demers and laughed like a maniac. He will have fun with the big jerk, Robert, and Doc Alex. Fortunately, some of Lefebvre's colleagues are slightly more reasonable, and they realize we were there to track down the kidnapped girl or girls. Or as one could say: to do their fucking job.

I haven't heard from Lafleur since our run-in. He's pissed off out of his mind, which eliminates him as a suspect in my book. Despite that, I'm wary of people who are overly fond of citrus. They are strange. I inform Phil that I am dropping the case, and he is furious, frustrated as he always is when I don't do what he wants.

"You can't do that," he tells me.

"Of course, I can. I can do whatever I want. And what I want is to get paid for my work."

He storms out of the office, probably to clear his head, or to smoke a cigarette and rant at me.

Nicole tries to reason with me, but I signal that the discussion is over. I keep hearing her squawking in the distance until she walks right back to my door in tears, and I am like, "Oh, my God!"

"Think about the girl, Martin. How can you leave a young girl behind like that? I don't understand your decision."

I sigh heavily and stare at her with a deadly look. I won't admit that I'm dropping the investigation because I'm scared shitless that the Big O's death is related to our case, and if someone has the means to kill the mayor and his wife, then they will do it even more easily with a minor private detective like me that nobody cares about. I'm not that negligible, but you know what I mean. I can only imagine what they would do to whiny Nicole. Her cream fudge won't save her, I think, laughing out loud. She watches me, wavering between despair and confusion. I calm down.

Then I hear the door open with a bang and footsteps coming in a hurry. For fuck's sake, will they kill me along with that silly Nicole for real? This must be a sinister joke. My time has already come?

Fortunately, I see Phil's face coming up behind Nicole.

"Watch out, Nicole," I say, yelling.

She panics and drops to the floor, and I laugh like a lunatic.

"False alarm, it's just Phil," I say.

If she could kill me with one look, I'd be dead a hundred times over by now.

"So, you want to quit the investigation, Martin?" Phil asks me unnecessarily, since I've told him several times, and I know very well that he knows that I know that he knows.

"We're not having this discussion again, Philippe."

"Then, tell them."

You son of a bitch. Lousy bastard. Instead of accepting my decision like a man, he ran to seek help from not only his girl-friend but also from Josiane, who stares at me with a sad look that would break your soul. It would break mine if I had one.

Flash news: I don't.

"Look ladies, I can no longer take on this case."

"Excuse me?" Melanie says, crossing her arms.

"What part of my announcement didn't you grasp?" I say, as seriously as I can.

"I heard it, but I can't believe you dare say that without feeling like the worst kind of trash."

A powerful surge of animosity climbs in me. Even Phil is uneasy with his girlfriend's acerbic response.

"I beg your pardon?" I say, in a rage-shaking voice.

"Don't you have any respect for your word? Where is your sense of honour?"

I look at her, dumbfounded.

"Is that a real question?" I say, giggling.

"Yes, it is."

"Honey, I don't have integrity, you fool. I only have a conscience for the things that bring me money. Did I tell you about the time I sold my mother for a toothless blowjob in the back of an old Econoline?"

"You're not half funny, Lafs."

She doesn't sugarcoat it. You've got to give it to her. Must be helpful in dealing with her fat, lumpy boyfriend. A more temperate and fragile Josiane approaches.

"Please, Martin. Do it for Lauriane."

I swear I came close to answering, "Why should I care? I don't know your daughter," but I refrained. Not least because I have an ounce of manners.

"You weren't too fond of me at first, sweetheart. And now I'm your only hope? Well, dear Josiane—"

"Do it," says a voice coming from behind the group, rudely interrupting me.

I lean over to see who it is, especially because it is a woman's voice. I see Anne-Marie, more delightful than ever. I glance angrily at my big, dumb assistant.

"Really, Phil? Anne-Marie? Really?"

He looks down. He knows I've tried to reach Anne-Marie more than once after she suffered the wrath of my foot ache. The last time she came to my house in a negligee still haunts my nights, when they're not haunted by the dead faces of Jean Ouellet and his wife. Anne-Marie comes towards me in a feline way.

"Do it for me."

"Presumptuous little brat," I say, sneering as I devour her from head to toe with my eyes.

"Do it, and I'll do what you want."

From that moment on, nothing else exists. It's as though I'm in a tunnel with just Anne-Marie. No more Josiane, no more Melanie. And good Lord, no more Nicole or Phil. Only the beauty and me. She bewitched me with her proposal. Suddenly, I'm not afraid of the pro-piranha zealot anymore.

"Anything?" I ask, with a lump in my throat.

She pronounces the word "anything" without a sound coming out of her mouth. She turns around and asks to be left alone with me. She comes back to me with her piercing gaze.

"Even that?" I say to make sure we are talking about "that".

She smiles.

"Even that."

Fucking hell. I won't disclose what it is, but you can imagine. Think of the dirtiest thing you've ever dreamed of doing, but never dared to ask, and multiply that by a hundred. You won't even come close to what it is. I'm all emotional, to say the least. She gently strokes the side of my face, knowing full well that she owns me, that she controls me. Then she walks out of my office and addresses the group, huffing, "he'll carry on" before taking her leave.

Melanie and Phil look at me, speechless, not believing what has just happened. Josiane smiles and Nicole giggles.

And I have sparkles in my eyes.

FORTY-SIX

I'm sipping one of the best cappuccinos I've ever had in my life while doing my favourite thing; observing and quietly laughing at people in my head. On the one hand, you have young college students doing their homework and drinking coffee they can't afford. On the other hand, you have struggling artists trying to make it big. Ernest Hemingway wannabes who have more in common with his alcoholism than his literary skills. I look at the side table next to mine, the one where Anne-Marie was sitting the first time I saw her. She didn't charm me at first, but since then, I've been unable to get her out of my head, incapable of picturing myself with another woman. You might say that I tried to screw with Serge's nurse only a few days ago. Yes, okay. You have a knack for bringing people back to reality, don't you? Romance is really dead in this rotten society.

Where was I? Oh yes, I am sorry for the way I reacted with Anne-Marie. I was the king of jerks. I'm obsessed with what she swore to do to me if I stick with this bullshit investigation, but I must admit I'm still petrified. Never tell that to anyone. I'll deny it to my grave. I was reluctant well before the mayor and his wife got killed. They died weeks ago, according to the coroner. I don't get it. I fought with the mayor days after his reputed date of death. Nothing makes sense in this damn shitty investigation anymore. Could someone be posing as him? But who? It was him, though, no one ever doubted it. But it would explain his change of tone towards me, and it would make me feel a little better. I don't mind being loathed. I even live with it quite well. But I need to know why someone hates me. And in this case, I didn't know. The only reason the Big O was standing there, before our stunned eyes, when he was supposed to be dead according to the coroner is that—oh no, it ain't a shitty The Young and the Restless episode, for crying out loud. The technology to get someone else's face transplanted on yours doesn't exist yet. Anyway, those who have tried it mostly look like Hannibal Lecter after he stuck a guard's face skin on his own to escape from prison.

I try to blend in when I see that asshole Marcel Lafleur enter the café. He scans the place and locates me easily. I stand out in this sea full of hipsters with my undeniable charm and great look. As soon as he sees me, his face hardens, and he turns to the cashier to order his coffee. Then he looks back at me, so I give him a tight smile that I immediately regret. I don't have to act like I'm trying to mend fences. He's the one pouting, not the other way around.

Shit, here he comes.

"Lafs."

"Lafleur."

He raises his eyebrows, staring at the seat in front of me. I nod, pursing my lips. He sits down.

"Do you have something to tell me, Lafs?"

He's not being as formal as usual. Something is broken inside him.

"No, what about you? Something to confess?"

He rolls his eyes.

"Mandarin. For the hundredth time, I'm not hiding anything from you. Think about it; why would I help you if I knew something that would incriminate me?"

"No idea, why?"

"No reason, that's why. Tangerine!"

"Tangerine all you want," I say, "there's something wrong."

"With your head, yes."

"Kiss my ass, nut job."

He looks down.

"I'm just tired of your allegations, Lafs. We need to trust each other if we are to work together, and for some reason, you blame me for things I haven't done. It just won't work."

"Fine."

"Fine," he says, before taking a sip of coffee, looking angry.

Maybe he's right after all. His dismay shows that he has nothing to blame himself for, right? Otherwise, he would fight back, body and soul. But he is more hurt than offended. I keep looking at him, bringing my coffee cup to my mouth.

"Anyway," he says, "maybe we're better off going our separate ways."

"Maybe," I say, letting out an expletive after dropping a little coffee on my beautiful white Calvin Klein shirt.

He snickers but doesn't fool anyone. His sad eyes betray him. He stands up.

"Goodbye, Lafs. And good luck figuring out what I've found."

He turns to leave.

"What did you find?"

The son of a bitch knows how to pique my curiosity. It better be linked to the missing girls, though. If he mentions that there's a new sandwich at the corner restaurant, it'll turn ugly really fast. The jerk keeps walking towards the exit, like he doesn't hear me. I sigh and go after him.

"Will you come back to your seat?" I whisper to him furiously, grabbing his arm.

He looks at my grip with a stern look, and I let him go, apologizing. He follows me to my booth.

"Why are you suddenly curious about what I have to say? Only interested when you can get something out of someone, eh, Lafs?"

"Stop whining and spill it out."

"Not until you apologize."

I laugh.

"Dude, why on earth should I apologize to you?"

He gets up; I stop him.

"Wait, okay. I'm sorry I suspected you had something to do with Lauriane Derome's kidnapping. Can we move on?"

I swear his intel better be good.

He sits back down and takes a long breath.

"After reading the coroner's report, I have to admit that I was a bit taken aback. How could it possibly… I thought to myself… but it was impossible."

"Would it be too much of a pain in the ass to come up with a full sentence?"

"Sorry. It's just that my theory is so far-fetched that—"

"The Young and the Restless?" I say, cutting him off.

"Exactly," he says as if I had just read his mind. "I still went through all the options. I flipped through all the publications about the mayor, watched all the interviews about his personal life, you know, monk work."

"All the shit I make Phil do," I say, chuckling.

"I read the newspapers, the gossip magazines—"

"I get it. And then what?" I don't have all day.

"The mayor often talked about his sister, as you know. A nincompoop, crystal meth addict turned nun in a village in Peru."

"The infamous Gertrude Ouellet."

"But nothing about other members of his family. I finally found a lead, a way, a sudden enlightenment, my eureka moment—"

"Please get to the point!"

Lafleur's eyes are round, and he stares at me in shock. Not everyone can tell a succinct story and get straight to the point, can they? Especially not this prick Lafleur.

"Lemon. If it's gonna be like that, Lafs, you can go fuck yourself."

The old Lafleur would never have dared say that to me. Something seems to have cracked between us.

"It's just that at some point, you have to give me something juicy, little buddy."

"Little buddy?" he says, insulted.

"Sorry Lafleur, I'm getting worked up."

He wriggles in his seat to, I hope sincerely, go on with his story and get to the goddam point before I jump at his throat to end my suffering.

"In a recent TV interview, he looked disturbed as he answered rather trivial questions."

I tap my foot impatiently.

"One reporter who noticed something was off asked him if he was OK. He said he saw a ghost. He didn't want to elaborate on the subject, and all assumed he was joking."

He looks at me with a smile, as if his story were intriguing. I grit my teeth because it isn't, and I widen my eyes to urge him to proceed, and especially to get to the core of the story, once and for all.

"It was two weeks before his presumed death."

There, now it's more interesting. Even if I hope there is something juicier than that coming.

"So, I questioned his immediate colleagues, those who knew him, to find out the name of the ghost he was referring to."

Give credit where credit is due; he worked much harder than I did. Whilst the chronology of events still baffles me, with the probable time of death of the Big O and his wife, Lafleur was going all Columbo on a fast track.

"Did you eventually find something?"

He smiles.

"I got a call one night. The person wouldn't say who he was but told me to check out a prison in Thailand for a guy named Rock Mercier. So, I did. Exactly six months ago, Rock Mercier broke out of that prison with three accomplices. I contacted the prison, posing as an Interpol agent, and to my surprise, they took my word for it. Or simply didn't care."

"Probably the latter," I say with a chuckle.

"I asked for a picture of all the escapees, the four guys. And I figured it out when I saw Rock Mercier. I knew it was him, the ghost Jean Ouellet was talking about."

He pulls a picture down in front of me, like a poker champion after going "all-in," and I almost choke. It's impossible.

"This is Jean Ouellet."

"More like his look-alike."

"No, it's him. It looks exactly like him."

"There's a reason."

"No, not The Young and the Restless?"

"Yeah, The Young and the Restless."

For fuck's sake, did the mayor have a twin? An "evil twin" like in a bad soap opera?

"Jean Ouellet's mother's name is Francine Mercier. His twin brother Rock thus took the maternal surname."

"Why was he in prison in Thailand?"

"Drug smuggling, forgery, threats, mischief and murder."

"Damn."

"He got a hundred and ten-year sentence."

"So, all this time it was Rock Mercier? But why pretend to be the mayor?"

"I learned he suspected his brother of betraying him all along. And Ouellet inherited his father's fortune. The old man was a textile tycoon. Mercier didn't get shit. That's when he allegedly changed his last name, to disassociate himself from his father and Johnny. The Big O found out what his brother was into and confronted him, because if word got out, it could jeopardize his political career."

"But no one even knew he existed."

"Indeed, Johnny Ouellet cut all ties with him. Mercier made his life easier by changing his name, which made it difficult to link the mayor to him. Especially since he was theoretically to die in prison. So, it was easy to pretend he never existed. I suspect Mercier paid Ouellet a visit the day before the press conference, hence the allusion to a ghost. Except that Rock Mercier is also wanted for murder in Quebec. So, by substituting himself for his brother—"

"He became Jean Ouellet," I say, amazed.

"Bingo. And Rock Mercier, although officially out of jail, would have vanished into thin air. What better hiding place than the body of another to avoid suspicion?"

"Indeed," I say, "but if it was the perfect hiding spot, why didn't he stay on as the mayor? Why resign and disappear? And why wouldn't he get rid of the heads?"

"Lemon, boss, you think exactly like me," he says, reverting to a friendly tone which leads me to believe that we're friends again. "I thought the same thing. I guess politics wasn't for him. So, he decided to slip away, thinking that they would find the bodies of his brother and sister-in-law and close the case. Jean Ouellet and Rock Mercier would no longer exist. He could become whoever he wanted. He probably already had a new identity. By putting the heads in a freezer, he probably thought that it would make it harder for the coroner to establish the time of the murder."

"I'm speechless, Lafleur. Great job. Honestly."

He smiles as proudly as humanly possible.

"Grapefruit, thank you, boss. But that's not all."

My God, how exciting this is!

"He was in Thailand for something else, too. More common for the region and one for which they did not charge him because of lack of evidence."

"Go on?"

"Statutory rape. Our friend Mercier is particularly fond of teenage girls."

"A damn pedophile? But how can anyone be so evil?"

"Tangerine, you're missing the point, boss. If he likes young girls, maybe he's behind Lauriane's disappearance?"

Holy shit, that's twisted.

"It would also explain why, as mayor, he was so adamant that we drop the investigation."

Lafleur sits back, folding his arms, proud as a peacock and smiling. I continue: "So, if we find Mercier—"

"We may find Lauriane."

And all the glory that comes with it. Can you imagine? Catching the mayor's killer and Lauriane at the same time. Getting her out of the clutches of a pedophile murderer?

"That's not all," Lafleur says.

"Will you stop being so interesting, for God's sake?"

He giggles like a goat as he expresses his undying love for lemons.

"What can I tell you, boss? I'm full of surprises."

"As long as they're not bad ones," I reply.

His face darkens.

"Don't start with that again."

I signal him to continue with his tale. For the first time, he is saying something interesting. I won't stop him in his tracks.

He clears his throat, smiles, and savours the moment as if he's going to propose to me. Dear God, he wouldn't propose to me, would he? What the fuck?

"Do you know what they called Rock Mercier in prison?"

Thank God. I was really afraid he was going to pull out an engagement ring right in front of my sorry eyes.

"No?"

"Plā pi rạn ỳā"

"In English?"

"The piranha."

"Is this a joke?"

He shakes his head vigorously.

"For fuck's sake. Even for The Young and the Restless, this is a stretch."

"But, lemon, not for us, right, boss?"

"No, not for us, Lafleur. Not for us."

I've seen a lot of dumb asses and cases that made little to no sense. But I must admit, this one is at the top of my list. I suddenly have a strong renewed interest in this whole thing.

Pro bono or not.

FORTY-SEVEN

James Romano paces around his shack. He casts furtive glances at the row of cottages housing the three girls. There are five of these tiny structures, but they still haven't found two other girls to live in them. The boss agreed three would be enough for now. They will find tenants for the other two later. But it will be without him. For the first time, he is in love. In fact, it's not the first time he's been in love, but it's the first time it's reciprocal. He's been waiting for a girl like Lea all his life. How to explain that it happens so late in his existence, and especially with someone so young? He has long since given up on the idea of a genuine love story, but now, God has sent him this goddess when he least expected it. This sublime young woman who loves him for who he is, who doesn't judge him despite his limitations, of which he is fully aware. It has been worth waiting for. He also realizes that Mercier will never allow them to live their passion as they wish, and worse, that he plans to have sex with Lea and the others so that they bear his children. Romano can't stand that. He can't bring himself to accept it. So, there are two solutions. The first is to kill the boss, but the thought of being separated from Lea forever by a prison sentence terrifies him. The other option is to run away with her. Out of here, he can better protect and care for her. Look forward and enjoy their life together. Lea has made it clear, though; she will only leave with the other two. He has no particular affection for Lauriane and Rashida. They can serve to give birth to the boss's offspring. He doesn't care about them. But Lea is inflexible on this; leaving her two friends behind is out of the question. Since he loves her more than anything in the world, he has agreed. It is a small price to pay to spend his life with her.

It will happen tonight. As usual, he'll do his last daily tour to make sure the girls have everything they need, but instead of going back to his cabin, he'll unchain them and walk them around the back of the buildings to bypass the ranch along the mountain, and then walk straight to the nearest road. He doesn't know many things in life, but his sense of direction is unfailing. He walks up to the boss's house as he always does. Mercier is listening to the news on the television, sitting on the sofa. The man looks at Romano curtly, as he always does. Despite all Romano's attempts to build a cordial relationship with him, it's no use. Rock Mercier is cold as a lizard with ominous eyes filled with all the nastiness in the world. But he pays well, and Romano has never had so much money in his life. That's legitimate, considering the boss's profession before he left. He treats James like an employee and leaves no room for a friendlier relationship. He has refused to give him access to normal television channels, limiting him, like the girls, to video-on-demand stations. Romano feels that his stay on the ranch is ending, anyway. He was supposed to stay there to help with the daily chores, shopping, and the girls, but the boss hinted that his contract might end sooner than expected, but he doesn't know why or especially when.

Romano couldn't have known that the boss had long since noticed his fondness for Lea. He would come back from his end-of-day tours with a smile on his face, thrilled like a teenager in love with his summer camp instructor. This exasperates Rock Mercier to no end, especially since it will become a problem when he sleeps with the girl, willingly or not. How will this big dummy react? Rock Mercier doesn't intend to find out. The question is whether he'll let the idiot go at the risk that he may rat him out to the law-enforcement authorities about what's going on here, or whether he'll just dispose of him. Either way, Romano has no one waiting for him in the outside world. No one will care what happens to him. That's why Rock Mercier chose him in the first place.

"What the hell are you doing?" Rock Mercier asks when he sees Romano standing there, waiting.

"I'll do my tour and go to bed."

Romano is about to leave when Mercier calls out to him.

"Wait a minute, you look weird. What's going on?"

Romano feels his legs getting weak. Is it that obvious? The boss suspects something, for sure.

"N—nothing, why?"

Mercier plants his stony gaze on Romano's and watches him in silence, as if he could read his soul.

"I don't know," he says. "You're not your usual self."

Romano bursts out laughing much harder than he would have liked.

"Come on, boss. I do my tour every night, don't I?"

"I know you do. But there's something weird about you."

Romano shrugs, expecting the boss to say something else, but he just stares at him with his cold, intense stare. Romano turns away after a few seconds, moving towards the exit with a muffled step as if he doesn't want to be noticed, waiting any moment for Mercier to say something else, but he exits without another word being spoken. Romano sighs and heads toward the cabins. He moves with a quick, nervous stride. He tries to walk as normally as possible, even though he has the grace of a newly born deer. He turns towards the boss's house, but no sign of him. This is reassuring. He goes first into Lea's house.

"Good evening, sweetheart. Ready?"

Lea smiles brightly. How beautiful she is! He feels his heart is melting every time she smiles. He approaches her leg and disengages the latch around her ankle. She smells like lavender. He wants to take her in his arms and kiss her, but they'll have time for that later. They must concentrate on the task at hand. Especially since Lea told him she didn't want them to kiss under these circumstances. She wants their first kiss to be perfect when they will be free.

"Let's get the others," she says.

"Wait for me," Romano replies, stopping her and heading for the door. He looks once again at the boss's house. He's not at the window. "OK, go out quickly and walk behind the house. Wait for me there, I'll free the others."

Lea grabs what few belongings she has and puts on her running shoes, then goes out and around the corner of the cottage to disappear into the darkness. There is light only in front of the door of each house. Romano enters Lauriane's room first, then Rashida's. He gives them the same directions as Lea, and they join her behind the cabins. All three hug each other, incredulous that their nightmare is about to end. Romano spies the boss's house one last time, then signals the girls to follow him. They walk into the twilight, doing everything in their power to avoid the glare of the lights and the full moon. The group moves slowly, avoiding making too much noise as they crush the gravel with their soles. The girls are quiet, but restless. Even Rashida seems to have recovered her energy, reassuring Lauriane. The night is cool and sweet at the same time. Lea is thankful that it is not raining heavily but that the weather is on their side. She watches Blondi walk ahead, hoping he knows what he is doing. They put their fate in his huge hands, despite his limited intellect. He is their only hope, so they don't really have the luxury to be picky. Lea will later clarify that she is not in love with him. Either way, he will face justice for what he did to them and will surely do time. Still, the help he's giving them could weigh heavily in his favour in court. She must always remember that he is partly responsible for their misery. She still feels bad about eventually breaking his heart, for abusing his gullibility, but she has no choice. She wavers between guilt and resentment, even though he is under the influence of the other basket case. She can't help but find him vulnerable and helpless, like a little kitten in the body of a Siberian tiger.

They climb a mound that leads to a dark, opaque forest. The houses get further away from them as they move forward. Romano's heart is pounding with each step, bringing them closer to freedom, to his life with Lea. He glances steadily behind to make sure the boss did not follow them. His suspicions leave him perplexed. What if Mercier has figured out what he is up to? Romano would have liked to instruct him to find other teenage girls, that nothing is stopping him from whatever he wants to do, but he should let him live his passion with Lea. Too bad he's had to drag the other two along with them. He would have liked to do it differently. He watches the full moon and pursues his breakthrough, followed by the three girls who still haven't said a word. Surely, they're as terrified as he is. They can hardly see two meters in front of them. The moonlight helps a little, but he should have brought a flashlight. He looks behind and smiles at Lea as he keeps going. He doesn't notice the shape in the shadow coming fast on his left. He feels a powerful push knocking him to his side as the girls scream in fear.

"Where are you going, you traitor?" Rock Mercier says loudly.

Staring at him with a furious gaze, he watches Romano, still lying on the ground. The latter feels like fainting, as he is terrified. He can't believe Mercier tracked them down so easily.

"N—nowhere."

Romano knows his explanation doesn't make sense, but he's not bright enough to come up with something clever. Mercier is holding the girls at gunpoint.

"Shut up," Mercier says to them, his voice trembling with rage. He turns the gun on his assistant.

"I asked you a question, you big moron. Where are you going?"

Without a word, James Romano quietly gets up.

"Did you really think you could fool me?" Mercier says. "Don't you know you're too dumb? That you could deceive no one, especially not someone such as myself? Get down on your knees."

"S—sorry?"

"I said on your knees."

"Don't do that," Lea says.

The boss points his gun at her.

"Back off and shut the fuck up. I won't even think twice about shooting you between the eyes. Do you understand?"

Lea steps back.

"Let him go," she says. "We will go back to the ranch. Don't hurt him. It's our fault."

"Oh, I know that, my dear. You've got him fooled, poor thing. You made him believe you were in love with him, but it was all a charade, wasn't it? Come on, you can tell him, he knows."

Lea looks at Blondi, who looks at her quizzically, as if he expects her to deny what Mercier just said, to assure her she truly loves him, that it is all nonsense, but she remains silent. She cannot lie at such a crucial moment.

"Lea," Romano whispers, "why don't you say anything?"

She stares at the ground, still not answering.

"Lea?"

"I'm sorry, Blondi."

Romano bows his head, finally realizing that everything he thought all along was a smoke screen, a masquerade, to get them out of there. That he put his life on the line for a girl who lied to him all this time. She looked so sincere, sobbing and smiling. He doesn't understand anymore. The pain he feels in his soul is more intense than his fear of Mercier. He has reverted to being James Romano, the one nobody loves, the one who is not entitled to anything. His eyes fill with tears.

"Shit, you won't bawl on top of that?" Mercier says with a disgusted look.

"Leave him alone, you scumbag," Lea says, sobbing.

She is sorry to see Blondi so helpless in his imposing frame. It breaks her heart that he has to find out like this. She would have liked to tell him more gently. Yet she should be angry with him, but all she feels is pity mixed with guilt.

"Run, Blondi," Lauriane shouts.

"Yes, run, Blondi," Lea adds.

But Romano doesn't budge. He stares at the ground, defeated. What's the point? Lea was his last hope for love, and she betrayed him like everyone else in his life before. Everyone abused his kindness and naivety. Like the boss, that dirty bastard responsible for his troubles. Suddenly, he's not afraid anymore. The rage that burns in his veins gives him a good dose of courage. He gets closer to Mercier.

"What are you doing?" Mercier says.

"Enough now," Romano replies.

"But... what—"

Romano lunges at Mercier and a deafening noise startles the girls as Romano tackles Mercier to the ground. He overpowers him, but instead of working to subdue and disarm him, he doesn't move.

"Blondi?" Lea says in a crying voice.

Romano is still inert. Rock Mercier pushes him away on his side after a few seconds and Blondi collapses on his back. His eyes are half-opened and stare at the full moon, impassive. Mercier gets up.

"Romano, you idiot," Mercier says in a low voice.

Lea screams as she sees Blondi's pale sweater darken as blood soaks into the fibers of the fabric. Mercier aims his gun at the girls.

"Let's go, you little bitches."

"You won't just leave him there?" Lea asks.

"I'll take care of him later. Go back to your houses and I swear that if one of you little dummies tries anything, you'll suffer the same fate as this asshole."

Lauriane must resolve to forget about her Plan B. She won't manage to escape into the full moon as she hoped. She couldn't take advantage of the confusion to run away. He didn't mind killing Blondi, he surely won't hesitate to shoot her in the back. They return from where they came from, and after a few meters, Lea turns towards Blondi, her eyes still wet. She observes his imposing inert frame lying on the leaves and the mud. She would so much like to see him get up and flee, but she knows he is dead from a bullet to the heart. The heart she broke a few seconds before. She's only happy about one thing, and that's that she apologized. She knows it's all over now. Their only hope is dead because of her. She sees Rashida and Lauriane moving forward like automatons, and she feels as responsible for their misfortune as for Blondi's. Hot tears roll down her cheeks as she walks back to hell.

FORTY-EIGHT

Philippe digs up everything he can find on Johnny Ouellet and his wife from public records. Since the mayor's brother vanished, he may have stolen his brother's real estate. They need to check whether any of the mayor's assets were for sale recently, whether someone used his bank accounts since the alleged date of his death, etc. The twin's thing is so far-fetched that they haven't bothered to tell anyone about it. A prankster who made up the twin thing could have duped Lafleur. On the other hand, Rock Mercier's prison break in Thailand is confirmed. But is he really Jean Ouellet's brother, or just someone who looks like him? After all, they say everyone has their perfect doppelgänger somewhere in the world. Phil wonders where his personal look-alike lives. Lafleur's story is plausible, if incredibly twisted. There are indeed transactions in Ouellet's bank accounts after his death, and there are several businesses in the name of JO Investments, his personal company which managed his holdings throughout his reign. He was careful not to own any buildings or land in the city he managed.

Phil feels they should start there; visit all of Ouellet's buildings and land, and see where it takes them. He has already confirmed that the shack where they found the severed heads does not belong to the company. It was a monthly lease in the name of James Romano, paid in cash six months in advance. Phil goes back to Chez Lise's room house to talk to the manager, but no one has seen Romano in weeks. Upon visiting Romano's room, which still smells like shit, they realize there has been no recent activity. Everything is still in the same place, except for dust gathering. Phil suggests they report Romano as a missing person to law enforcement, but the manager says that isn't his job. He isn't liable for the fate of his clients, and Romano is free to do whatever he wants. He is a grown man, after all.

"Was he paying his rent by the month?" Phil asks.

"Yes, that's usually how it works."

"But since he's been gone for weeks, how could he have paid his last month's rent?"

Robert Roy admits he doesn't know. Upon Phil's request, they check with the accounts receivable clerk, who states that the room is paid for the next ten months. Phil asks if this large payment was recently made.

"It was," the ginger-haired woman corroborates. "He paid for twelve months a few weeks ago."

"A little less than two months ago?"

"That's right."

"It must be rare for a resident to pay upfront for the year, right?"

"Yes and no," the accountant says, "some have relatives who settle the bill annually for their brother or uncle. But that's not the norm."

"And as for Romano, he used to pay by the month until that instalment two months ago, right?"

The little woman looks at her records. That is indeed the case.

"So, something has changed recently for him," Phil says to himself.

"It's getting interesting," the manager says, hanging on his every word.

"And no one has seen him for weeks," Philip went on. "Whereas those I spoke to this morning said he was always around, rarely went out. That's a lot of new information, don't you think?"

The woman nods, gazing at Phil as if she wants to rip his clothes off and do him, right here on the sparse office carpet. Phil thanks them and sneaks out before being forcibly grabbed by the middle-aged woman. The only assumption he can make is that Romano is acting as a front man. He can't afford to pay his rent in cash for the house where the mayor and his wife's heads were discovered. Nor can he pay for his own room for the next twelve months. There is no way he can afford both.

Back at the office, Lafs listens carefully for a rare occasion, and they agree to get Lafleur involved in a tour of JO Investments' properties. Phil talks with the company's employees but has learned nothing new. They are appalled at what happened to the mayor and his wife but know nothing useful. Lafleur will tour the two large uninhabited lots about an hour outside of town. Phil will target the residential buildings owned by Ouellet, and Lafs the commercial buildings. They will then reconvene at the office the next day for debriefing, hoping to gather information leading them to Rock Mercier, or James Romano. Or anyone else who might have a stake in the mayor and his wife leaving this world dead.

FORTY-NINE

Rock Mercier has no other option than to lock the three girls in their houses. He thought he was doing the right thing by letting them socialize on the veranda, but they took advantage of the situation to hatch their plan with James Romano and jeopardize everything he built. Once the adrenaline wears off, however, he realizes that Romano's death was inevitable. The more he thinks about it, the more he can't see how it could have been otherwise. If Romano was corrupted so easily by a young scatterbrain like Lea Briand, then the police would have had no trouble getting him to disclose information after a few seconds of tough questioning. He said he was in love. What an idiot. Mercier knew Romano was dumb, but not to this extent. In what world could he ever conceive that a 16-year-old girl would be infatuated with a pudgy, mid-forties-looking nincompoop? Mercier doesn't care if the girls like him. If they do, that's a bonus. He'll do what he needs to do, anyway. He wants them to do what he planned all this time in the slammer, hoping he'd get the chance to carry it out one day. So, when the opportunity arose to make a run for it, he didn't think twice. He befriended some highly intelligent Kazakh prisoners who were in jail for fraud. The guys had offshore bank accounts and the smarts to escape. But they needed a henchman, someone brave and skilled with weapons and tools. When Mercier exposed the huge security holes in the

Thai prison, the Kazakhs exploited it. They perverted guards by promising them money. Mercier does not know if they eventually paid them. He begged them to let him in on their plan, and that once he was out, he would go his own way. No money or anything else. He would vanish forever.

Once outside, he did some unnoticed petty theft on citizens, and he collected enough money to bribe a cargo captain to shelter him in a storage room while they crossed to Chile. There, he smuggled his way back to Canada. He'd tampered with the documents of an American tourist he killed in Thailand a few weeks earlier. The end justified the means, as with the three girls, and as with Romano. He walks with a swagger towards the cottages after strapping his gun holster prominently to his waist, like a cowboy seeking to scare off his rival. He gathers the girls on the long veranda in front and explains how things will be from now on. He is in his late fifties and lacks the time for what he wants to accomplish, so the girls will be put to good use as a group. As a survivalist, he knows the self-reliance basics and how to live on virtually nothing. He wants to raise his children free of society's contamination. He has read extensively about births so that he can deliver the newborns safely. Soon, there will be five teenagers, and at this rate, they will bring as many children as possible into the world every year, for a total of fifteen kids in three or four years. That will be plenty. He will tutor them personally on the ranch, so they will develop into powerful citizens of the world and bring balance back to this broken society. They will be entrepreneurs, politicians and lobbyists. They will share his life philosophy, and together they will reshape society. Mercier may not be around to see the shift take place, but at least he will have put together an army of unstoppable powerful soldiers dedicated to the cause. He will then kill all the girls. But he will never tell them that. He needs them to behave and trust that if they do what he wants, they'll have a chance to make it out alive.

They watch him with such animosity that it's laughable. These silly little girls actually think that he has a soul? That he cares about their feelings? He can't wait to see their faces turn from hatred to horror as he goes through what he has planned for them. Not only will he force his spawn on them against their will, but they will be his slaves. They will work on the land, growing fruits and vegetables, harvesting eggs from the coop, cooking livestock that he has slaughtered, etc. They already have cows, rabbits and pigs. They have everything they need to sustain themselves and live for a long time with limited external support. With the internet today, one can get groceries delivered online. He has rented a house near to the ranch to secure the items purchased online, instructing the couriers to drop the supplies and victuals in the backyard. He'll pick it up himself, incognito. His plan is perfect. But it is imperative to restrict his movements, hence the need to maximize self-sufficiency. Every time he orders stuff online and wanders away from the ranch, it's just one more chance to get caught. He smiles as he finally sees fear on the three girls' faces. They are incredibly pretty and sexy, but also unbelievably gullible. Two of them are crying, begging him to let them go, promising not to tell anyone, not to go to the police. He closes his eyes to enjoy his victory. Desperate girls put him in such an exhilaration that he feels extremely powerful. The only one not to speak, Rashida Lafleur, stares straight ahead, totally oblivious. He's noticed she's been like this for weeks. He doesn't care. If she doesn't step up and doesn't fear him anymore, he'll use her as an example and shoot her dead in front of the others, to further cement his dominance. And then he'll just need to kidnap three more teenage girls instead of two. Easy peasy.

He says that if they don't figure out what he is trying to do now, they will come to agree with him that this broken society needs a serious overhaul. They will realize that they are part of something great, that they will be talked about as Linda Kasabian, Leslie Van Houten and Susan Atkins of the Manson Family are still talked about today. They will be remembered and become stars. Together, they will change the world. As he takes each girl back to her respective house, he slaps Lauriane Derome hard for calling him a creep.

"Don't ever insult me again, you dirty whore. Next time, I'll have you join Romano."

Lauriane holds her cheek while looking at him in fury. She is proud that she challenged him, even with that slap stinging her face. She is serious when she says that she would rather die than indulge his fantasies.

FIFTY

I finish my circuit of the commercial buildings owned by Jean Ouellet, finding nothing of substance. The tenants do not know that their landlord was the former Montreal mayor. They never met him. I spend a little time teasing a cute girl at a construction company's reception desk, but she is aloof, and quickly instructs me to get lost, especially once her boyfriend, the president of the company, comes to inquire about the situation. Since his shoulders are as big as my head, I leave without question. I come back to the office, only to find Nicole in a frenzy, eager to tell me what her Oreo-cookie-loving husband did wrong. Nicole has the unfortunate trait of expecting that I am some psychologist paid to let her bust my balls with her bullshit stories. Someone will have to pay me at some point in this goddamn story. Pro bono and passive listening to co-workers is all well and good, but I'm not a charity worker, for Christ's sake. I nod at every intonation, as if I'm listening. I add a "well, I'll be damned" or two, and a heartfelt "indeed," so she can wrap her story up, and I can go fuck myself elsewhere. Although I'm sure Nicole would like to do it for me, naughty woman. I've always thought her complaints about her husband are just a pretext for trying to screw the boss. But no way, I'm not so desperate.

"Where the hell is Phil?" I say, interrupting her rudely.

Phil is her second favourite topic of discussion. These two are like the fingers of one hand. A hand that a trash compactor has crushed, but a hand, nonetheless.

"He should be back any minute now."

"No shit," I say, to emphasize the obviousness of her answer. Of course, he'll be back eventually, you silly woman. But what else?

"He just grabbed a cup of coffee."

"See? Not that complicated."

"I beg your pardon?"

"Have you seen Lafleur? He was supposed to meet us here this morning."

"No, I didn't."

"Lemon," I said, with a playful flash in my eyes.

"What's that?"

I sigh. She never gets my jokes. I shoo her away with a wave of my hand and go back to my office.

Later, when fucking Phil comes back, I urge him to sit down, which he does, still sweating and breathing as if he had just fled a herd of hungry hyenas. Surely, there would be enough meat to feed a family of twelve with Phil's carcass.

"Why are you smiling?" he says.

"I was thinking of a herd of hyenas."

"What?"

"Never mind. What do you have for me?"

He informs me he talked to the Big O apartment building's tenants and got the same answer I did. The occupants didn't know the mayor owned their building. Phil looked at the company's records, and as expected, Ouellet and his wife were the only shareholders.

"What about his bank accounts?"

"Empty."

I look at him, not sure I appreciated the magnitude of what he just told me with the casualness of a guy reflecting on the weather.

"What do you mean by empty?"

"The accounts are empty, money withdrawn with certified checks."

"Who made these transactions?"

"According to them, the mayor did."

"And according to you?"

"Probably his evil twin."

Nicole intervenes, still sitting at her desk.

"Are you talking about Bryce's twin from The Young and the Restless?"

Phil is about to say no, but I shush him with my hand.

"Yes Nicole," I say, yelling across the room, "we're talking about Bryce's damn brother from The Young and the Restless. We have nothing better to do. It's not like we are looking for a missing girl or something."

Of course, she does not catch the sarcasm in my retort. Her face hardens.

"That son of a bitch. After all Bryce has done for him," she says, mumbling.

Disappointed that she didn't get my joke, I turn back to Phil, who probably got it, but doesn't give a shit. I'm surrounded by people with no sense of humour. It's depressing.

"What the hell is the citrus lover doing?"

Phil shrugs. He hasn't heard from him. Nicole laughs several seconds later.

"Are you talking about Marcel Lafleur?" she asks with all the insight of a wildebeest quenching its thirst in a crocodile-infested river.

"You're quick, Nicole," I say, winking at Phil, who smiles tightly. Nicole's irritating voice comes from afar.

"Hey, Martin. Lemon."

She giggles like a horny mare, and I rub my eyes, annoyed that she has just made the exact same joke I did a few minutes earlier, and she didn't get it. If she didn't exist, I would have to invent her. Or not. I call Lafleur on his cell phone, since we're waiting for him, and above all, I don't have all day. I get his voice mail, but it's full.

"Strange. Lafleur normally rushes to take his messages, right?"

"Yes, he is afraid of missing a job," Philippe says. "He doesn't stand for the little red light blinking on his phone."

I sink into my chair, surprised to be worried about him.

"Do you have the addresses of the land he was supposed to check out?"

"Of course, I do."

I'm thinking out loud that maybe we should see what it's all about.

"Do you want me to call Claudine?"

I take a few seconds to figure out who Nicole is referring to. Lafleur's office receptionist, and her likely replacement if I ever partner up with him.

I chuckle.

"Yes, good idea. Call her," I say, a tad in awe that Nicole took an initiative that isn't completely lame.

Claudine hasn't seen Lafleur either since the previous day. She, too, has tried to reach him unsuccessfully. I sigh as I look at Phil, who knows what we need to do. He gets up to fetch the land addresses from his folder. I put on my jacket and wait for him next to Nicole's desk. I stare at her with an inquisitive look.

"Hey Nicole."

She has a slight smile.

"Lime."

I laugh like a bovine, but her face shows she doesn't get the point once again.

Holy shit, she can be such an idiot sometimes. And God knows it happens more often than not.

FIFTY-ONE

Phil is pissed because I stopped to buy peanut butter on toast from a local restaurant. What can I tell you? I'm hungry. Why the hell does he care? He's driving.

"It reeks everywhere in the car," he says, teeth clenched. "I hate that smell."

"Well buddy, I couldn't care less," I say with my mouth full of this delicious nectar.

We arrive in front of a railing blocking the way, with a sign instructing us to leave or else we expose ourselves to a shower of bullets with no further notice. As Phil and I have seen it all before, it will take more to impress us.

"Mha fawar eets," I said, my mouth still full of peanut butter.

"Could you please finish your bite before you speak? You look like you're eating for the first time in your life."

Phil is really getting on my nerves. Enough with the adolescent tantrum. "I said we have to walk," I say, even though it's obvious.

"You're a genius, Lafs."

"Yeah, fuck off, man."

Right after that, hot, melted peanut butter drips through my fingers and onto my jeans.

"What did you say?" Phil says, smiling for the first time in ages.

"Damn it."

I lick my fingers, trying to limit the damage, but I feel like a circus tightrope walker about to lose my footing. Phil opens his door.

"Where are you going?" I ask, realizing the question is rhetorical.

"To Cuba, I'll be back," he says with all the sarcasm he can muster.

I giggle and show him my middle finger.

"I'll meet you at the other side of the—"

He slams the door without letting me finish my sentence. I swear to God, one day, that little bastard… I look for paper towels or tissues in the glove compartment, anything to get that brownish, milky stuff off my hands, but I can't find any. Phil's car has a huge amount of junk in it, but nothing useful. I'll settle for licking my fingers, even if it gives a half-assed result. I grab my gun and sigh with rage at the sight of peanut butter on the butt of my gun. That fat bastard was right. The peanut butter toast was a shitty idea.

I get out of the car and wince as I stretch out my legs. Getting old is a real bummer. I look forward, but don't see that jerk Phil. I whisper loudly,

"Phil?"

No answer other than the wind in the leaves. I grumble as I close the car door and walk furiously toward the field. I told him to wait for me, didn't I?

———

Farther on, Phil walks through the long grass, following the path traced by the gravel. He takes to the meadows so as not to attract attention. Then, in the distance, some shady shapes emerge. They look like houses stuck together, or a farm with several enclosures. He wonders what the mayor intended to do on this land. Was it his retirement project? After all, many people return to nature in the autumn of their lives. He wonders if it will be the same for him. He doubts it, as he's more of a city boy than a country boy. Not to mention that Melanie also favours the city, although she certainly enjoys the outdoors.

On the face of it, the place seems deserted. There is no one within sight. No animals, no humans. He stays on his guard, though. You never know. He does not think that Lafleur is there. They will certainly have more luck at the other address. But since his rigour dictates that he must make sure the buildings are indeed vacant, he moves on to two medium-sized houses on his left. In the distance, a series of shacks reminds him of a vacation spot in Gaspésie, where he used to go with his parents when he was a child. It remains one of his youth's fondest memories, although he never went back to the beautiful region. He would like to look at the sea on that side of the Atlantic one more time, and dream about how far the body of water could take him if he were a sailor.

He strolls to the first house on his left and knocks gently on the door. No answer. He knocks two more times with more authority, but still nothing. He bends down to look through the window but sees no one there although there are belongings strewn about the furniture, as if someone is living there. He knocks on the pane carefully, hoping without really believing that a distinct sound will draw the occupant's attention. No luck, nothing. He surveys the surroundings, and especially the small houses further away. They are small and beige.

They are quite recent constructions, but Phil keeps wondering what the mayor expects to do with them. The land is in the middle of nowhere. He can't see why tourists would rent these shacks. There's no river nearby, so it's not a good place for future vacationers. All this is very curious. The cottages also seem uninhabited. The curtains are drawn, and there is total silence. It's like a ghost town in an old western movie. Phil goes to the second house, which is bigger than the first, and knocks on the door. Strangely, it gives way after two knocks and opens softly. He peeked through the small doorway and sees a dining table with four chairs and a picture of Lenin on the wall. He didn't know the mayor very well, but he would never have thought him a Marxist-Leninist.

"Hello?" Phil calls out, blankly.

He pushes on the door and moves gently into the room. In front of him, an open door leads to an adjacent room, probably a bedroom. He looks to his right where a kitchen and a dining room are, then to the left where there is a sofa facing a turned-off television. He proceeds cautiously toward the bedroom and then —damn it.

"Lafleur?"

Philippe doesn't have enough time to hear his gagged-up colleague's answer. He falls to his knees after an enormous blow to the back of his head. Then, the room waltzes around, and he sees nothing but darkness.

FIFTY-TWO

Rock Mercier realizes now that his plan won't work. He has learned from the news that the police found the heads of his brother and sister-in-law, and a few days later, two strangers have showed up at his house, and a third one is wandering around the property. He saw him on his surveillance cameras, but he's too far off for Mercier to see who it is. Mercier will have to leave quickly, but first he has to clean up after himself. Leave no embarrassing witnesses behind. He will go back to the drawing board and plan his next move more carefully. He doesn't recognize the two idiots he knocked out, tied to a chair and gagged, nor does he know how they tracked him down. He doubts they are cops, so it can only be a coincidence. Probably a couple of overly nosy weirdos who will pay with their lives for their curiosity. Everything started so well, though. He was nervous on his first day at City Hall, taking over from his asshole brother. He thought it was too much and feared he'd be exposed if anyone were to notice the small mole next to his eye, the only differentiating feature between him and his twin. His voice was also raspier, and his personality was the polar opposite of Johnny's. But nobody took notice. He was called Johnny from the start, given top secret files, and he did a much better job than he expected. Some people thought he was rougher than before, but no one thought he wasn't the same person. It wasn't enough to raise serious suspicions.

He knew his brother had cut him out of his life when he was in a Thailand jail for the rest of his life. He unwittingly helped Johnny by changing his last name. The connections were more difficult to make, despite their near perfect resemblance. It wasn't the first time his brother failed him. Johnny was their father's favourite, even though they were born within minutes of each other. Their father saw Johnny as the elder and treated him as such. Despite their indistinguishable physiology, their personalities could not have been more opposite. Johnny was the scholar, the schemer, and the coward. He was crappy at physical and manual activities. Rock is just as intellectually gifted, but he is courageous, persistent, cunning and excels in sports. He is also very good at manual labour. When their father died of a heart attack, Johnny was the more afflicted of the two. Their mother didn't really love her husband anymore, staying by his side only because it was the right thing to do for people of their generation. Rock didn't have a good relationship with the old man either, always up to his mommy's neck. But his passing devastated Johnny, the darling. He wept for days, not figuring out why his brother was insensitive to the patriarch's demise. It all shattered when a notary disclosed details of their father's will. Johnny got everything, with Rock only getting a few scraps. As for their mother, she could keep the house until she died, and she got a certain amount of money, just enough to support her. Rock realized that day that he never meant shit to his father although he'd made efforts to grow closer to him.

He expected his brother to rectify the damage done by his father and give him a portion of the family fortune, if only out of good faith. But Johnny didn't want to hear about it, only mentioning that he honoured the deceased's wishes, that he couldn't do otherwise in good conscience. Rock punched him in the face and left the family home. He can still see his brother lying on the floor in tears, stating he never wanted to see him again.

That he would sue him for battery if he came back! Rock left and never looked back. His lack of financial means caused him to get involved with the wrong people and fall into crime. Meanwhile, Johnny was using the family fortune to invest in real estate and the stock market. He cowardly bought his way into the mayor's office, using every resource at his disposal to lure voters into electing him. Rock knew his brother stashed a lot of money in offshore accounts. He expected a scandal to erupt one day and expose him as a thief. But no, everyone admired him, they worshipped him, and no one saw his ugly side. Then Johnny married this woman Pauline, heir of the inventor of a supposedly healing necklace that took the world by storm. This was too much for Rock, and he vowed to get his hands on what was rightfully his. He had to right the wrongs of his dimwitted father. Except he was caught red-handed acting as a middleman in a mega drug deal. He even got a life sentence for child sex trafficking. This was a lie. He was never involved in that. Sure, he was a customer. He spent sleepless nights with underage girls, but he never made money off of them.

Sentenced to over a hundred years in prison, his only salvation was to figure out a way out. He thought about what he would do if given another chance. However, if he broke out, he would be hunted all over the world. He couldn't live with a sword of Damocles hanging over his head for long. All these years, he'd plotted to steal everything Johnny owned. Just like that. People would think Rock Mercier vanished, and no one would ever hear from him again. He would become Jean Ouellet, and would get all his money, all his accounts, his papers, his passport. He would get back what they took from him. His wealth and his freedom, of course, but above all his dignity. For once, it was practical to look like this bastard. He might as well make the most of it. They looked so much alike that even their own parents sometimes confused them. The only time his father gave him any affection was when he thought he was Johnny. It happened rarely, but it happened. And when his father realized he was actually Rock, his face would harden to the point where it broke Rock's heart. Because of his prison sentence, he couldn't even attend his mother's funeral, and she was the only person on earth who truly loved him. He had nothing left to lose, so he focused all his energy on getting back as much as he could. He remembers his brother's bleak look when he saw him after all these years.

"You thought you got rid of me, didn't you, Johnny?" he said before beating him so badly that he knocked him unconscious.

Johnny was equipped for political battles, but inadequate for back-alley brawls. Rock subdued him with consummate ease. He had no intention of living with his brother's tart, so he kidnapped her too, injecting her with a powerful sedative while she was sleeping. He locked them up in the house's basement he was renting, a former Chinese-owned clandestine cannabis greenhouse. Then, after gathering all the information he needed about his brother's bank accounts, properties and offshore accounts, he simply shot them. His intention was to take his brother's place as mayor while he set up his pawns. Then, he'd announce his retirement from politics to set his other plan in motion, namely, to replenish the earth with super-powerful offspring. He would do this with the help of young girls who would be his sex slaves for the rest of their lives. He carefully chopped up his brother's and his wife's carcasses and disposed of their body parts in separate and distant locations, so as not to cause alarm with the discovery of an easily identifiable corpse. No one would ever link it back to him. He was supposed to return once the ranch was settled to take the two skulls out of the freezer and close the book, but he didn't have time. Someone slipped into the house that no one knew about except for Romano and the moron doing their shopping. Surely it wasn't them who called the police, the same police who made no effort to track down the teenage girls. He'd clarified that this wasn't a priority. They barely had the manpower to investigate murders in the territory. They had little time and fewer resources to put into finding girls who probably ran away, anyway. So why the sudden twist of fate? Surely it wasn't that bastard Martin Lafs who tracked him down. Mercier had convinced Lauriane

Derome's mother not to trust this loser, so it certainly wasn't him. From his three small black and white surveillance televisions, he scouts the movements of the other individual on his property, quietly approaching his residence. He can't quite see who it is, but he suspects he'll go the same way as the two other jerks. One more or one less to dispose of isn't a big deal.

Philippe Lavoie realizes what is going on as he regains consciousness. He notices the carbon copy of Mayor Jean Ouellet standing in front of them with a demonic smile on his face. Of course, it is his brother Rock, the fugitive. Phil's head hurts like hell, but he still runs through the options, and there aren't many of them. It's not the first time he's been in a precarious situation. Rock Mercier, in a sinister Rambo-like disguise, watches Lafleur and him now and then. He has painted his face in camouflage, and wears a red bandana around his head. This man has a crazy look in his eyes that doesn't sit well with Phil, especially since Lafs is their last hope of making it out. It's enough to make Phil tear up. He can't believe that this dummy has their lives in his peanut butter-stained hands. He hopes with all his heart that Lafs wouldn't get caught like them. Lafleur is in a terrible shape. He has been badly beaten, and only has one eye fully open. His face is swollen, like someone who boxed twelve rounds with an opponent far too strong for them. Phil wonders if that's what's in store for him, too. Mercier looks very nervous, glancing furtively at something on the other side of the room. Then he shuts the door and quickly heads to the other end of the house. It could only be Lafs following the same path as Phil did earlier.

Lafs usually carries a gun, so Phil prays he had the presence of mind to grab his revolver although it won't do him any good if he gets knocked out from behind as well. He feels tears of despair filling his eyes as he reflects on Melanie. They parted this morning with a quick, casual kiss and wished each other a good day. Had he realized it was his last day on this planet, he would have at least hugged her for a long time, expressed all his love, and made her swear she would never forget him.

The problem with death is that you rarely know when it's coming.

He recalls the first time he met Melanie, how beautiful she was with her long brown hair and her mischievous look. He fell in love at first sight, but never thought for a second that he stood a chance with her. She was completely out of his league. But for some reason, the feeling was mutual. On each of their early dates, he expected she would suddenly realize who she was dealing with. That she would see that she could do much better, and she would drop him like a hot potato. But every time a date ended, when he drove her back to her apartment thinking it would be the last time he would see her, she would still call him back, cheerful as if she didn't realize who he was.

He knew what her family and friends thought when they saw a girl like her with a big loser like him. Phil couldn't blame them since he was exactly of the same opinion as them. Even so, Melanie stayed. He doesn't have a lot of money; he doesn't have any particular talent besides putting up with Martin Lafs and being good at sifting through evidence, but otherwise he has nothing. So, if she's still with him after all these years, then she really loves him for who he is.

Against all odds.

He shakes his head. This can't end so foolishly. Lafs must fight that poor man's Rambo, and free them. Be a hero for once in his fucking life and save the day. He hears Mercier mumbling something. Then someone knocks on the door before opening it.

"Hello?"

It's Lafs voice. He's gone the same way Phil did.

Phil closes his eyes and prays for a different outcome.

FIFTY-THREE

There's a song that goes "I've got a feeling". Right now, I do not have a very good feeling. The closer I get to the first house, the more pressure I feel, like Big Antonio is standing on my shoulders. For those of you who didn't know Big Antonio, he was big, and his name was Antonio. I don't know what else to tell you. An annoying cross wind throws dirt in my eyes to where I feel like I'm in a bad western on this damn shabby ranch, even though there are some fairly recent shacks. There seems to be no living soul here, yet I have the awkward feeling that someone is looking at me. I look towards the top of a big wooden electric pole and notice that there is a surveillance camera. I look around and spot a few others strategically set up to cover most of the area. If there's no one on site, someone at least wants to know what's going on. Shit, what I'd give to hear that bastard Lafleur screaming a citrus name right now! And where the hell is Phil, for heaven's sake? My intuition leads me to start with the biggest house on my left. If there is someone in charge of this damned place, he or she lives there. The others are much smaller. Or should I start with the beige houses further on?

What the hell, let's go with instinct. The old bugger hasn't let me down very often. I approach the door, which is half open. It's darker than in a bear's ass, or it's the external/internal light contrast that isn't letting my pupils adapt. In any case, I can't see shit.

"Hello?" I say with no real expectation of a reply.

Indeed, nobody answers. I move a little closer. I take another look as shapes start to reveal themselves. I push on the door, which creaks like my grandfather's knees when he stood up from the dinner table.

"Hello?" I say again.

Yes, I know, I'm not original. But since this is not a stylistic experiment, you'll have to make do with it. I see an aquarium on my right, with a multitude of small, nervous fish swimming around. Piranhas. If it's Mercier, this guy has a sick obsession with these ugly little fish. A wallet lies on the floor, turned on its side, as if someone has dropped it. I bend down to pick it up while being on the alert, and I see it holds Philippe Lavoie's cards. My Phil. I hear muffled noises in the room across the hall.

"Phil? Lafleur? What are you doing here?" I say after opening the door to the room.

They fidget in their chairs, widening their eyes.

"Hmmhdnhhmmhhggg," Phil says, shaking his head vigorously.

"What do you mean "Hmmhdnhhmmhhggg"? I say, giggling.

Except I stop giggling. It takes me too long to realize why these two were freaking out, and to appreciate that they didn't gag and bind themselves to their chairs. So, I'm not surprised to feel a huge blow on the back of my head and collapse like a rag doll. I have time to see Phil lower his head in dejection before I lose consciousness.

I wake up, sweating, strapped to an upright chair with tightly bound ties. We are no longer gagged, but we are all in the same awkward position. Phil is looking at me furiously while Lafleur is, by golly, bruised like a grapefruit. I laugh at my citrus reference to his Tourette's.

"We're screwed," Phil says, shaking his head.

"Of course not," I say with a wince. My head hurts so badly.

"Shut up," a voice from the other side of the door shouts.

"He's not very kind," I say, chuckling in a whisper.

Phil and Lafleur look at me as if they can't comprehend how I can make jokes at such a critical moment. I mean, to pretend that Lafleur is looking at me is a stretch. Let's just say he does what he can with what's left of his functional eye.

"Man, he beat the crap out of you," I tell him, almost admiringly.

He sighs in disgust, then tells me that when he arrived, he walked in on Mayor Ouellet, and the mayor lunged at him. Although he got the upper hand at one point, he was knocked by what he refers to as a "lucky punch" that smacked him off balance. And then Johnny Ouellet beat him until he lost it.

"There must have been some citrus names thrown around, right?" I say as I wink at Phil, who shakes his head.

I turn back to Lafleur.

"But you know he's not the mayor, right?"

"What do you mean?"

I look at Phil, seeking support. Phil frowns, looking at the poor guy.

"What Lafs is saying is that the man who beat you up is not Johnny Ouellet."

"What are you saying?"

"OK, we're going in circles here," I say with a touch of frustration in my voice. "What we're telling you, dumbass, is that this guy isn't the mayor. He's his twin brother. You're kidding, right?"

Lafleur looks at me as if I just asked him to fix a trigonometry equation.

"Remember the house we went to together? Down in the basement, the freezer?"

"That sounds familiar."

"Do you recall what was in the damn freezer?"

"Yeah, fishes."

"Yes, but under the fishes?"

"I don't know?"

I look at him, expecting him to say he's bullshitting me, that he knows very well this jerk is not the mayor because we have discovered his head and his wife's head under a pile of piranhas. But he doesn't.

"Johnny Ouellet and his wife's severed heads? You're screwing with us or what?"

Lafleur widens his only eye that opens.

"Are you kidding me?" he says.

"No, we've talked about it several times."

"I thought it was a figure of speech."

I frown.

"What do you mean, a figure of speech? Why did you throw up then in the house after looking in the freezer?"

"Because it was full of dead fishes. Dead fishes are disgusting."

I chuckle.

"Well, buddy, you haven't seen the worst of it. The guy on the other side, his name is Rock Mercier. Remember we talked about a Rock Mercier?"

"Lemon."

"There you go, lemon. You even did the research and told us about him."

"Oh, yeah!"

"You got it hard on the head, huh?"

"Grapefruit, boss, I swear I have blackouts. I can't remember anything."

The door opens suddenly.

"Will you shut the fuck up already?"

I turn around to look at this Rambo wannabe who's foaming at the mouth.

"Who's talking?" I say, looking at Phil.

Phil looks back at me, wondering if I'm rambling.

"I hear voices behind me, but I don't see anyone."

Still no light in my colleague's eyes.

"Damn it, Phil, he wears camouflage. That's the joke."

Lafleur laughs as Phil rolls his eyes.

"You want to play games, Lafs?" Mercier says.

I don't have time to reply before he hits me in the back of the head again. The pain is too much. It infuses an uncontrollable fury in me.

"You bastard, I will kill you, I swear I will kill you, fucking asshole. Fight me like a man. Or can you only take men from behind, like in prison?"

He moves his face closer to mine, the big vein in his forehead threatening to burst at any moment.

"What did you just say to me, you son of a bitch?"

"I said you were taking men from behind in prison, you know? In Thailand?"

He stands up with a terrifying smile on his paint-blackened face. He leaps back to smack me in the face.

"No, wait—"

But he doesn't wait. His fist smashes my nose. Holy shit, I'd be crying like a child if I wasn't so busy suffering.

"Anything more to say, funny guy?" he says, shouting much too close to my ears.

I shake my head.

"That's what I thought, you coward. Anyway, your graves are dug. It's over. Tonight, you will be history."

"Where are the girls?" I say with a trembling voice.

"The little cunts? No better than dead. I'm packing up in a few hours, and I don't intend to bring any baggage, if you know what I mean."

I know what he means. It's not so clear to Lafleur, who looks at me with question marks on his face. I signal to him to let it go. The multiple blows he got to the head have really made him dumber than he was before. Let's just say it wasn't a luxury he could afford. Mercier leaves the room, slamming the door. We must find a way out of this mess. Because I hate to agree with Phil, but we're in trouble. There's not much time left.

FIFTY-FOUR

Lauriane Derome is anxious because she hasn't seen her girlfriends since their failed escape. Luckily, since her cabin is between Lea's and Rashida's, she can talk to them individually through an air vent on each wall. In Lea's case, she has to climb on a chair to reach the grill, whereas in Rashida's case, the vent is in her bedroom, so she only has to climb onto her bed. She communicates with the girls several times a day, if only to know their state of mind. Lea is doing well, given the circumstances, but Lauriane is deeply concerned for Rashida. She told her several times that she won't last much longer. Things have gotten worse since the madman reiterated the terrible things he has in store for them. Lauriane says she would rather die than go through all this, but as time goes on, she wonders if she will be brave enough to take action. Rashida has a similar speech, but in her case, Lauriane is convinced she will do it. She must not give up. All is not lost. Lauriane keeps thinking about what they can do to get out of this. And even if she doesn't know how, maybe they will find a way out through working in the garden. Who knows if someone will show up at the scene by chance? The police will eventually track them down. That's what she keeps telling Rashida, who doesn't consider it anymore. But as long as Lauriane stresses her optimism, she feels she is gaining time. Rashida has just enough faith not to hang herself with her chain or fool around with the kitchen's sharp utensils. Lauriane climbs up on a chair and asks Lea how she is doing this evening. It's dinnertime, and she wants to make sure she gets something to eat.

"I'm having eggs," Lea says in a monotone.

She still blames herself for Blondi's death. Lauriane knows this because Lea has told her multiple times. Lauriane keeps reminding her he kidnapped them and was not their ally, that he only wanted to be in a relationship with an underage girl, which is also a crime. But Lea is adamant that they were better off with Blondi than without him. He had a kind soul, although intellectually challenged and influenceable. If she hadn't seduced him to help them, he would still be alive today. The logic is compelling, and Lauriane knows it. But she doesn't have the same sympathy for Blondi as Lea does. Although she feels sad that it ended this way, she would do exactly the same thing to break out of this mess. She would exploit his intellectual shortcomings to manipulate him again and again if she had to. In this situation, the end justifies the means. The only thing she is sorry about is that she couldn't vanish into the darkness like she planned to. She hopes that a passerby, or someone on a quad bike will find Blondi's corpse and notify the police, but the likelihood of him still being in the same place is slim, Rock Mercier said he would take care of him, so he probably dug a hole to bury him in, or dissolved his corpse in a barrel of acid. Whatever that crazy bastard did, Blondi's body is probably not there anymore.

It was the first time she saw someone die, and it traumatized her, but she needs to snap out of it to focus on her primary goal, leaving this damned place.

She heads to her bed to talk to Rashida, but the other girl doesn't respond.

"Rashida? Please talk to me."

No reaction.

Having called her several times with no reply, she knocks hard on the wall they share.

"Rashida, this is not funny. Please answer me. Tell me you are still there. Don't go away."

Nothing.

She screams, hitting the wall with all her might. "Rashida, say something. Rashida, for the love of God, answer me."

After several minutes of this merry-go-round, Lauriane collapses, sobbing on her bed.

"Rashida, you gave me your word. What did you do?"

The memory of her lively friend when she first came to the basement comes back to her, and she cries even louder. Seeing Blondi die was certainly horrible, but she will get over it. She has seen no one die as slowly as Rashida did. Lauriane won't eat, staying in her room to stay with Rashida, so she won't be alone.

Lauriane touches the wall with her hand, hoping that somehow Rashida will sense it, and know that she is not alone, that someone who loves her will stand by her side until the end.

FIFTY-FIVE

I don't know how much time I have left, but I've loosened my ties a bit. With some effort, I might even be able to untie myself. I see the sun setting through the window. I also hear Mercier moving around. He goes in and out with gusto. So, I guess he's getting ready to leave. But he won't go anywhere without killing us all. He's said that several times, and I believe he will. If you can cold bloodedly kill your own twin, then you don't value human lives at all, and you're a fucking psychopath. Anyway, who would dress up like Rambo and not be missing a few bolts in the head? Even for Halloween. I look over at Lafleur, who's asleep, head bent over his chest, snoring like a buffalo.

"Hey, grapefruit," I say, for him to stop busting our balls with his snoring, which is worse than a torture round in Guantanamo. He doesn't wake up, though. I see Phil is as annoyed as I am.

"Death suddenly seems more bearable, doesn't it, Philou?"

He laughs at first, but then his face darkens.

"Thinking about Melanie?"

He nods. I don't know if I'm imagining things, given the low light in the room, but it sure looks like tears rolling down his chubby face. I pinch my lips together. I won't lie to you. It breaks my heart. The guy finds a girl who is way hotter than him, and he can't enjoy it any longer than that? I understand why the poor guy might be depressed. I've now come to regret that Melanie turned the Martinator down the other night. What am I saying? She's my employee's girlfriend. I need to stop rambling and figure out a way to get us out of this. After all, I'm to blame for this mess. Actually, you know what? This whole thing was Phil's idea, so he's got his share of the blame, too. And Lafleur insisted on joining us, so he bears some of the burden too. Subsequently, you are right. I'm not responsible for what happens to us. Not for a second. But when I see how these guys are doing, I feel I can only count on myself.

"Phil, follow my lead," I say.

"Wait, what?"

"Hey, Mercier, get your mother-fucking face in here, presto," I shout, winking at Phil.

He looks at me, wide-eyed. I don't know if it's because of hope or because of incomprehension of what I'm about to do. The door opens with a bang.

"Good timing. You were next. Have you done your prayers, you morons?"

He sneers like a goat caught on an electrified fence.

"God cannot exist, you stupid bum, or you would have died ages ago, and your brother would still be alive."

He comes towards me.

"You will be the last to die, and you know why?"

"Because I am beautiful?"

"No, you are ugly as fuck. You'll be the last one to die because I want you to see your friends die while you watch, and then I'll take my time with you. I'll make you wish you were never born, you'll see."

"Your brother should have eaten you in the womb while he had the chance."

"Wow," Mercier says, standing up. "Even for a guy like me, that's heavy stuff."

"Yeah Lafs, I know we'll die, but let's not overdo it," Phil adds.

Mercier points his knife at him, and stares at me. "See? Even the fat fuck thinks you're pushing it."

"Fuck you like in Thailand," Phil says through clenched teeth.

God in heaven, I'm proud of him. I look at Phil, tears in my eyes, contemplating my work as if I had been sculpting him in clay for all these years.

"Come again?" Mercier says as he moves towards him.

Since my bonds are not so tight, I slide horizontally enough on my chair to extend my leg and trip him with my left foot. Mercier wobbles, then crashes into the cherry wood dresser to his left. He falls heavily alongside Phil, like a sandbag. I wriggle vigorously to get loose from the chair. Mercier is on the floor, groaning, blood dripping from his head.

Obviously, he fractured his skull when he hit the corner of the cabinet. I manage to free myself, and I jump at him just as he opens his eyes and rolls over onto his back. The pain I feel is overwhelming. Even Phil clenches his teeth in disgust. At first, I thought he struck me with his fist on my shoulder, but I see his switchblade handle resting between my chest and my shoulder, going through my collarbone. I know very well that the blade went through my body and came out the other side. This jerk tries to pull the blade out of my chest, but I cling to him to take away any leverage he may have, only for him to push the dagger deep into my flesh and twist the blade into my wound. I'm about to pass out. I try to gouge his eyes out in a last desperate attempt, but my fingers slip and land in his mouth instead. He bites, and I can't take it anymore.

I pass out.

———

I wake up startled, my face pressed against the floor. Mercier is gone, but I feel his liquefied blood still under my cheek. I almost throw up. I try to push myself to turn around and check if Phil and Lafleur are still there, but my right arm refuses to comply. I can move it a little, but it has no strength. Finally, I turn my head enough to see Phil looking at me anxiously. And I get nervous.

"Where is Mercier?"

"Over there," Phil says in a steady voice, pointing ahead with his chin.

Too calm for someone who is about to die.

I get up to kneeling using my left arm and my steel abs. My right arm is shredded, totally inoperative. I turn around and see Mercier's army boots on the ground. I also see his pants attached to the boots. They're also on the ground. But I have a hard time spotting him because of the darkness.

"Lemon, boss. We thought you were dead."

I look at Lafleur and scowl.

"Thank God you stopped snoring."

He giggles and faints once again. I get up and stagger to Mercier. I turn on the light and close my eyes. It feels like someone has just stabbed my eyeballs with needles. I keep my eyes closed, waiting for them to adjust to the ambient light before opening them completely. Mercier is lying there, half out of the room. He passed out. I walk towards his body and kick his knife away, the object of my suffering, which slides several feet away. I think Maradona would have been proud of my free kick. I grab the gun lying on the living room table and walk up to Mercier again. I hit him over the head with a joyous slap.

"Come on, scumbag. Get up."

I quickly lose my strength.

"He's dead, Martin," Phil says in a calm voice.

"How can you be so sure?"

"Details, I guess. Like when he said, "Damn, my throat's swelling. What was on his fingers? Peanut butter?" or when he went forward looking for his EpiPen, I suppose, or when he collapsed in there and made funny noises, like someone drowning. Ha, and also that he hasn't moved for at least two hours. So, my educated guess is that he's dead."

I scan Mercier as I move the arm covering his face. Holy shit, that fucker is really dead. His face is all swollen and purple. His bloated, oversized tongue is sticking out of his mouth. I look to my right and realize he was about a foot away from reaching for his medicine. We were this close to dying. This close. Okay, you can't see it, but I'm showing you a small gap between my index finger and my thumb. I can't believe that jerk was allergic to peanuts. Well, buddy, not even your ridiculous Rambo disguise could save you from that.

"Hey Lafs?"

"Yes," I say weakly.

"Since you're as pale as a ghost and threatening to collapse at any moment, can you cut us loose?"

"Yeah—sure."

The floor spins dangerously under my feet.

I stumble over and point the gun at him.

"Hey Ho, Lafs. No. The knife. It'll go better with the knife."

"What? Ha—m'kay."

I drop my gun and barely make my way to the knife, which is rendered much too far away, along the edge of the wall. I move back to Phil even though the floor tilts forty-five degrees to one side, then the other, as if I were on a small sailboat in the middle of an ocean storm. I cut Phil's bonds enough to get him to break free.

"Can you... lemon... him...," I say, pointing my knife at Lafleur.

"Yes, Lafs, I'll do it. Go lay on the couch in the other room. I'll call an ambulance."

"No .... not... bulance."

I sit down painfully on the old sofa after stepping over Mercier's corpse, and my head is so heavy that it falls backwards. After a few minutes, I see Phil dragging Lafleur with his arm wrapped around the helpless guy's neck. He sets him down next to me.

"Phil... girls... search.... probably.... here...."

"Yes, I will search for them."

"And Phil—"
"Yes Lafs?"
"The…bulance... good idea...."
"I'll make the call."
I pass out again.

FIFTY-SIX

Phil hears the first vehicles approaching the ranch in the distance and sees the flash of their sirens illuminating the night. He sits on Mercier's front porch, gathering his thoughts. He is truly concerned about Martin Lafs and Marcel Lafleur. Both are terribly injured. For the couple of hours that Lafs was unconscious after being stabbed by Mercier, Phil thought he would die right there in front of him. He feels grateful that he made it out so well, even if emotionally he's not okay. He called 9-1-1 after retrieving the cell phone Mercier took from him, then called Melanie to reassure her he was alive and that he loves her. She didn't have time to worry since he regularly works long hours, so it was natural that she hadn't heard from him by then. But once she realized the magnitude of what had just happened, she broke down in tears. Phil tried to hold back his own tears but could not. She asked him whether this time he would consider changing careers, and for the first time, he didn't shut the door. After all, is it worth it? It's his passion, but other things in life are more important than work. People often undervalue the comfort of a nine-to-five office job.

He then called Nicole, who also wept. She was worrying because, unlike Melanie, Nicole is in constant contact with either Lafs or him. She asked him about Martin and Marcel, and Phil just said they were with him. He didn't tell her about what happened to them. She's already upset enough as it is. She'll soon find out what really happened.

He glances inside the house. and Lafs and Lafleur are still as he left them twenty minutes earlier, unconscious on Mercier's couch. Mercier is still lying flat on his stomach. Phil wonders what will happen to his piranhas. He can't help but link them to Mercier, which was his nickname in prison. He did not know how he got this nickname, but he can conceive why. Apparently, Mercier was proud of it given his aquarium, and especially the amount he used to cover his brother and sister-in-law's heads. Phil doesn't venture out to the cottages further on, but he stares at them, hoping that Mercier didn't have time to carry out his Machiavellian plan. Phil would have a hard time living with himself if the girls' bodies, or anyone else's are found. The paramedics are first on the scene and quickly process the three men in the house. Phil does not know why, but he feels relieved that they have left Mercier lying in the same spot, draped in a yellow plastic tarp. That seals his death, although it was clear just by looking at him. Lafs screams in pain while being carried on a stretcher, cursing everyone as he goes. Same for Lafleur, who runs through the whole citrus family. Phil smiles at how his two colleagues are being true to their image, despite the circumstances. But the greater relief comes when the cops show up and head for the small cottages. When he sees the first girl come out, a pretty blonde with ginger highlights crying and trembling uncontrollably, he seriously hopes that Lauriane will follow suit, and that there will be no dead body.

His legs soften and his eyes fill with tears as he sees Lauriane limping out of the second house. Her left ankle has wounds, similar to deep scratches. She yells, trying to reach the cottage to her left, but the officers won't let her in. As they drag her to the emergency vehicles, she keeps looking at the cabins. Then she sees Phil and knows that her nightmare is over. They've met a few times before, but it is as if Phil is the person she is most happy to see right now. He stands up and hugs her, kissing the top of her head. She mouths a thank you and asks him to call her mom and check on someone named Rashida, then goes with the cop leading her to the paramedics. Phil knows they will undergo a battery of tests, but from what he can tell, both girls seem to be in decent shape.

There are few words spoken between Phil and Josiane Derome. She bursts into tears when Phil tells her the good news, after that, she keeps crying with little room for conversation. Phil waits patiently for her to overcome it and says a few words as he watches the cops go in and out of the cottages. They buzz around the two at the end that are uninhabited, but they have been in the middle one for several minutes. Phil is nervous that there might be a problem. Then a cop calls over the radio for paramedics to be dispatched with a stretcher. Phil wonders if it is another girl, dead, or if it is James Romano. The last thing he wants is a dead body. Other than Rock Mercier's, of course. He hangs up with Josiane, who has thanked him a thousand times, and he keeps looking at the third house, afraid to get closer. He is standing in the middle of this vast ranch and fears what the police have found. Then the paramedics emerge with a third girl, an oxygen mask over her face and a blanket up to her shoulders. She stares straight ahead, emotionless. She's in worse shape than the other two, but she's alive. And that's what matters. Phil is heartbroken to see the lack of a glint in this girl's eye as she passes by him. She barely blinks. The cops offer to escort him back to his car parked at the trailhead, and he agrees, considering that it is dark, except for the many lamp posts illuminating the ranch like a baseball field.

He thinks back to the cottages he visited once he was sure they were empty. They're tiny houses with a boat anchor screwed into the floor, and probably into the cement slab. A heavy chain at the end of each anchor was a metal tie with a padlock obviously used to hold the girls captive. The last two cottages were untouched, as if no one had ever set foot in them. Phil gets a chill down his spine as he realizes that Mercier's original intent was to kidnap even more girls. He hopes the girls know what Mercier had in store for them, because it makes no sense, and he'd like to understand. Since Mercier is dead and Romano is nowhere to be found, they are the only ones who hold the key to the mystery, unless they can find the big knucklehead.

On his way home, Phil's hands shake on the steering wheel. He can't get past how close he came to being killed. And that if it weren't for Martin Lafs's brave gesture, they would all be dead by now. He replays the scene over and over in his head. Lafs tripping Mercier, Mercier falling to the ground, blood pouring from his head. And Martin launching himself at him, but Mercier turning to counter. Phil didn't realize at the time what was going on as he heard Lafs scream in agony, but he soon realized when he saw the blade of Mercier's knife sticking out just beside his shoulder blade. But Lafs fought on bravely until he noticed the blade spinning in the wound. When Mercier pushed him away to stand up, Phil thought it was the end. But Mercier quickly grabbed his throat. Phil and Lafleur glanced at each other, seeing Mercier panic and stagger slowly. His lips were swelling rapidly as he stood up and headed for the door. He lost his footing as he slipped in his own blood and struggled to his feet. Phil clenched his jaw, looking at him on his way out of the room. He hoped he wouldn't find what he was looking for. Then Mercier collapsed again, passing out. And he laid flat on his face, convulsing. He fought for every ounce of air in his trachea, then a few more jolts, and nothing.

After about twenty minutes of him lying still, Lafleur laughed gently. He didn't understand what was going on, but Phil did. Mercier had a severe peanut allergy and Lafs must have stuck his fingers full of dried peanut butter in his mouth. As Phil watched him eat his toast with concern and rage, fearing that he would soil the seat of his car, he couldn't imagine that his sudden craving for the damn toast would save their lives. In the end, Lafs was luckier than he was good, but nothing could take away his bravery in charging at Mercier, unarmed, driven only by his courage, and probably also a bit by his recklessness.

FIFTY-SEVEN

I woke up here, in this hospital bed, not sure why I was here. Even though I had scattered memories from the last days, I wasn't sure of what was real and what was my imagination. I asked Phil to narrate several times the account of my bravery in saving everyone. Strangely enough, I can't seem to get enough of it. I was even prouder knowing that not one, but three girls were found in the cottages, including Lauriane. I cried when I heard the news. Of course, I was happy that it ended well. But mostly because it marked the end of the pro bono bullshit. Never again, do you hear me? Never again.

The girls said that Rock Mercier killed James Romano as he attempted to save them. My opinion of him changed, but his room's foul smell will always be etched in my memory.

I struggle to move my right arm, and I'm terrified I can never use it again. Also, I'm right-handed. All to make it worse. What will I do when no one is available to entertain me on dreary November nights, and my right hand is not an option? Desperation brings tears to my eyes. Phil informs me the doctor is optimistic about the recovery of my arm. He says it will take a lot of physical therapy because nerves and muscles were severed. I smirked at the mention of my muscles, which didn't go unnoticed by Phil, who rolled his eyes a bit. For a guy who owes me his life, he could spare me his childish manner. He thanked me so many times for bailing them out that I stopped counting. At first, I cherished it, imagining how much it must hurt him to give me credit, but now it's just too much. Speaking of too much, I see Lafleur and his bruised face coming along slowly, dragging his pole and his solute bag with him. It's my turn to roll my eyes. I just want to go back to sleep and be left alone. Phil realized this when he offered to come back later, to which I retorted it was very kind, but really unnecessary.

"Hey Lafleur. You didn't win that fight, did you?" I say with a chuckle, seeing his basketball-sized bluish face and puffy eyes.

"You should see the other guy, boss," Lafleur says, grinning and grimacing.

Indeed, no one would want to be the other guy. I groaned out in pain as I moved my body half an inch.

"Lemon, boss, are you okay?"

"Sort of," I say with a grunt. "I think the morphine, or whatever they injected me with, is losing its efficacy because I feel a twinge in my arm."

"Do you want me to call the care attendant?"

I look at him sternly.

"Come on, Lafleur. Don't you know people don't say care attendant anymore? What is this, 14th century London? Jesus."

He is stunned.

"Dear Lord, excuse me. What should I say then?"

I admit I don't remember what the word is.

"You don't know what the term for that is? Really Lafleur? I'm disappointed."

I keep talking to buy myself some time, hoping the word will come back to me, but probably because I'm drugged up enough to overpower a herd of elephants, I can't remember it for the life of me.

"Something that ends in urs."

Fortunately, people show up at my door. It's Phil again.

"Phil, guess what? Lafleur said care attendant."

He looks at me mockingly. I give him a stern look that puts him right back on track.

"You mean nurse?"

I snap my fingers with my left hand.

"That's right, nurse."

I see Melanie appear behind her boyfriend. She smiles at me. I'm surprised. Probably Phil told her about my act of heroism.

"Hello, Martin, how are you?" she asks in a tone of voice that leads me to believe that she is really interested to know.

"Well, I fucked my arm up, but otherwise, I'm fine."

She comes closer and grabs my left hand, tells me how grateful she is that I saved her lover's life, that she'll always be grateful and that of course I'm invited to attend their wedding. I look at Phil. Wedding?

"Yes, we decided to get married in a few months. We figured there was no point in waiting. What just happened showed us how fragile life is."

"And how peanut butter toasts are underrated," Lafleur adds with a laugh.

I look at him with resentment.

"You're pretty cocky for a guy who looks like he spent the night getting his ass kicked by Mike Tyson."

He pouts. I turn back to Melanie.

"Count me in. Congratulations, lovebirds."

If they only knew how much I hate weddings and how much it pisses me off to attend them.

They finally leave, and I urge Lafleur to do the same. He thanks me again for saving him and walks away much too slowly.

"Hopefully, you don't have to go too far. You'll be here all night," I say with a chuckle.

He pulls off his hospital gown, exposing his hairy ass. I almost throw up.

"I didn't want to get to know you that well, you disgusting bastard," I say, holding back a severe gag.

The feeling fades when the beautiful nurse shows up, the same as with Serge. Damn, she's hot. What if my courage makes her receptive to getting laid now? I need to look as miserable as possible.

"How are you, Mr. Lafs?"

"Fine," I say in a weak voice.

She looks at me sternly.

"You just yelled at Mr. Lafleur a few minutes ago. You can stop your act."

I stiffen up and frown.

"Compassion isn't your forte, huh?"

She smiles, and her face softens.

"I heard about what you did. Everyone in the hospital knows as well, even the news shows are talking about it."

"No kidding? That's awesome," I say, turning on the old, dingy TV set hanging on the wall.

I'm foreseeing all the beautiful girls who will want to get a piece of the hero I've become. My God, it will be like fishing with dynamite.

"Why are you laughing like that?" she asks.

"Never mind."

She smiles at me.

"Anyway, you're not the filthy, artificial jerk I thought you were."

Well, a little bit, yes.

"Does that mean that—"

"No, it doesn't."

"You don't even know what I was going to say."

"Yes, I do, and the answer is no."

"What was I going to say?"

"If I would date you."

"Who the fuck do you think I am?"

She crosses her arms.

"Okay, then what?"

"..."

"..."

"Yes, that is what I was going to say. The dating thing," I say, glancing down.

"The answer is still no."

I'm kind of offended, though.

"Am I a goddamn hero, yes or no?"

"Yes, you acted heroically"—enjoy the detour she takes to not dignify me with the term hero—"but that doesn't mean I will leave my husband and children for you."

"Of course, I hadn't thought of that. A pretty woman like you was bound to be in a relationship."

"Not necessarily, but I am."

I watch her for a few seconds, thinking.

"Are any single colleagues of yours as gorgeous as you?"

"No."

"But—"

"No."

I sigh, irritated. She laughs and instructs me to rest, then leaves with her feline wiggle that keeps making me swoon. If I were the least bit suspicious, I'd swear she was doing it on purpose. I close my eyes, enjoying the minutes of rest I have to imagine all the things I would do to this beautiful babe if only we were both in my warm bed, exposing the Martinator before her astonished eyes, and to the clamour of the crowd.

"Hello, Martin."

For fuck's sake, leave me alone, people. This place is worse than a train station.

Josiane Derome comes in, hushed as if she is afraid to bother me. Too late.

"We wanted to thank you personally, Martin. For Lauriane."

As she speaks, I see a pretty blonde standing next to her, a stunning young girl with a bright eye and a genuine smile. I smile back at her.

"I guess you are Lauriane?"

She nods as she gets closer. She puts her hand on my arm and struggles for words. I look at her, candidly. I know what she wants to tell me, and I feel a little embarrassed thinking I wanted to drop the investigation more than once. But seeing her in front of me puts a face to it all, and I'm glad I persisted. That and what

Anne-Marie promised to do to me if I kept going, but I won't mention that, as you can imagine. Tears run down the teenager's cheeks as she can't find the words she so desperately wants to tell me, but I smile at her and assure her I get it. Strangely, I don't feel any embarrassment that she is so emotional. Normally I deal poorly with crying, but this time I feel nothing but gratitude that she is alive. I recall other girls were with her at the ranch, according to Phil. I ask her if she has any news.

"Yes, we talk every day. Lea is fine. She's a little shaken up, like me, but she's getting on with her life little by little. For Rashida, it's more complicated. Though we've had brief conversations, she is undergoing treatment at the psychiatric hospital she has been staying at since our rescue. Doctors say it will take a long time for her to get back her former self, if she ever gets it back, but they will work with her to make it happen."

She explains how things were for them over there, and I am totally stunned that they went through that, and she can tell me about it with so much assurance, just days after they got out of that hell. I glance at Josiane, who nods in frustration as she hears the story for probably the hundredth time. Thankfully, Mercier never had time to defile them before he died. If there's a silver lining to all this, it's that he couldn't have done more damage.

An hour later, I see hospital employees bustling down the hallway just as the TV talks about a man running down the side of the highway, naked in his hospital gown. They show us a cell phone video of a jerk, ass to the wind, staggering by the cars that are slowly driving by. Thank goodness they blurred out the part where you can see this moron's butt that—God in heaven. I roar with laughter in my room. I'm laughing my ass off. They just showed freaking Serge's face running barefoot on the shoulder of the freeway, gratifying everyone with his old man ass.

Later in the evening, Annie-Marie comes to visit me and tells me she will keep her promise, but not here, in the hospital, silly me.

Lea Briand's and Rashida Lafleur's parents also came by to thank me, and they did the same with Marcel and Phil. Those two were also brave to venture out on the ranch. I didn't do it all by myself even though, as you will agree, I am the main hero of this story.

You don't? My name is on this book's cover, isn't it?

Whatever, leave me alone. I need to get some sleep.

Visiting hours are over.

I look at Philippe and Melanie as they exchange vows to be there for each other through thick and thin, and I have to say I'm a tad jealous. I never intended to get married, and let's face it, I am commitment phobic. But every time I attend a wedding, it highlights my emotional shortcomings in bold strokes. This union happened very quickly. Only eight weeks after what happened at the ranch, here we all are at Phil's wedding. They've managed to do it in such a short time. I smile at the sight of Phil in his tuxedo, looking like a penguin who ate too many cheeseburgers. And the elegant Melanie, looking absolutely stunning, staring at him like he's one of the wonders of the world.

Anne-Marie is by my side since we keep in touch with each other from time to time. I don't think this is a major love affair, but we enjoy each other. She lives in her apartment, and I live in mine, but we see each other on weekends. She has told me that as long as she is happy with the arrangement; it is fine. If that ever changes, she'll let me know.

My right arm is still in a hitch, limiting some of my movements, but I feel that it's getting stronger. I should be okay soon, don't worry. Don't be fooled by how much I wince with pain every time I reposition my arm, either. It's all part of the act. I'm pushing it because it draws me sweet glances from the opposite sex. I'll milk it for as long as I can, but you already know that, since we've come to know each other rather well. I groan as I settle my arm and glance at Anne-Marie on my right. She looks at me with an "oh, you poor thing" look on her face, and I smile, downplaying it. See? Don't tell me you wouldn't take advantage of it too.

Phil's family has shown a great deal of compassion and appreciation for me, but not as much as you would expect for a man who saved the life of one of their own. I guess all of Phil's complaining about me at family gatherings in the past still weighs heavily on the clan's opinion of me. I swear I grimace with pain every time I sense them peering at me from afar. They will eventually give me the respect I deserve.

I flinch as Anne-Marie's hand lands on my thigh. It makes me realize she hasn't yet done what she promised to do to me if I agreed to carry Lauriane's investigation on. She says she just wants to wait for the right moment. So why do I feel like she's messing with me and had no intention of keeping her word? I almost died and—I can't stress this enough because people are quick to gloss over this—I wasn't paid.

Of course, I'm glad we found the three girls at the end, but would it kill people to make me a national hero for a day or two? I expected to get multiple interview requests, naughty letters from a swarm of beautiful creatures with well-rounded butts offering to do many unimaginable dirty things to me, but none of that happened. I did an appearance on a community radio station and was interviewed by a local TV station, but no major networks showed up. I guess saving two men and three girls from a sure death isn't enough. They would rather talk to talent-less singers about their last album. Anne-Marie asks me if I saved the girls because it was the right thing to do, or for my own personal fame. Of course, it was the right thing to do, but at the same time, the exposure would have helped the agency. Despite that, I hope someone will make a movie about my adventures. Somebody will eventually wake up. I taunted Guy Lefebvre and his colleagues once I was out of the hospital. I was happy to rub their incompetence in their faces and tell them that without us, three young girls would have been raped and probably killed. For a rare time, Lefebvre was silent. He looked at me coldly, but I know that, deep inside, he was embarrassed. Commandant Tremblay also got a piece of my mind, even though I still respect him. I did this hoping that next time they would help us instead of putting up roadblocks and endangering people's lives.

Lafleur is sitting next to his wife, who is as grateful for what I have done for him as Melanie is for Phil. But that's it, a similar gratitude to the one I would have had if I had lent him a couple of hundred dollars to get him out of trouble. Marcel Lafleur's face is back to its original colour and shape and, except for a few bruises here and there, there are no more signs of his troubles. I would have thought that after this, he would want to move on to a less precarious job and spend the rest of his life in a safer setting. But no, the guy still wants to partner up and have other ventures like that. Even Phil, who at some point questioned his career after the events at the ranch, no longer talks about quitting.

When I saw Nicole back at the office on the first day out of the hospital, she wrapped her chubby arms around me and told me how scared she had been. I was feeling special, but she did the same to Phil, who had already been back at work for several days. I see her sitting close to us next to her husband Gilles, who attempted to dress appropriately for the event by putting on a clean pair of pants and a loose shirt, refusing to tuck it into his pants as his wife suggests. She is much more chic than he is, which is so off-putting that it's laughable. It looks like a mother who couldn't get her sulky teenager to dress up for the occasion. Me? Well, friends, you'd be happy to see my blazer, which is perfectly tailored. I'm the star of the day, just not very stylish with my arm, but as Lafleur would say, "If life gives you lemons, make lemonade." Well, he never said that, but he said "lemon" so many times it's like the quote came from him.

The mayor and his wife had a civic funeral. News of the evil twin made headlines around the world, putting Montreal on the map for all the wrong reasons. Media outlets acknowledge that, occasionally, reality is more than fiction. Many snarky analysts wonder how no one could tell the difference between the twin and the mayor. Other than the change in attitude and tone, I didn't see it either. I swear the resemblance was striking, especially when nobody knew about the twin brother Johnny Ouellet had carefully suppressed from his life, as if he didn't exist.

I spoke with Josiane Derome a few days ago, mostly because I needed to be commended again for my bravery, and she told me that Lauriane is doing fine. She went back to school and has a new outlook on the world. She is making the most of every moment, and even has a new boyfriend, Samuel, a guy from her improv class. She occasionally has nightmares, but they are much less frequent than in the early days. Of course, she gets weekly counselling to help her come to terms with what happened. Lauriane remains in contact with her two friends. Lea Briand, who is also back in school and seems to do well, and Rashida Lafleur, who returned to the family house a few weeks ago and is getting back on track. Her road will be long and arduous, but she should soon be back in school too. Lauriane talks regularly to her and helps her as best she can. Rashida was the first to be taken, and therefore the one who has lived through this ordeal the longest. She is well cared for, according to Josiane. She has a solid family. She will get through this. Incidentally, Josiane is in constant contact with the Briands and the Lafleurs, since they have a powerful bond that unites them through their daughters' misfortune.

There are horrific events that bind people together for life.

"Are you all right?" Anne-Marie asks, with a worried look.

"Yes, sorry, I was in my head."

A mischievous smile lights up her face.

"What were you thinking about?"

"That you still haven't kept your promise!"

I know it's opportunistic. It came out of nowhere.

"Don't worry, now is the day."

My eyes widen.

"Oh, yeah?"

"Follow me," she says as the ceremony ends, and the party begins.

She leads me to a remote place in the middle of nowhere. There is a small wooden hut which is used for who knows what. I realize the little rascal has been scouting the place.

"Here?"

"Of course, Martin, you like to live dangerously, don't you?"

I look at her like, "Is she really asking me that question?" as I show her my disabled arm.

"Then, let's go!"

We enter this empty room that feels more like storage than anything. The octagonal structure and the white backdrop curtains give it a dreamy look. Anne-Marie locks the door with the latch and lunges at me like a panther at a baby giraffe. I grab her with the only hand that has enough strength, and we embrace in a powerful grip where our tongues fight for every square inch of our respective mouths. And that's when she goes for it. At first, I surrender to her. Dear God, it's amazing.

Oh, baby Jesus!

I don't feel any more pain. I feel nothing but pleasure all around. No normal man can go through this without completely losing his mind.

Hey, what's wrong with you, peeping Toms? Can't you see I'm busy?

Come on, beat it.

WOULD YOU LIKE TO SUPPORT THE AUTHOR?

First of all, thank you for reading the second novel in the Martin Lafs series. We hope you enjoyed it. If you did, we would really appreciate it if you could take a few minutes of your time to leave your review where you bought this novel. Reviews are really important to authors and allow other readers to discover them.

If you would like to receive two FREE short novels, introducing you to two more of the author's literary styles, sign up for Sebastyen's newsletter and download your starter library.

https://link.sebastyendugas.com/backlafseng

ABOUT THE AUTHOR

Sebastyen Dugas is an author from Montreal, Canada. He started his career as a journalist and then switched to a career in computer science.

Writing has always been a passion for Sebastyen for as long as he can remember. He loved to write for his own pleasure as well as contribute to blogs for other publications.

In his spare time, Sebastyen enjoys reading, photography and film. He loves to travel and has already visited more than twenty countries.

In the coming years, he wants to continue to travel the world, write more fiction and enjoy life.

You can reach Sebastyen on his website or on social media.

facebook.com/sebastyendugaswriter
twitter.com/TalkWithTheY
instagram.com/sebastyendugas

ALSO BY SEBASTYEN DUGAS

Martin Lafs Series

Epiphany From a Broken Camera

Don't Find Roger

Brevis Series

Death Ride

Stockholm

Abygaelle Jensen Series

The Wooden Queen